REMEMBER TO LOVE ME

A Ghost Story

BECKY WRIGHT

Published by Platform House
www.platformhousepublishing.com

Copyright © Becky Wright 2021
All Rights Reserved
www.beckywrightauthor.com

Third Edition
ISBN: 9781977925374

First published 2008

Book & Cover Design © by Platform House
www.platformhousepublishing.com

For my sister

PROLOGUE

People die every day. We mourn the same.

We concern ourselves with how to continue without their counsel, friendship — their love.

We grieve for ourselves. We long for our lives to be as they were, with them as a part of our daily routine, however mundane or insignificant. We crave a life that once was, longing for a constancy that has passed on with them. In turmoil, we are left empty with a cavernous hole to fill only with a consolation that they have gone to a greater place — now at peace. We take solace that they are freed of life's pains and are indeed safe and content.

But what of our dead?

Do they miss our touch, comforts and haven of home?

Do they long to embrace, to converse on the ordinary?

Are they left in a dark lonely place where they view our images through a veil of haze, them, moving beyond time at an endless pace of continual emotion? Left only to watch their loved ones grieve, long for the missing links in their living moments. Are they in a new existence of not peace, but torment, fuelled by an eagerness to return to the warmth of family?

What if this were so?

Would they do whatever it took to remain, even to torture their unfading souls with the imagery of their once-living selves? Would they, if indeed possible, return to us, to the bosom of kith and kin, a new life with an old soul?

CHAPTER ONE

The Past

I would have been happy to stay here forever. The young lady gazed up at the afternoon sun. It no longer warmed nor dazzled. ...*forever and a day.*

She hitched her blue lace dress, revealing her ankles, and wandered through the grass with bare feet. She made her way around the headstone and traced each newly carved letter of her name with her forefinger.

No, I was happy to stay here, but now I am dead, you are taking me home.

~

'No!' Her voice cracked under the weight of tears. 'It was not meant to be like this. How can I go on without you?' Annabelle's plea splintered the afternoon calm, but there came no reply.

Early September heat warmed her dress; sunrays glorified the words before her with a beam of divine light.

Wearily, her head sank into her palms; her fingers skimmed down her tear-stained cheeks as her arms wilted beside her. Softly, a hand slipped into hers, familiar and warm. Annabelle closed her eyes, savouring the moment.

Time paused as her heart lay spellbound — Oh, how she wished it to be real.

'I love you,' she whispered.

Her knees crumpled to the grass in a tangle of petticoats. Beyond the echo of her sobbing, she faintly heard someone's approach, but she did not glance; instead, cradled her face.

'You all right there, Miss?'

'I...' wearily she took a handkerchief from her pocket and dabbed her eyes. 'Thank you, Albert, yes.'

Her gaze remained locked on the headstone.

'I'm sorry to disturb you,' he said, moving to leave.

'No, that is… I mean, you did not disturb me; I was just…' Annabelle hesitated. 'Please, do not go,' she urged.

The young man knelt beside her; his brown tweed knees close to her hands. She idly played with the grass; each long blade brushed over her fingertips as she coiled and entwined intricate green ringlets.

'I've watched you from the beach,' his voice sang gently. 'I watched you both. I used to see her up there… sitting.' Albert cast an eye across the churchyard towards the dunes.

'You watched us?'

Discreetly, her eyes followed up until they reached his familiar face. He was young, the same as her early twenties; however, the elements had begun to betray him. The tanned skin around his eyes thinned with lines of his contented smile; his bronze cheeks dappled with freckles. Yet, as he spoke words of condolence, as so many had done, she saw it, new light, a truer light.

'Perhaps, you should go home. There is nothing here for you now. You belong at home,' Albert nodded.

Squinting, she faced him straight on. The afternoon sun flushed her cheeks; she could feel herself slipping, hypnotised by his deep blue eyes. Finally, there was the tranquillity she had been searching for. His hand tenderly reached over to hers.

'You cannot find what you have lost, for what you have lost is still with you.'

Albert rose to his feet and softly squeezed her shoulder. Annabelle remained kneeling but listened to the muffled tread of his boots, the crunch on the dusty gravel and the light tapping of the horseshoes on the cobbles as he left.

Then it came — hush. Stillness once more left only with her forlorn regrets and the headstone. With her forefinger, she traced the words:

This lovely bud, so young, so fair,
called hence by early doom,
just came to show how sweet a flower,
in paradise would bloom.

With no conscious thought for where she headed, Annabelle walked, leaving her lost love behind — silently passing the cottages in a blur of memories. Those sweet childhood recollections carried her off on their musical voyage of love and laughter.

Moments slipped through her hands as the grains of sand underfoot. Annabelle stood on the dunes, high above the village, staring out at the North Sea. Intense and vibrant, the dusky sky reached down to kiss the dark horizon; the sea undulated at the line of her eye.

With a yearning to fly, soar on gull wings, her body numb with pain and defeat, her soul wished to escape. How could she return to a life of routine and constancy when life had become something so vastly different?

The world appeared infinite and majestic from up here, the all-powerful elements relentless in their custom for change. She felt insignificant to the task ahead, a young woman with a fear of the future, the changes that had been, and those she had yet to face.

CHAPTER TWO

The Present

Steeped in history, the Suffolk market town of Bury St Edmunds offered a rare, rural beauty. It was not too dissimilar to Norfolk, to the coastal village April had loved. Adjusting and the reality of *finding her feet* was hard to fathom. Change never sat well in the pit of her stomach but was all she seemed to have endured of late — graduating and now the upheaval of moving house. But the relocation was her parents' choice, not hers.

At least here in Bury, April had her grandmother, her one constant stability.

December was upon them, with the festive season peering its frosty warmth around the corner. Christmas and Nan, the two went together. Her thoughts always returned to her favourite visit. Dad had dropped her off, and she had spent three weeks with Nan — just them. A little before her eleventh birthday, life had been so uncomplicated. Leaving home for the whole of the school holiday had been an adventure. Bury held magic; its buildings were imposing, more majestic than home. There, she worshipped the natural glory of the horizon, where the sea and sky merged.

New Year's Eve, they had sat snuggled outside in thick blankets on padded garden chairs and hugged mugs of hot chocolate. April had lost herself then, utterly captivated as fireworks painted the pitch sky, great explosions of vivid colour that crackled and hissed.

Now they were in Bury St Edmunds, to live. There would be no more visits, no more going home. This was *home.*

~

April closed the back door of their new place, an antique shop in the town centre, close to her grandmother's house. She wandered towards the cathedral, recalling the churchyard behind it, and could not help but wonder where that magic had gone — that flutter of childhood excitement. On the surface, it was still apparent, the beauty and glory of the ancient, but her heart bore an emptiness.

April reached for the brass knocker as the door opened; she pushed on the glossy black paintwork to reveal her grandmother.

'I knew it was you; I just knew it. There you are, my Little One. Come in, come in,' Sarah said as she stepped aside.

'I didn't even get a chance to knock. So, how'd you know it was me, Nan?'

'It's been two days. I knew you couldn't wait much longer; I've been so excited to see you.'

April entered the front room down three steps, glanced at her trainers and jeans and thought how out of place she looked in the old-fashioned room.

'I knew you were *feeling ill*, Mum's words, not mine, so I thought I'd leave it a couple of days.'

'It was only a momentary ailment, and I'm perfectly fine, as you can see. But you know full well, there's nothing I enjoy more than spending time with my favourite granddaughter.'

'I'm your *only* granddaughter!'

'Cup of tea, oh, and some cake too as it's a special occasion. It's so lovely to see you. I have missed you so much.' The tiny, immaculate lady reached over and hugged her.

April inhaled her grandmother's perfume; the familiar childhood scent conjured idyllic memories. She knew the

5

story of how her grandfather had bought her a bottle of expensive fragrance from France; from then on, she never wore another. As a child, April would creep to her dressing table to admire the bottle pride of place next to their wedding photograph and a single baby photo of Aprils' mother, Julia.

Her grandfather, Edward, had passed away many years before she was born, although his presence was still solid in a plethora of framed memories that speckled the house. He had stood tall with his military authority; his time in the Royal Air Force had given him a dominating presence, with a hint of wit, April always thought, beneath his thick silver moustache.

'It's good to see you, Nan,' April said as that missing magic spread through her body, '…and cake sounds great.'

Sarah looked timeless in a long skirt and silk blouse, the shade of Parma Violet sweets she had stored in the pantry when April came to stay. Diamond earrings glinted under her long white hair she tied back with a ribbon. April would never have known she was *ill* unless her mum had said.

'Sit down, sit down; I'll warm the pot.' She hurried off to the kitchen.

April rubbed her hand over her favourite seat's dark red velvet upholstery. The antique settee sat under the window with a deep-buttoned back and intricate wooden arms and legs with a matching one, the other side of the room near the fireplace. The fire crackled, hissed, casting the room in a warm amber glow.

Sarah returned with an enormous tea tray; her arms outstretched; she placed it perfectly on the coffee table. A china teapot, matching cups and saucers and iced cakes neatly on a plate. Sarah sat in her chair opposite; its wings of pink velvet wrapped her in a hug.

'Shall I be Mother?' She chuckled as she reached forward to pour. 'So, tell me, how are you settling in the new house?'

'Nan, this is lovely; the cakes look delicious as always; Mum's aren't quite the same.'

Sarah paused, cocking her head to one side. 'You haven't answered my question?'

'All right, I suppose. It's not the same, but no doubt I'll get used to it.' April reached for a cake, '…not like I have a choice,' she uttered.

Sarah ignored the comment, casting an eye her way. April shuffled in her seat.

'So, how's university?

'Finished; you remember the graduation?'

'Oh, yes, of course, of course. So that is it now; you are a qualified historian then.'

'Well...' April hesitated. 'Not really, but I do have a degree in Art History...'

'Well, there you are then. But the question is, what are you going to do with that knowledge in those brain cells of yours?' Sarah sipped her tea and stared intently.

'Not sure. I didn't have a plan or any real idea of what to do afterwards. Which leads me to... thank you, Nan, you know, for paying for everything.'

'You had a desire that needed fulfilling,' she laughed. 'Your university fund had been there since you were born. So, there is no need to thank me again. You have thanked me already; look at you. I never had that delight; times and our priorities differed when I was young.'

April smiled and took a bite of the cake.

'So, any plans for your birthday then? A party?'

'No, I really don't want to make a fuss, Nan.'

'Twenty-one, it's a big deal,' Sarah sat back, eyeing her granddaughter.

'I know, but honestly, you know I'm not one for all that fuss, maybe just a quiet dinner,' April sighed, her shoulders easing a little, although she hadn't realised she had been so tense.

7

'I agree, that would be lovely. It has been such a long time. It's wonderful to have you here, finally, where you belong, where you have always belonged.'

'I have missed you. I wasn't pleased about moving to be honest. I'm sorry. I know it sounds selfish,' April shook her head, heat rising in her neck. 'I had just got home after Uni only to find another upheaval,' her cheeks flushed. 'Sorry, I just hate...'

'Change.'

'Exactly…' she faltered. 'But I am happy to be near you, Nan, truly.'

'I get it, darling. But this is your home. Things will change now, though; I do not doubt that. But that is not to say it's a bad thing. On the contrary, the time is right, more so now than ever. I've waited so long to have you back.'

'The time is right?' April leant forward, sweeping back her long auburn hair.

'Our fate, our destiny, it's mapped out in front of us, you know. Even if we stray off course, whether we can help it or not, sometimes, it just takes a while for us to find our path, but when we do,' Sarah paused, sipped her tea and sighed. 'When we do, we know. We just know.'

'Know what?'

'We know who we are. When I was a young girl, I always knew where I belonged, but… well, something just wasn't quite right. A piece of me was missing, if you like. Although, of course, back then, I didn't understand or know what it was, what it could be, of course not, I was only a child, how could I?'

'Nan, I don't have a clue what you mean. What was missing?' April quizzed, brow furrowed, her lips pursed.

'Oh, I was about your age. I wish I'd been younger, though, so I could have made a difference. But, unfortunately, by the time I understood everything, it was too late,' Sarah took another sip of tea and smiled. 'That's a lovely cuppa,' her voice was sentimental, '…regrets.'

'What?

'Something was missing, and when I realised, there were... regrets.'

'Missing, what was missing?' April shook her head.

'Just me. Never mind; how's your cake? Pink, I know it's your favourite. You always loved pink icing. When you were young, you made such a fuss if I did them white. A proper little girl, pink every time.'

'Yeah, I remember...'

April carefully raised her teacup, holding the saucer beneath to catch stray drops. The smooth bone china and sweet tea filled her head with more memories. She eyed her grandmother over the rim of her cup.

'What happened, Nan? You wished you'd been younger before what?'

'Before it was too late, Little One, before it was too late.'

'But for what?'

'To say sorry. When I realised it was far, far too late, then I just had no way of saying it. Too late for sorry,' Sarah sat nodding, her eyes staring out through the window to the cold street beyond.

'Why, what had you done?' April put her cup down, clanking the saucer as it toppled, spilling tea.

'Nothing, nothing at all, that was just it, I hadn't done a thing. If I had known back then, I could have done something, said something. Make amends, make up for lost time.'

Although intrigued and equally confused, April pressed her grandmother no further. Instead, she sat watching her with a concerned eye.

CHAPTER THREE

Low winter rays seeped through the window, bleaching April's bedroom in sunlight. Along with the rest of the house, it was now neat, except for some stray moving boxes of odds 'n' ends that no one had the heart to throw out.

Next to an antique wardrobe, along one wall, a tall shelf housed her library of books. On the opposite side, a matching dressing table with a tilting mirror now had pride of place, with her favourite framed photos. In the middle, a black enamel frame with a photograph of a young April and her Nan; taken one summer in her grandmother's garden under the colossal tree, thick with leaves.

April watched the icy-blue sky, desperate to conquer the last few dreary clouds. Sunday morning, no work, she mused, stretched and pushed her hands on the polished headboard, sinking her deeper into the warm pillow.

Work was in her parents' antique shop — their retirement plan. So, it would do until she decided where life would take her, and she had to admit she loved it.

April hauled herself out of bed. Then, after dressing in a sweater and jeans, headed for the kitchen.

'Morning, sweetheart, how'd you sleep?'

'Morning Mum, cosy didn't really wanna get up,' she replied, yawned deeply and grabbed three mugs.

'Will you call your dad for breakfast? He's downstairs with a box of stuff he bought at the auction,' Julia asked as she reached for the breakfast plates.

'Dads in the shop already?'

'It was so busy yesterday; he didn't get time to do it. So, he thought it was better to spend half-hour early this morning. Although I must say, we've had an incredible response. We didn't think we were going to be so busy so quickly. And, with Christmas just around the corner, it couldn't be better.' Julia flipped crispy bacon onto each plate, then cracked eggs into the hot frying pan.

Descending the staircase, April entered the antique shop from behind the old mahogany shop counter. She glimpsed her father, standing in front of a bookcase near the shop door. He perched on a wooden crate with shredded newspaper by his feet.

'Morning April, breakfast ready? I'm almost done... the last one; there we go. I'm pleased with them. Candles are *back in vogue,* so your mother tells me.' Michael placed the last candlestick neatly on a shelf next to its identical porcelain twin. 'And if not... I'll be blaming her,' he chuckled. Then, switching off the light, they headed up to the kitchen for breakfast as the coffee aroma wafted down the stairs to greet them.

~

April sat on the sofa researching a date of a bowl from its maker's mark, flicking through the pages of a book on 18th-century silver. The peal of the church bell chimed through the house, so loud, it seemed futile owning the grandfather clock stood beside her. Centre stage, it kept a watchful eye over the hi-tech gadgets of modernity — the room a juxtaposition of contemporary and antiquities. Finally, April closed the book, resting the bowl on top leaving them on the coffee table. Sunday Lunch with Nan; her heart warmed.

~

Michael reached for the knocker, the brass lion's eyes level with his own. The door opened.

'Quickly, come on in before you let all the warmth out,' Sarah said, ushering them through.

April admired the holly wreath as she began to close the door. The silk leaves glistened with droplets of morning frost, and the crystal berries glittered in the sunlight, framing the brass knocker in greenery.

The festivities had cast their annual magic. A giant Christmas tree stood ceremoniously in the far corner, bushy, full, and thoroughly out of proportion with its top branches sprawled across the ceiling. With the scent of fresh pine needles and heirloom adornments, her heart soared. Near the tree sat an upright piano, so close April imagined it almost impossible to play without being jabbed by stray branches.

April ran her hands over the white linen runner that lay neatly across the top. Her fingertips tingled, darting shudders up her arms that reached the nape of her neck in a frenzied shiver. Her mind dazed, it swam in a dark mire of mixed flashes.

Memories?

The room spun; April clutched the smooth wood of the piano, leaning her arm across the top to steady herself.

Then a voice. Inside, and yet not inside her head whispered in her ear. *My love.*

She shuddered, stepping backwards, hitting the tree, causing it to sway, the glass baubles clinking; a sharp branch stabbed her cheek.

April rubbed her eyes, pressing the heel of her palm to block out the visions. Swirls of blinding colour, vibrant yet blurred, with no clear definitions. And the pain.

As sudden as it arrived, the pain vanished, leaving a peculiar sensation that draped her like a veil. Akin to pulling back a stage curtain, the recollection of singing carols at this piano danced vividly before her eyes. Unable to recall how or when, yet the sensation was unmistakable.

She was standing beside the piano, the spicy taste of warm wine on her lips.

April clenched her eyes tight, desperate to summon the memory in greater detail. Instead, it weakened and faded, leaving her dazed, with a thick, dreadful feeling of loneliness — a sensation of loss.

Deep breaths.

Deep breaths.

April staggered to the settee, dropping her head, resting it on her knees. She rarely got a headache, let alone a migraine. That must be it.

Darling, are you coming?

'I'll be a minute…' she called back. Then, as she raised her head, listening, it slowly dawned that the voice was in her head.

Still giddy, April carefully made her way to the dining room, gripping the door frame then wall as she went. She passed a half-moon hall table, where a citrus scent attacked her nose, oranges and satsumas. Next to the fruit neatly sat a festive ornament, a frosted glass Angel. She had played with the trinket as a girl. April carefully leaned against the table, dizziness still threatening to take her legs from under her. Slowly she passed the staircase to where a matching table stood, including another fruit bowl, this one with apples. However, it was the photo frame that stole her attention. Clearing the muddy mire from her mind, she stared closer.

The silver frame was inlaid with mother-of-pearl and ornate scrollwork, rising to an intricate bow at the top between the two oval apertures. A row of silver beads encircled each photo. Beautiful, she thought.

This house was untouched by time; it had always been its enchantment. April knew every piece of furniture, book, and painting, having studied them all closely as a child.

However, not these, these photos she had never seen.

April paused there a moment, delving into her memory, impatient to recall. The two young women within the images were beautiful; she was positive she would have remembered them. Both, in turn, sat upon a light-coloured wicker chair with a scrolled fan back, around the age of eighteen or nineteen, surely no older than her. The younger had dark hair and wore a light dress. The other, slightly older, was fair. From the depths of her memory, she recalled having seen the fairer woman before but much older than she looked here.

Sarah appeared at the dining room threshold.

'We were wondering where you'd got to. Dinner's almost ready,' she beckoned.

For a moment, April was motionless, her eyes closed, still perplexed by the photos and the dazed memories of the piano. The was something else, too, another memory or thought that clung to her ribs until her heart stung.

Come, sit next to me, my dearest.

CHAPTER FOUR

As delicious as lunch was, roasted lamb with mint sauce, followed by homemade apple pie, April spent most of the time pushing it around her plate, mindlessly lining up peas along the gilt edge of the china. Her mind had wandered off into the front room with those whispers that still lingered in her ear. Julia cleared the table while April was lost in thought. Then, she followed her family back into the front room.

Michael sat on the settee beside the fire, Julia on the other under the window next to April; the velvety fabric and warm glow of the open fire made her mother drowsy. Julia puffed a gold cushion behind her and settled into it, closing her eyes. April glanced at her father, who'd dozed off as soon as getting comfortable.

'Nan, that photo frame on the hall table?' April shuffled her way to the edge of the settee, taking advantage of the quiet room.

'Yes, I know the one,' Sarah replied quietly.

'I don't remember seeing it before. Where did it come from? Do you know who they are?' April spurted, almost waking her parents.

'One thing at a time,' mouthed Sarah. 'Come with me.' She rose from her winged chair.

April, already on her feet, followed into the hallway. Sarah took the frame from the table and walked to the foot of the staircase while April stood in the doorway, curiously watching.

'There are some things I had put aside for you. I found them a few weeks ago.' Sarah said with a creased brow. 'I didn't know they were there, not a clue, it's the strangest thing,' she sighed, shaking her head.

'What are they?'

'I'll show you.'

April followed up the staircase, climbed the patterned carpet as they passed panelled doors, paintings and gilded mirrors on the immaculate papered walls.

Something glinted at the corner of her eye — only small — but it snatched her attention. April paused on the turn of the stairs. A gilt frame hung at eye level. Swift defined brushstrokes swept the canvas in a surging tint of blue; the sea and dawn sky blushed with pink. It made her heart hurt, and her eyes weep. April felt the passion and fury of the seascape, the command of the waves, the forever vastness of the sky. Yet, in the foreground, the fresh newness of the grassy dunes, so crisp, she felt her hand reach out to take a blade of grass. Her fingers hung in the air, their tips skimming the canvas.

She shook, first her hand, then her body trembled with a deep sadness. Inside her, an inconceivable familiarity tore at her heart. Then, as her eyes closed tightly to stop the tears, her fingers began to move as if holding a brush. She swept it through the air, great sweeps of colour in her mind, muted blues, greys, and flashes of white, then her mind was black, darker than night, as dense and endless as a hollow soul.

'April?'

With a start, she opened her eyes, the painting filling her view. Her grandmother stood a step up, her hand on her shoulder to steady her.

'I found that too,' Sarah said, nodding to herself, her hand patting April's back. 'Come on.'

That painting.

The words never materialised; they hovered somewhere behind her lips. Eager to look away, she stared down at her feet, following her grandmother.

Sarah stopped at the foot of a narrow staircase leading to the attic. They climbed the last few steps. April trailed behind through the small door. The space opened into a large room with small windows set in the roofline, funnels of afternoon glow cast to the floorboards. But it was the shadows that drew her in as if tugged forward by a beckoning hand.

This was the one place in the house April had never been.

'Let's sit over here.' Sarah pointed to the large gold chaise lounge near the doorway, putting the photo frame down on the padded seat.

April sat, her hands running over the silky upholstery, her fingertips skimming the silver frame, while her eyes never left the far corner drenched in darkness.

Sarah lifted a box from a battered tea chest, bringing it into the dusky light. Aprils' eyes flitted to the small leather case; the low sun's golden rays shone on its surface.

'Here it is,' announced Sarah pacing back to the chaise.

April pulled herself from the shadows, daring herself not to look back. Next to where they sat was a disturbing elephant foot umbrella stand. April hadn't ever seen it in the house but remembered a picture of her late grandfather, standing in a dignified pose, holding a walking cane next to the distasteful object. Sarah sat beside her, the leather case on her lap. Getting darker by the minute, she reached behind and pulled a tassel cord on a barley twist floor lamp, topped with a pink shade.

'I was up here having a tidy and found this in that tea chest. The frame and that painting were in there, tucked under everything else,' Sarah said, gesturing to the wooden chest in the corner.

That corner. April ran her fingers over the back of her neck, then her hands down her jeans to her knees. She sat hugging them a moment, rocking gently. Then, a pain, so deep inside, it had no defined place, swamped her.

'Who were they, Nan?' she said through gritted teeth. The importance of the question left a mark on her tongue, hollowness in her stomach, where the pain settled. April felt that inside she should know the answer, that it was clear.

'You don't look well; this can wait for another day,' Sarah said, her words soft.

'No. No, I need to know. I'm okay; it's nothing,' April lied.

'One of them is my grandmother, so your great-great-grandmother.'

April nodded, 'and the other?'

Sarah shrugged.

'Can I have a look? I'll be careful.'

'Of course,' Sarah carefully handed her the case. 'Come down when you're ready. I'll put the kettle on for a pot of tea. And I'll find you something for that, headache.' Sarah slowly stood up, rubbing her back. 'Don't be too long, mind, I don't like how pale you are. You need to eat something.'

'I'm okay. Honestly, it's nothing,' April insisted. Sarah gave a soft nod and headed down the stairs.

It had nothing to do with not eating dinner, and no matter how she tried to wave it away, Nan knew it too. The air had altered; the house felt different today. As soon as she had closed the front door, April had felt... What had she felt? Someone, something? Memories? No. It must be that — a migraine. She had had one once; it had stopped her in her tracks, a desperate aversion to light and pain so intense she had felt her skull split in two. But this pain was not in her head. April pressed her fingers to her temples. No, this pain was entirely different.

Leaning back, looking up into the lampshade, April clenched her eyes.

I am here.

Her eyes darted open. She was alone; she knew she was. April heard Nan shuffle down in the kitchen, the water running in the sink, the click of the kettle. But she had heard it; she was adamant. She shook her head, rolled her shoulders and turned her attention to the case.

The leather was a rich tan, the surface mottled with age. April pushed with her thumb, sliding the old clasp, flicking it free and the lid lifted. On the top was a white handkerchief embroidered with pink roses and the initials ERW. Folding it, she placed it beside her on the chaise. Neatly wrapped in a linen cloth were three silver items, a large hairbrush, an ivory-toothed comb and a hand mirror. All were a little tarnished with age, though the simple swirl of engraving was still visible and the same three initials.

At the bottom of the old case lay a wooden box, the size of a shoebox with marquetry inlay of coloured woods and mother-of-pearl. Dad had one similar in the shop but a lot smaller and nowhere near as intricate.

She turned the box, the front face towards her. A silver lock on the front sat empty, devoid of a key. April rummaged in the bottom of the leather case, but no joy. She tugged at the lid, slid a fingernail gently along the seal between top and base. It would not give; the box was locked.

April gathered up the silver frame, replacing the items one by one into the case. She recognised her now, the fairer of the two, her great-great-grandmother. She was beautiful. But the other?

April's eyes darted back to the far corner. It grew darker, denser. Eager to pinpoint a movement, a sound, any reason for the swathe of anxious energy that crept its long fingers up her spine, threatening to strangle her. She was transfixed, sewn to the very fabric of the chaise, unable to move for fear of ripping the stitches.

I am here.

An icy chill slowly snaked the air, touching every part of her body. April pressed her palm to her chest, hoping to ease her rapid heartbeat. Cold wisps tangled about her planted feet like knotted tree roots — she could not move. The lightbulb hissed, crackled, flickered rapidly, plunging the attic into soft darkness, with only the dim afternoon light seeping in. Quickly adjusting to the dark, April leaned forward, eager to focus on the shadows. Then, a distant echo, a voice, soft at first, then building, whispered from the darkness.

Do not leave me.

She needed to move, to run. Yet, whatever was telling her to leave was also keeping her there — compelled to stay — an invitation.

The whispers stopped, making her ears ring, and plunged April into a deafening stillness that reverberated off the rafters. Then, as if drowning in the silence and pain, it threatened to rip at her insides again.

Her heart thudded erratically — faster and faster, it pounded, fit to burst from her ribcage. Her breathing grew heavy. The churning pain in the pit of her stomach leapt to her chest. She tried desperately not to panic as the inexplicable feeling pumped through her veins. April's eyes wandered the room looking for a logical cause, her gaze intent on the dark corner.

Her body shuddered, and her skin tingled with a swathe of goosebumps as April took a breath. She took another, deeper this time, drawing the frigid air into her lungs. Then, something curious. Her nostrils grasped at a scent, a sweet fragrance, a delicate, floral perfume. Bewitching and bewildering. Where was it coming from?

In the mounting darkness of the attic was a glow. A flicker. For what seemed minutes, it danced and darted, quivering in the bitter air, gradually becoming brighter. Then, as quickly as it had arrived, it was gone. The attic room was still, eerily silent. April held her breath, not daring to move.

Gradually twisting and coiling, the air grew misty. The old floorboard swirled with a thin white mist as the fog rose from the floor. Steadily it grew defined, curled with more substance into a shape — a vague willowy blur of a figure.

Paralysed, April watched.

She stared hard at the hallucination, amazed and stunned but strangely no longer afraid. Her fear had drifted, swept up by the mist, dispersed into the ether. All that remained was a female form.

April gasped. That unknown woman from the photo now stood before her — an impossible vision in a long dress and dark hair that bore a translucent gleam. She did not move or speak, yet life shone from her eyes. And she smiled.

Clutching the frame, April felt herself drifting, her vision blurred. Her mind was dizzy, light-headed. April could hear whispering memories worrying in the corners of her mind, but with her head too heavy to steady, she swayed, and her eyes drooped. She was gone, floating. No, she was falling. Down and down, further she fell until the *thud*. She hit the bottom.

~

With an impulsive breath, fragranced air filled her lungs. Balmy summer sun warmed her cheeks. A moment passed. Slowly and tentatively, April gathered her bearings

The sun shone through April's tightly gripped eyelids. Cautiously opening them, she saw a garden. Her grandmother's garden, but not how she knew it. It had an abundance of flowers in full bloom, and where she stood, sweet-smelling lavender. In total dismay, April thought of having died and gone to heaven, a heaven that felt like home.

She scanned the vista, standing on the top step. From here, she could see the whole scene.

The garden was blooming; borders of rose bushes in shades of pink and flourishing lavender shrubs paved the way deep into the grounds of the Victorian house. The far corner of the garden, a shaded area under the large tree that spread its boughs across the grassy walled enclosure, casting a vast dappled shadow, under which settled a scrolled fan backed wicker chair.

She became aware of whistling. Anxiously, she watched her feet as she walked down the steps, not sure whether she could move at all. A middle-aged gentleman, bald and round, entered her view. He carried a large leather case. Transfixed to the second step, unable to move, she watched in astonishment as the man assembled his photographic equipment.

She stood in silent contemplation. What was happening? She knew where she *believed* she was, but everything was wrong. Lavender and roses? It was December. Nothing made sense.

'Oh, do come along; the gentleman is ready for you.' A man's voice boomed through the warm air as a female reply came from deep inside the house.

'Please wait, Father. I shall return momentarily!'

April swung round to see an attractive middle-aged gentleman with white hair and moustache in a light-coloured suit. A gold pocket watch hung from his waistcoat. April stood glued to the spot. He gracefully stepped down into the garden. But, to her dismay, he seemed oblivious to her presence.

'Ah, Captain Warner, good morning. Everything is ready when the young ladies are,' announced the photographer loudly.

'Ah, yes, Mr Brown, so I see. My daughters shall be ready in just a few moments.'

'It surely is a good day for it, Sir. It sure is....'

'Yes, yes,' interrupted the captain, waving a dismissive hand.

The photographer went back to rummaging in the bottom of his bag before standing upright next to the captain. Then, taking a deep breath, he filled his waist-coated chest in the hope of giving himself some air of authority but falling short of the task.

April turned on her heels to gaze back into the house. Heavy lace curtains swung gently in the summer breeze, through which she caught sight of a female figure in a delicate lace gown, high at the neck, with her auburn hair elegantly up, wisps caressing her face.

'I could not have the photograph taken without this,' exclaimed the young lady, holding a cameo brooch.

The captain was now in conversation, despite his tedium, with the photographer over the weather. He seemed unaware of the young lady's comment, simply gesturing to her to quicken into the garden.

April edged as far to the boundary of the step as she dared, pushing her way into the lavender, trying not to sway and tumble down the remaining steps. She steadied herself as the young woman drifted by; she too made no acknowledgement. But as she passed, a sweet scent lingered under April's nose. That same perfume.

She swayed, giddy and woozy. Once again, she felt the frigid chill on her cheeks as she drew in a deep breath. Her hands shook from her tight grip as she clutched the frame tightly.

'April, darling, wake up, wake up!' She opened her eyes slowly to see her mother, 'Are you okay?'

April nodded, her head threatening to fall and roll off her shoulders.

'You must have fallen asleep, sweetheart. Do you fancy a cuppa now?'

April sat up, debating this, as she looked over at the tea chests. The room was black; the lamp was still out, and the only light glowed from the hallway down the narrow staircase. The garden and its ghostly occupants were gone.

'A coffee please,' she replied, rising to her feet, steadying herself on her mother's arm.

'Are you feeling all right?' Julia said, cautiously looking her over. 'Your nan said you came over poorly, so I came up and found you asleep.'

'I just need a drink, don't worry!' April reassured.

~

When April took her usual seat in the front room, no one spoke for a few moments. She watched, digesting their faces and expressions, savouring the normality. How could they be so calm after what she had just seen? Sublime ignorance.

April turned, looked at the tea laid out on the table, thankful for the afternoon tradition, and reached for her coffee. She sipped, lost in thought, savouring each mouthful, allowing conversation to drift off, swallowed by the walls.

Sarah rose from her chair and lifted the tea tray.

'Nan, let me do that!' April stood up, taking the tray before she could argue.

'All right, you can help me wash up.'

'Nan?' April hesitated. 'I'm not sure what happened earlier. I felt a little strange in the attic.' What she wanted to say was she believed she'd seen a ghost.

April stood at the kitchen sink, carefully washing the delicate china teacups, trying to find a way to broach the subject without sounding crazy.

'When you say you felt strange? What do you mean? I've also experienced very odd feelings since I found the case. Nothing I can be certain of. It may be my imagination.' She said this in such a way; it seemed she could read April's mind.

'Have you seen? Err... what I mean, do you...' April couldn't finish her sentence; she felt too ridiculous thinking it, let alone saying it.

'The marquetry box, yes, it is lovely, and before you ask, no, I don't know where the key is!' replied Sarah.

The marquetry box: she had forgotten about that.

'Yes, the box. So, you don't know where the key is?'

'No, as I said, I only found the case a few weeks ago. I'd never seen it before then. I've never seen photographs of my grandmother that young before, either. Wasn't she lovely?'

April knew this was going nowhere fast; she could almost taste the continuing circles of conversation on her tongue. The only thing she could think to do was to have another look through the box.

'Nan, any chance I can take the case home? I'll be careful?'

'Do you know? I think that's a splendid idea,' she smiled, her expression calm and clear. 'Shall I get it for you?'

'It's okay,' April started. 'I'll come with you.'

April followed her up the stairs to the attic door; it was still open after her abrupt exit.

'Oh, I left the lamp on, Nan. Sorry, I didn't think it...' April stood, looking for an explanation, hoping her grandmother had one. 'I thought the bulb had blown...'

'Never mind, there's no harm done.' April tentatively followed her grandmother over to the chaise. The old leather case sat on the floor, the silver frame on the gold upholstery. Sarah lifted it and placed it next to the box at the bottom of the case, then reached across and pulled the cord on the lamp. The attic room was dark once more.

'It's quite heavy, Nan. Let me carry it.'

April timidly took the case, unsure what effect it would have. For an instant, she stood rigid. Nothing: April analysed it for a second, just a box of bits and bobs. What had she expected?

They headed down the stairs, closing the door behind them.

Kissing her grandmother goodnight, she walked the two-minute journey home, wandering behind her parents, unaware of her movements, occupied by her thoughts. She climbed the staircase to her bedroom, closing her door behind her, encasing herself in her protective shell. Then placed the leather case on the floor beside her bed and undressed, continually watching it.

April drew her bedroom curtains and lay cocooned in her bed. All that occupied her mind was the thought of the young woman, her ghost, and her life form. Yet, all of that was impossible. Ghosts are not real. This wasn't a novel or a movie. She had been dreaming, surely? The whole thing, some strange concoction her mind had conjured. It must be the migraine.

April reached inside the case, taking out the silver frame, staring deep inside the photographs, studying them. There, worn on the high-necked dress, was the cameo brooch. April had seen it.

Unable to look anymore, her eyes stung. April closed them and drifted.

June 1900 — The smooth, black ink noted the date onto the back of the two photographs. Next, carefully, he pressed the rolling blotter to seal them, locking in the memories. Meticulously, he inserted the pictures in turn into position, stood the frame on the writing desk, viewed his masterpiece — the silver frame, with its intricate inlay of shimmering iridescent mother-of-pearl.

The captain rose from his leather chair and with military precision, replaced his pen onto its rest and flicked the lid of the inkwell. The desk overlooked the garden. A red velvet settee sat on either side of the window, flooded with light spilling through the large sash. High shelves reached the ceiling, holding leather-bound volumes, books on art, poetry and history. Between them, bookends of framed memories, seaside trips and lost loved ones.

The captain left his study. As he reached a half-moon table in the hall, he cast another admiring glance at his daughters, then lovingly positioned the frame pride of place on the table's polished surface.

April awoke with the church bells ringing in her ears, striking her skull in waves. Groggily her eyes roamed her bed; on her pillow lay the photo frame. She held it close and remembered her dream. She drifted with her mind wandering through the rooms of her vision, her grandmother's rooms, so alike and familiar but so wrong, everything laced with another era.

The bell struck again. Opening her lazy eyes, she heaved herself up and opened her bedroom curtains, allowing the morning sun to seek every part of the room behind her. Bright but bitterly cold, frost clung in natural sunburst flakes, decorating the windowpane like a gift. April held the frame in the light and looked at her great-great-grandmother, a bracelet around her wrist. Then her eyes travelled once again to admire the cameo brooch. April pressed her forehead to the glass, expelling her drowsy thoughts as she recalled Nan's jewellery box. As a child, she had been allowed to admire the heirloom pieces. Had there been the cameo or the charm bracelet?

April turned, leaned back against the window, clutching her stomach; the ache was back. Yet with it a dark feeling of emptiness.

CHAPTER FIVE

The town bustled with shoppers. The Antique Shop burst with customers; the family worked flat out to cater for the stampede. April had not allowed herself to think about her dreams or the ghost — if indeed that is what it was. Though now, as the festivities had crept in like the ghost of Christmas present, vibrant and jolly, April allowed herself the same joy.

April lifted the lion doorknocker as the door opened.

'There you are, Little One. I've been looking forward to this for days,' Sarah ushered April in.

Sarah wrapped her long scarf around her neck as April noticed the emerald brooch on her coat lapel.

'Nan, when I was little, I remember a jewellery box?'

'Ah, yes. You used to sit on your mum's lap in front of the mirror, trying on all the pieces. One was never enough. You had to have everything on at the same time.' Sarah beamed as she tucked the scarf under her collar.

'Can I have a look again, later? I don't have to go back to work; we've got the entire day together.'

'What a wonderful idea,' Sarah beamed and tucked her arm under her granddaughters, pulling her close.

The bitter air chilled their faces as they eased through the humming crowds, ticking gifts off the list.

'I have one last thing, something for Mum, any ideas?' April asked as she tucked the folded paper back in her pocket. 'She is always the hardest to buy for.'

'I'm not quite sure. How about jewellery,' Sarah smiled, rubbing her hands together, 'I know the perfect shop.'

Arm in arm, they meandered the busy streets. The Abbey Gate was visible from the top of the road; it stood majestically against the icy sky. The chorus of carol singers travelled the air that hung with the aroma of hot roasting chestnuts. Halfway down the street, they reached the jewellers. Mounted on a wrought bracket hung a clock, proudly over the door. April gazed up; the winter sky flashed from icy white to vivid blue.

Gripping the deep window frame, April squinted. A young man in a flat cap stood at the top of a wooden ladder, polishing the clock face.

'Be careful up there…' April called as a young couple bustled past her, heading straight for the ladder. 'No!'

'Whatever is it?' Sarah clutched her elbow. 'What's the matter?'

She had no answer. April could do nothing but watch the couple walk through the ladder, the rungs vanishing, melting into their coats, then appearing again, solid.

The young man in the flat cap frantically rubbed the last of the roman numerals, pushed the cloth into his back pocket, readjusted his braces and carefully descended the wooden struts.

'There you go,' he politely said to a portly gentleman with a large moustache, who stood within the shop doorway. The young man took a battered pocket watch from his trousers and flicked open the case.

'Yes, perfect time. Two minutes past the hour, precisely.'

'That's an excellent job. Yes, a job well done,' replied the shopkeeper as he paced backwards into the cobbled road in the middle of the street. The jeweller admired his new clock, fists on hips, his paunchy belly before him.

April looked back up at the wrought iron bracket, the sky wintry and icy again. The clock had aged, the face dappled with time. Stunned and confused, April stood mute.

'I think we should go inside, see if they have somewhere you can sit down. You look white as a sheet. Heavens, you look like you've seen a ghost.' Sarah pulled April to the doorway. 'Excuse us, please,' she said, brushing past the young couple.

The lights dazzled inside the shop, glinting off reflective surfaces and mirrors. April shielded her eyes and leant carefully against the glass counter.

'Excuse me; my granddaughter is feeling unwell. Do you have a chair so she could sit a moment, please?'

April heard the words and the eager reply as Sarah ushered to sit on a plush chair at the end of the shop. She remained sat, sipping a glass of water that had been thrust in her hand. The feeling had finally eased. The same dizzy sensation that veiled her senses to a dull glow and yet at the same time cast a stark glare to her vision. Like she was looking at the sun through a lace curtain.

April finished the last of the water, carefully putting the empty glass on the long counter next to her. Nan was busy chatting to the jeweller whilst casting a covert glance every few seconds her way. April nodded and stood.

'How about those?' Sarah's finger hovered over the glass, pointing to a pair of drop earrings. 'Your mum loves amethysts, what do you think?'

'Yes, they're lovely.'

'Good. Thank you, we'll have those please?' Sarah nodded to the jeweller. 'We need to get you home,' She mouthed, squeezing April's hand.

The shop was brimming with customers now, filing in and out through the small doorway. Panic had started in her cheeks, flushing her face hot until it burned. Suffocating, the other patrons were closing in on her. She needed to get out.

'Nan, I'll wait outside if you don't mind. I...' the words were muffled as she tried to catch her breath.

April clutched the edge of the counter to steady herself, stared down through the glass, desperate to focus her blurred vision. Beneath her reflection, silver hip flasks, letter openers and fountain pens hazed in and out of view. April's ears felt numb; only the pounding of her heartbeat echoed through her skull.

Deep breath. In. Out. In. Out.

Gradually, careful not to hyperventilate, April slowed her breathing, rolled her head, and eased her shoulders. She opened her eyes. The silver items were gone. In their place were brooches pinned to a green velvet tray. White knuckled, she gripped the counter.

'Yes, I must agree, that one is delightful. An excellent choice if I may say so.'

The air hitched in her throat. She looked up.

A portly jeweller stood on the other side of the counter, beaming from beneath his moustache. He reached down, took out the green velvet tray. April hadn't seen the antique pieces there before, not that she'd had much opportunity to have a good look, but she was adamant that tray had not been there. The jeweller removed a brooch from the bottom.

'This one is solid silver and set with Wedgwood, a blue Jasperware cameo. It is extremely individual, as you can see, with the flourish of silver foliage surrounding the cameo, perfect for a special birthday gift.' The jeweller offered the brooch in his plump hand.

April paced back a step, staring at the proffered brooch.

'What do you think, darling?'

Shaking her head, April turned to her side. It wasn't her grandmother. She knew it wasn't, but still, her mind struggled to grasp it.

A tall gentleman stood close. Impeccably dressed in a beige summer suit, dark hair and well-groomed, she could feel his body heat. April blinked, rubbed her hand around the inside of her collar. His green eyes drilled into hers as he smiled. An unexplained familiarity lay within the handsome features. He nodded, beamed, turning to the jeweller as he took the brooch.

'I must agree, it is perfect. Wedgwood, you say?' The gentleman studied the silver design, checking the security of the clasp. 'Such a lovely piece. I think it will do beautifully. Would you like to take a closer look?' He turned back to April, offering the brooch.

April's legs crumpled. She closed her eyes tight, gripping the counter; her fingertips drained of blood and numbed under pressure. Then, slowly steadying herself, she daringly opened her eyes. The antique brooches gradually transfigured back to the modern silver items, reflected in the glare of the contemporary lights.

'April? April?' Her grandmother's words, faint, faded in and out. She gathered her bearings to find herself back on the plush chair at the end of the shop.

'I'm feeling a lot better now. Thank you, just a little faint.' April smiled at the jeweller and turned to her grandmother.

'We are going home, right now,' Sarah ordered. 'We've finished shopping anyhow. And you need something to eat and a good sleep by the look of you.'

'Nan, I'm all right now, honestly.'

'Thank you very much for your help,' Sarah said as she swept April out through the door.

The cold air hit her square in the chest, but she couldn't help but look up at the clock. All normal, as it should be.

April took her grandmother's arm, and they both headed back home. The carollers were standing around the Christmas tree on the hill, crowds gathered. Sarah kept a tight grip on her arm. Neither spoke a word. April could not remove the image of the gentleman, his green eyes still drilling through her.

CHAPTER SIX

'I'll go warm the pot,' Sarah said as she draped her coat and scarf over the high back of her chair.

April nodded, unable of more and slumped onto the settee. The gold cushion behind her head, cradling it as she sat spellbound by the tree lights and the amber glow of the fire. April tried to soothe herself with thoughts of Christmas, the simple delights of caramel-filled chocolates and sticky dates, anything, to release her mind from the shopping trip. But, no matter how she battled, she lost.

What was happening?

Where was the lateral thinker she'd always been, the mind that relied on facts, evidence? Now, she felt her soul had split; part of her was drifting, weightless, floating like a leaf on a cool breeze. Angry with herself, April stood and paced the floor, her feet, one after the other, following an invisible line, a timeline she had somehow crossed.

April had stood in that jewellery shop as if it wasn't the first time. And those green eyes — she had felt — well, she couldn't begin to fathom how she had felt.

She came to a sudden halt, dropped back to the settee, her hands worrying themselves in her lap. The man with the green eyes, she couldn't decide if he seemed familiar. In those few moments, something had stirred.

She was just tired, had allowed her subconscious to play tricks; it was the book she'd read on the town's history. Yes, it was a picture she had seen. That was the most obvious explanation unless, of course, she was going mad.

April gasped, dug her fingernails into her palms, watched as her nail beds whitened, then inspected the eight neat arc imprints on each hand. How could this mean anything other than she was going mad? She rested her head back against the settee, trying to calm down.

The distant crackle of the logs on the fire began relaxing her. The tick of the mantle clock's hypnotic chant deep inside her consciousness made it impossible to keep her eyelids open. April drifted.

'Darling, will you come outside? Some fresh air will do you good; you have been sitting in this room all afternoon,' came a voice from the doorway.

Annabelle raised her head from the book. 'In a while, I am comfortable in here. Please, let me finish,' she lifted the book a touch. 'Then I shall join you all,' she said in a sweet but resolute tone which she followed with a smile. The man nodded acquiescently. Not saying another word, he turned on his heels and silently closed the door behind him.

Annabelle sat on her favoured velvet settee beside the window, the heady scent of her mothers' roses floating in through the sash. The light was softer here, gentler, kinder for reading. Disturbed, having lost her place, she now closed the book, holding it to her chest while she lounged, watching the billow of the drapes. A gentle murmur of distant voices crept in.

'Annabelle,' the sweet chant carried on the breeze.

Annabelle rose, replaced the book on the shelf and headed back to the open window. Her blonde hair whipped her fair cheek. She brushed it away so that the sun could warm her face. Today the garden was bustling with her family.

'Oh, do come along, are you joining us?'

'I am on my way,' she called through the open sash. 'Patience is a virtue, sister,' she muttered to herself.

'I heard that.' Emily stood at the bottom of the stone steps, hands on hips, her auburn hair amber in the afternoon light. She wore a blue dress with lace sleeves, high at the neck, sat a Wedgwood cameo brooch. Smiling, her sister turned and walked back down the garden.

Annabelle laughed, 'good; you should not be so impatient.' Then left the study and followed the laughter down the lavender lined stone steps and into the garden.

'Mary has made some lemonade, and I am beating Richard at chess!' Emily announced.

Emily and Richard sat opposite one another, with the old family chess set between them; its slightly discoloured ivory pieces mid-game. With a face devoured by concentration, Richard deliberated his next move. Emily scanned the chessboard, looked at her sister, raised her eyebrows and beamed, with a suppressed giggle.

'Your husband is becoming increasingly frustrated. He was expecting to win, as usual.'

Annabelle reclined on a chair under the tree canopy, her eyelids closed, soaking up the warmth as she relaxed in the mottled shade. Birdsong travelled, lulling and hypnotic.

'Annabelle, how are you feeling this afternoon?' Her father descended the garden. The captain sat next to her, then reached for her hand.

'My dear, it is good to see you outside. The air will do you good.'

'I wish you would not worry so.' She squeezed his hand in reassurance.

'Both you and your sister are my most precious things. I could not bear to...' A solemn look came over his face, an expression she knew.

'I am resting. I do little else,' she assured again.

Patting his hand, Annabelle pulled hers away and closed her eyes. In truth, she had no desire for the conversation to find her mother, as it always did. Annabelle was four the last time she saw her mother. It had been early June; Annabelle lost her mother and gained her sister — a cruel twist.

Her father restated his concern with a sigh.

'Please, everything is going to be fine. When the baby is born, Richard and I shall be a complete family, and nothing is going to take that away.'

Emily squealed and jumped to her feet, her face a picture of exhilaration.

'Well, I never; your sister has finally beaten me. But, Emily, I did think you could have won before now,' Richard said sarcastically.

'You are just sore that you lost. Father has been teaching me.' Emily danced around the table, then gracefully sat next to Annabelle.

'My dearest, how are you feeling? You gave us such a fright yesterday.' Emily's tone was serious now.

'Please, not you, too.'

'Would you like me to fetch your book? Or I can read to you, as you did for me when I was little?' Emily clasped her sister's hand.

'I am happy enough sitting here.' Annabelle glanced over to where Richard was resetting the chessboard.

'Belle, how about a game?' Richard balanced the chess set on the folding table as he carried it over.

'I am not sure I am a worthy opponent for you, Richard. Perhaps you would rather a re-match with Emily to regain your title?'

'I see your condition has not affected your sense of humour.' Richard lowered the table onto the grass and knelt before her.

'Belle, is there anything I can get you?' he said, gently placing his hand on her stomach.

'I shall go and see Mary, and we shall have some tea.' Emily jumped to her feet and strolled up the stone steps to the house, followed by her father. Richard got to his feet and sat on the chair beside his wife.

'To think, I shall be a father,' Richard mouthed as he gently rubbed her stomach.

'You shall be a good father. I know it.'

'And you, a mother. I am sure that you were born to be so,' he paused, smoothed his large hand over her hair. 'You are a mother to Emily.'

'Even when I was young and no more than a child. It is my purpose deep down.'

'Belle, you have far more purpose than just to be a mother,' Richard paused.

'You do not understand. To me, it means everything,' Annabelle sighed; her heart ached at the thought. 'I do not expect you to understand.'

'My Belle, please forgive me; all I meant was...'

'It is me, who should apologise,' she shook her head.

'Well, now you should be resting.'

'I do not do anything to put our baby in harm's way.' She closed her eyes, lifting her face to the sun, absorbing, recharging with its energy.

With a sudden wail, she gripped Richard's hand, clutching at her lower abdomen.

'Whatever is it?' She did not answer. 'Please look at me. What can I do?'

She looked away, hands tightly clenched and doubled over, her blonde hair draped across his arm.

'Belle! Annabelle! Please, darling, what is it?' Richard pleaded.

Annabelle pulled herself upright, her pain-stricken face clear in the sunshine. Then, slowly, he took his hand from her belly and stood.

'Richard, please! Please do not leave me!'

'We must get the doctor quickly! The doctor, get the doctor!' Richard shouted up into the house as he dashed across the grass. Within seconds, Emily rushed down the garden steps and was at her sister's side.

'Father is getting the doctor. Annabelle, everything is going to be fine. I promise,' Emily said, her voice strained.

Running down the steps, Richard returned with a blanket. Wrapped Annabelle in it, whisked her up in his arms and carried her quickly into the house.

She closed her eyes, too much to bear; the pain blackened her thoughts. Everyone became immaterial. This misery was all too consuming; it pulled her into her thoughts, lost memories, forgotten ones that had fallen between the floorboards, and those she had tucked away safely.

Mother — she was holding her hand. *Stay with me*; she beseeched, d*o not leave me again.*

~

The doctor reached the bottom step, a tired expression on his aged face; he took a deep breath and entered the dining room with his bag in hand.

'How is she?' Richard sat at the table. Not wanting to hear the reply, he covered his eyes with the heel of his hands, long fingers brushing the front of his dark hair.

'I am sorry. There was nothing I could do; it just was not meant to be…' he paused, arranging his words. 'It may affect future pregnancies. For now, she needs rest, Richard. She should stay here for a while; I do not want her moved. I shall check on her again in the morning,' he nodded, stepping further into the room. 'I have given her something for the pain; it will let her sleep if nothing else,' he said softly. 'She is strong.' Dr Hickson placed his hand on Richard's shoulder.

Emily stood cradled in her father's arms, her sobs muffled by his shoulder, both speechless.

'She had rested just as you had instructed. So why did she lose the baby? It is only a few weeks!' Richard's despair hit the doctor square in the back.

'The Lord only knows why these things happen. But it is better for Annabelle that it was at this early stage. Believe me, Richard, it could have been far more detrimental to her health. She will need you to be strong,' Dr Hickson replied.

'Wasn't there something you could have done? You are the doctor, do something, damn it!' Richard held his breath deep in his chest as it burned. 'The Lord can jolly well explain to my wife why she has lost the one thing that meant more to her than anything, even me.'

'Richard, now there was nothing I...'

'This was our baby, and that is my wife lying up there,' Richard bellowed as his anger grew.

'Now, Richard, you must keep your voice down.'

'Does she know? Does Annabelle know it is lost?' Emily asked, her voice low and strained.

'Yes, she knows; she already knew before I arrived.'

'Will everyone stop referring to our baby as *it*? Have you no decency at all?' Richard demanded. 'And I will not keep my voice down,' he said as he lowered his tone. He looked at the doctor, pleading.

'I shall see myself out.' Dr Hickson nodded with a sombre smile.

All was still in the house, the atmosphere thick with misery. The cool air of the late hour travelled as they sat silently at the dining table. The teapot stood cold and untouched.

CHAPTER SEVEN

April awoke to the sound of clinking china, opened one eye and found her grandmother pouring tea. Sarah perched on her winged chair, leaning forward to serve. She raised her head, and their eyes met.

'All that shopping must have exhausted you.'

'How long have I been asleep, Nan?' April sat upright, leant forward to retrieve her teacup.

'Not long, maybe half an hour or so, I gave your mum a call at the shop, just to let her know we were home.'

From her tone, it was plain she had called to inform her of the incident in the jewellery shop.

'Oh, what…what did she say?' April asked uneasily.

'She thinks you should take it easy. Perhaps, you're coming down with something.'

'Nan, what do you think?'

April fidgeted, running her fingertip around the edge of her cup. Did Nan know what happened? What about in the attic that day?

Sarah said nothing but continued with the tea, arranging the china items on the tray, searching for the right words. April slumped back on the settee; the cushion again cradled her head. Instantly, her thoughts were on the dream, not wanting to recall it and yet desperately needing to. That deep sadness: she could still feel the desperation, the agony in the pit of her stomach.

'Nan, I need to talk to you. It's important, well, I just need to talk to you.' She had spurted the words before her mind caught them. Was she ready for this? She had no choice.

'I think that's a good idea; I can see it in your eyes. But, first, I have something for you to see.'

Sarah stood, heading out of the room. For a few moments, April sat fixed; all energy drained from her body. Tentatively, she closed her eyes.

April lined up all the day's events. Why? Why was she having these visions, if that's what they were? Was it just her imagination, or did they mean something? She lay back, trying not to fall asleep. The last dream had been too disturbing; didn't care for another; her body still ached.

'Here we are.' Sarah returned, carrying a leather jewellery case.

April opened her eyes, and they sat together on the settee.

'Your jewellery, I'd forgotten.' Relief swamped her.

'Do you know, I haven't had this case out for years, probably not since the last time you looked through it when you were tiny.' A smile crept across Sarah's face.

A key hung from a red cord tied to one of the brass handles. The case was square and slightly larger than a chocolate tin. Sarah inserted the key, with a click, the lid sprung open, revealing a hoard of heirloom jewellery.

It always had held an enchantment. April ran her fingers over the items. Long strings of pearls lay entwined with lengths of amber beads, an Art Deco bracelet with brilliant-cut rubies and baguette diamonds set in platinum. As she lifted it, the gems glistened, reflecting the twinkling lights.

'This is stunning!'

'My mother wore that on her wedding day, 1926, I think it was. A wedding gift from her mother, my grandmother.'

'Annabelle,' April announced.

'Yes.'

'Annabelle!' She repeated, her eyes fixed on the ruby and diamond bracelet in her hand.

'Yes, Little One, the blonde from the photo…' Sarah reached into the case, pulled out a leather drawstring pouch, casting a sideways glance at April.

'It just feels…' April paused, wondering, how did it feel? 'It feels good to make a connection, you know, the photo and the jewellery,' she added, putting the bracelet back in the case. 'She feels so real.'

Sarah gently pulled the cords of the leather pouch and tipped its contents into her hand, a gold watch on a heavy chain.

'This pocket watch belonged to Captain Charles Warner, my great-grandfather. He was an elegant and proud gentleman, very sophisticated.'

Sarah's eyes surveyed the antique watch. 'There, look on the back, his initials.' In scrolled engraving were the letters CW. April leaned in for a closer look; the initials were faint now, rubbed smoother with years of handling, the caress of sweeping fingers.

'Captain Warner, Annabelle's father…' April muttered, gathering the family tree in her mind.

'Yes, she was a Warner before she married my grandfather,' Sarah glanced at April. 'My grandfather, Richard Hardwick. He was quite a catch in his day, handsome, and came from a very well-to-do family.' Sarah was still admiring the pocket watch, 'Yes, Annabelle was quite the envy of all the local ladies.'

Blood rushed to April's cheeks. A flash of green eyes, a touch of his hand. The man in the jewellers. Instinctively, she pressed her palm to her stomach — the man from her dream.

Sarah held the watch up in the afternoon light. It dangled, like a clock pendulum, glistening, as the low sun caught it while it swayed from side to side.

'Richard.' The name felt intimate on her tongue. 'I mean, the Hardwick's, what sort of family were they?'

'Oh, I don't know a great deal about that side of the family. They were landowners, had a large country house and estate a few miles from here; it'd been in the family for generations. Richard was either an architect or a solicitor, something professional like that. My mother wasn't able to give me much. She never really spoke about him at all, come to think of it.'

'What about the captain and his wife?' April pressed, desperate for every scrap of information, eager to piece together, make their connections with one another — and her.

'My great-grandfather had joined the army when he was young. He came from a comfortable family, not rich, not like the Hardwicks. The captain made his money later in life, investments and the like. After about twenty years or so in the army, he retired and found employment as an engineer in a local business, and that's when he married my great-grandmother, Rose. She must have been quite a bit younger than him. Now, Rose was well educated, having gone to a private girls' school. Her family were very well off; her father was a factory owner, cloth or wool, I'm not sure.' Sarah smiled and nodded. 'It was Captain Warner who bought this house when they got married in the 1870s.'

'Nan, I don't suppose there are any photos of the family from around that time?' April asked, not overly hopeful; she had never seen any.

'I'm not sure if there are any that early. I hadn't seen my grandmother looking so young until I found that photo a few weeks ago. But why don't we dig all the albums out tomorrow after Christmas lunch? Your mum and dad will probably fall asleep after dinner anyway...' she chuckled.

'That would be a treat.' April kissed her cheek and continued rummaging in the depths of the jewellery case.

The image of Emily, as if sweeping in on an afternoon breeze. 'How about brooches, Nan? Do you have any cameos?' April carried her eyes across the contents.

'Let me see, maybe under here.'

Sarah placed the watch back into its pouch, lifted a tray from the middle of the case, revealing a tray of rings, and lifted it to reveal another compartment. April reached inside to retrieve a black velvet cushion, a dozen or so brooches pinned to it. April scanned them all, but no cameos.

'No,' April said. 'How about Wedgwood jewellery?'

Sarah looked slightly mystified, 'Wedgwood jewellery, no, definitely not. I do have a collection of Wedgwood but no jewellery.' Sarah shook her head. 'Sorry. Any particular reason?'

'Umm… I've seen one, a brooch, silver with a blue cameo. I just wondered.'

April sat a while, running her fingers over gemstones. She was stalling; there was no way she could keep it to herself. She had to tell her, ask her. Finally, April took a deep breath and gulped.

'Nan, do you know who the younger lady is in the photo, the one with the dark hair?' April slowly lifted her gaze from the diamond and pearl earrings she held.

'I did wonder how long it would be before you asked me again,' Sarah said calmly in a matter-of-fact tone. 'I've been waiting.'

'Well, Nan, do you know who she is? Do you know her name?'

Of course, April already knew, had seen, felt them both, but hearing it spoken aloud; she hoped it would make it real and not in her imagination. April still doubted herself. The past few weeks had been so peculiar that she felt her entire world was evaporating; she had entered a life that wasn't hers, a window to another time. But the emotions felt so real.

'I'm afraid I don't know much about her at all; maybe she was Annabelle's sister. Apart from that...'

'Do you know her name, Nan? Are there any other photos of her?' April was impatient.

'I don't know her name. I'm only guessing she's Annabelle's sister by the age and resemblance between them. I've never seen a photo of her before; certainly not to my knowledge.'

April hesitated for a second as she studied her grandmother's expression.

'Her name was Emily, and yes, she was Annabelle's younger sister. Her hair was auburn like mine, and Annabelle's was very blonde. They were both beautiful.' April knew how ridiculous she sounded, but she kept her eyes fixed on her grandmother's face.

'Ah, Emily.'

'Yes, those things you found up in the attic were hers. I think she was ERW, Emily Warner. I'm not sure what the R stands for, though.' April's voice was confident, and she spoke adamantly, with conviction. There was a short pause.

'Maybe the R stands for Rose,' announced Sarah. 'My mother was Rose, and I imagine she may have been named after her aunt. It was the sort of thing that happened in families. Names were passed on through generations.'

'Well, it certainly makes sense because if she is Annabelle's sister, then her mother was Rose. But, Nan, I know this is going to sound as if I've lost it. Like I've gone crazy, but...' she hesitated as she tried to gather the words; they were scattered, whispering in every corner of her brain. Her grandmother's expression was normal and not at all surprised, as April assumed it would be.

'Nan, the thing is...'

Then, Sarah interrupted, 'I know, you don't need to tell me. You've seen her, haven't you? You saw Emily. That afternoon you were in the attic, you saw her then...' she clasped April's hand with reassurance.

It was not the response she'd expected. Unable to react, April sat for a minute, contemplating the situation.

'Nan, so, did you see her too?'

'When I was giving the place a general tidy up, I did see something... But it was getting dark, and maybe my eyesight isn't what it used to be, you know?'

'You know as well as I do that there's nothing wrong with your bloody eyesight. It's as good as mine!'

'As I said, it was getting dark, and I can't be sure what I saw really. It was over quickly, like a flash, or when you see something move out the corner of your eye, you know?'

April nodded.

'The afternoon had flown by; I had been in the attic for hours. For years I've been meaning to clear those old tea chests, your grandfather never got to it, and one year rolls into the next, and well…' Sarah stopped, looking at April.

'Nan, what is it?'

'You.'

'What? What d'you mean? Are you okay?' A rumble of panic shot through April.

'You look just like her.' Nan sat back in her seat, examining her granddaughter.

April gave no response. She couldn't find one among the rubble of memories and emotions. So, she had seen her.

'I found the case in a chest in the far corner, smaller than the others, tucked away behind everything. I mean, nestled under the rafters.

'As if someone had hidden it?'

'Perhaps.' Sarah gave a quick nod with a raised eyebrow. 'I could barely see in that corner, so I took the case, sat on the chaise and switched on the light. I have lived in this house my entire life, not once, not once in all that time had I seen, or felt…' Sarah let out a long breath. 'She was before me in a flash, one moment nothing the next a girl was sitting on the chaise with me. I could smell her.' She closed her eyes, pushing her hand to her heart. 'Cold. That is what I remember. A desperate bone-chilling coldness and the deepest feeling of loneliness I've ever felt.'

April leant over, resting her head on her grandmother's arm.

They remained quiet for a while, swaddled in the warmth of the fire and Christmas lights.

Sarah shuffled, lifting April from her, gazing directly into her eyes.

'I don't remember much after, not until I came to, down here on the settee, with your mum running a hand over my forehead, smoothing my hair. Then, all I can recall is darkness swamp me, cover me, then nothing. As if I was no longer there. As if I no longer existed. I have never been so afraid in my life.'

April frowned. 'I don't think Emily is bad. I don't think she meant to hurt you. Do you?' She shook her head. 'No, none of this feels right.'

'Hey, it's okay, Little One. No, I don't think she means harm. But I think she needs something, or, to tell us something.'

They sat, staring at one another for what seemed an age. Neither knowing what else to say, April took a gulp.

'A ghost. Emily is a ghost!' It sounded ridiculous. 'That's not all. I've *seen* others too.'

'Other ghosts?'

'No, not really. Dreams, but not like normal ones. They are like *I am* there. I can feel the sunshine, smell the flowers; even the feelings are real. I don't understand it. I'm dreaming about a family I know nothing about. Memories, that's the best way to describe them, only not ones I know, but like looking at a photo or a scene and putting yourself in it.' April's eyes cast to the piano. The voice, the whisper in her ear. 'Nan, I think, I think I'm going mad!' Tears were building in April's eyes. She looked away, desperate not to cry.

'Everything is going to be okay, mark my words. We need to keep a clear head, though. I'm sure there's a reason for all this. Perhaps it is meant to be. Perhaps...' Sarah hesitated for a few seconds, then continued with a jovial tone. 'I don't know, *a haunted house*; well, I never!' She smiled, then winked.

This wasn't Nan making light of the subject; but rather, easing the mood, April knew that. Yet, that cold despair was settling in her stomach again.

'What happened in town earlier? I know; I'm now certain that you felt something at the jewellers, didn't you? Was it Emily?'

'No, it was…' April wanted to say his name, but for some inexplicable reason, she couldn't. She hadn't known who he was at the time. Now recalling the dream in the garden with Annabelle, she could give him his name. 'Richard.' April smiled.

Sarah said nothing, just smiled in return.

With a sudden rush of reality, April wiped the smile from her face, replacing it with an expression of embarrassment. Sharply, she stood, uneasily straightening her clothes, running her fingers through her hair.

'I think I'll go home, get some rest. I'll be back with Mum and Dad later, ready for dinner.' April took the few short steps to where her coat and bags lay, grabbed them, coyly smiling at her grandmother as she opened the front door. 'I love you, Nan.'

CHAPTER EIGHT

In tradition, the family gathered around the tree as the captain reached high, placing the angel on top. Protruding pine needles prodded his chest as he stretched to reach the top branch.

'This is going to be the best Christmas. Oh, I do so love Christmas Eve; it is for sure my most favourite day of the year,' chanted Emily.

Annabelle laughed. 'Not forgetting your wedding day. I believe we shall have snow. So, you shall have the most wonderful wedding day anyone could wish for.' Annabelle sweetly leant over towards Emily and squeezed her hand.

'I cannot wait to marry James.' Emily pressed her palm tightly to her breast.

The captain turned to face his family with a joyful smile.

'There, the angel is on the tree, and all is complete. It is set to be the perfect occasion with my daughter's wedding.' He looked over to Emily with a nod to James. 'And I'm sure the New Year will bring us hope, maybe, a new addition to the family,' switching his gaze to Annabelle. 'We shall say goodbye to the old and welcome in the arrival of the new century. 1900 is sure to be a year of change for us all. So, a toast.'

The captain raised his glass of mulled wine.

'Merry Christmas,' they sang, sipping the spicy wine.

Emily eased herself closer to her fiancé, James. They stood near the tree.

Lance Corporal Wright of the West Suffolk Regiment's Second Battalion. He was a gracious man, steadfast and loyal. The outbreak of war in South Africa earlier in the year had created a real threat. With it hanging dreadfully over their heads, they had brought the wedding forward to 27th December. The first Battalions had already been mobilised and sent to the Cape in early November, with growing fears of the inevitability that more troops would be needed.

'Emily, how about a carol?' requested her father.

Emily sat at the piano close to the Christmas tree, her blue dress hung to the carpet, covering the stool.

'Very well,' she declared as she opened the piano lid. The sweet melody, the pure clarity of her voice travelled the room. Spirits high, all worries of war dispersed, as the room overflowed with joy.

Annabelle clutched Richard's hand. They stood beside the fire; logs crackled and hissed, casting a rich ambient glow. Richard turned and kissed her cheek, trailing his lips over her warm skin. His arm wrapped around her waist, with his hand gently caressing her back.

'My dearest Belle. You mean the world to me,' he said, squeezing her hand.

'I do believe you are holding my heart right here.' She ran her thumb across his palm with her delicate fingers. She looked at his hand, remembering the first time she touched it, how it had stirred every emotion in her body.

'Then my Belle, this must mean that you are mine, to do with as I please,' Richard hushed the words lightly into her ear.

She blushed.

'I think you will find that I have belonged to you since the first time you touched my hand.' Her cheeks flushed. 'How could any woman have resisted those green eyes?'

'No other woman has ever been offered them, never having the inclination before I met you,' he added. 'I have a special gift I would like to give you, but in private,' his emerald eyes glinted as he winked.

Annabelle, taking a deep breath as her heart pounded with the memory of that first encounter, answered, 'I shall delight in it, I am sure. I would give you the world if you wished for it, darling.'

'Belle, I shall only ever wish for you. You are my world,' he replied, his green eyes flashed, and he took her in his arms and held her tight.

CHAPTER NINE

It was half six before April awoke, hot, flustered and holding the frame tight to her chest. She hadn't planned to fall asleep; it had taken her like a great wave, consuming her whole.

'You ready for dinner, darling?' Julia called through the door. April jumped, sat upright and looked at the carriage clock on her dressing table.

'Almost, give me fifteen?' Flustered, she rummaged through her wardrobe, searching for something suitable to wear for dinner. Christmas Eve was a tradition, first, dinner, then at eleven-thirty, the service at the Cathedral.

April pulled on a new pair of dark jeans and a beaded sweater she'd been saving for the occasion. Dressing quickly, she slipped on a pair of heeled boots and placed the frame on the drawers beside her bed. In front of the mirror, she combed her hair, brushed a little colour to her cheeks, then closed her door and headed for the lounge.

'Got everything? Are we ready to go?' I thought we'd take the presents over tonight and put them under your Nan's tree, ready. What do you think?' Julia asked as she pulled the curtains closed on the dark evening.

'That's a good idea, Mum. Oh no!' April dashed for the door. 'I'll be back in a min.' She grabbed her shopping bag on the way. She quickly wrapped her last-minute gifts in metallic silver with red bows.

~

Carols boomed through the house as they stepped down into the front room. They seeped from a mahogany cabinet that hid the stereo. Festive aromas radiated through the space, pine needles and the lush woodland scent. The coffee table was laden with silver trays and glass bowls, fruit, nuts, and dates, and amidst it all, a large bowl of hot spicy wine.

'Anyone fancy some mulled wine? Dinner is going to be ready at eight o'clock sharp, so we have time to enjoy a treat first.' Sarah took her seat in her usual winged chair as she reached over to the crystal glasses.

'Mmm, mulled wine, it smells... intoxicating. You'll have us thrown out of the church for being drunk and disorderly!' Michael chuckled as he reached for a date.

'Not too much wine! Just one bottle, some orange juice, and the traditional spices, it must be the splash of brandy I put in that you can smell!' she replied while she poured it from the large silver ladle.

'A *splash* of brandy, Nan, are you sure it wasn't the whole drinks cabinet?' April took her glass from the tray.

They sipped and listened to the choir-sung carols. April sat back on the velvet upholstery and watched her family as the tree lights twinkled and the mesmerising glow from the fire bewitched the room with their magic.

April scanned the room, the hissing logs as the flames danced, the carved mahogany mantle, the old gilt clock. She blinked, her heart leapt; there, for a moment, stood.... No, she blinked and looked away. Holding her breath until it burned, April counted to ten, but impulse dragged her eyes back to the fireplace. Richard stood by the crackling fire, sipping wine, his long fingers wrapped around the cut crystal glass. He lifted it to his full lips and smiled.

Standing sharply, April dropped her glass; rich wine seeped into the carpet.

'What on earth is the matter?' Julia dashed over to retrieve the glass.

'Oh, I'm so sorry, Nan. I nearly broke the glass.'

Embarrassed, mortified, her pulse rapid in her throat. Tingling whips sent shivers down her spine as she fell back on the settee, her swirling head repeating flashes of his image.

'The glass is fine; there's no harm done.'

Although Nan wore that all-knowing expression, it did not make April feel less embarrassed. Her mother fussed at her feet, mopping and scrubbing at the red stain.

'Oh, don't fuss, there's no harm done, it's only a little,' Sarah interrupted, as the colour had drained from her granddaughter's face. She then turned to the clock as it chimed the hour, eight o'clock. 'There, dinner is ready. Come, let's go into the dining room.'

April followed. Julia and Michael took their seats on opposite sides. April pulled out the chair near her mother; still slightly shaking, she sat down on the pink upholstery.

The view of the garden, visible by day through the glass doors, now reflected April like a mirror. The outside was almost impossible to see; the darkness was dense, thick, only the dining room interior with its large chandelier. April looked closer into the glass, past her reflection.

'It's snowing!' She darted over to the doors, unlocked, and slowly opened one ajar. She took a deep breath. The chilled air filled her lungs; she held it for a moment until the coldness made her chest burn, then exhaled and filled her lungs once more. Finally, it cleared her head. Large snowflakes drifted down to the ground; the grey, stone steps quickly transformed into a glistening white carpet. It brightened the entire view with its reflective finish: the sky full of snow clouds, the atmosphere thick with frosty flakes.

Michael dimmed the chandelier and, striking a long match, lit the new wicks. A display of five tall candles set in a wreathe of greenery twinkled in the dim light.

'That's perfect. Come on, Little One, sit down next to me,' Sarah fussed with a sprig of holly, pushing it back into the arrangement. 'See, Christmas wouldn't be the same anywhere else, now, would it.'

April closed the glass door and returned to the dining table. The surface was full, the table hardly visible beneath; white china serving dishes with large silver spoons, crispy roast potatoes and an array of seasonal vegetables.

'I've never seen such a feast, Sarah. You've excelled yourself; it all smells so delicious.' Michael took a long-handled spoon, started to serve.

All bar a couple of carrots and a drop of gravy, the rest was spent, the satisfied family sat back in their chairs, nothing was said for a while, a few grateful sighs, and sips of wine.

'That was delicious, Mum, thanks. There isn't anything quite like your cooking.'

'It was rather lovely, wasn't it? Now, before we have dessert, I have a special gift.' Sarah rose and wandered over to the sideboard, opened a long drawer and took out a wrapped box.

'Now, April, as you are my favourite granddaughter, and as you will soon turn twenty-one, I've a special gift for you.' Sarah reached across the table, handing her a long, wrapped present. 'I want to give it to you tonight rather than waiting until the morning.'

April sat holding it. This was not normal for Christmas Eve; gifts were strictly for Christmas morning. But then again, this was rapidly becoming anything but ordinary. April slipped her fingernail under the tape, eased off the gold ribbon and pulled away from the shiny paper. Before her lay a long red leather box with gold swirl inlaid around the edge. April moved her dinner plate, rested the box on the table in front of her.

'Nan, I don't know what to say,' she said, shaking her head, then rested her hands on either side of the box, fingers spread wide flat on the table. She drummed her fingertips, not sure whether to look inside or not.

'Of course, you don't know; you haven't opened it yet,' Sarah replied and gestured to the box. 'Open it, go on; the suspense is killing your mum.'

She took hold of the box and lifted the lid; its long hinge squeaked as it revealed its contents. April sat transfixed, gazing in amazement at the treasure. Finally, she looked up, and her eyes met her grandmother's.

'When I found it, I just knew it was yours! It's a special gift to celebrate you being back here, where you belong; a sort of coming home gift if you like.' Sarah's face beamed with delight as she clasped her hands together and pressed them close to her lips in anticipation.

'But Nan...' her words were stuck somewhere between her pounding heart, eager to burst from its confines, and her throat, so dry she merely sat, mute, with a heavy stirring sensation in the pit of her stomach. She had seen it before, but this was the gift she never expected. April reached inside the box.

The silver artwork draped across her hand; the bracelet was heavy with charms; diamond-set hearts, a cross, keys, a myriad of glittering gem set charms.

'It was my grandmother's. It now belongs to you, April. Merry Christmas,' Sarah looked at April; her eyes twinkled in the candle glow as she winked, 'It belonged to Annabelle.'

'Oh, Nan, I can't believe it. It's Annabelle's charm bracelet.' April's eyes filled; the emotion that had been building all day burst through the barrier in a torrent.

'No, it is *your* charm bracelet. It belongs to *you* now,' Sarah said, tears streaking her cheeks.

Composing herself, April wiped her face with her napkin. Thoughts spread; she felt excited, confused — she was holding Annabelle's bracelet. Where had it been all these years?

'Where was it? I didn't know you, had it? It wasn't in your jewellery case, was it? I know, I would have remembered.' Emotional, the words rambled from her lips. She took a deep breath and sat teary-eyed, gazing upon her shiny treasure.

'I found it in the leather case with the photo frame. I knew then that you must have it,' Sarah got to her feet and wandered around the table, 'I thought I'd wait till Christmas,' Sarah beamed. 'Here, let me put it on you.' Sarah took the bracelet and fastened it about April's wrist.

It felt familiar now; the heavy sensation pulled her to another time. April rested her head back on the dining chair, silently counting until the dizziness passed.

Snow had fallen through the night. Christmas morning was crisp and glistened with a crystal carpet. The bright sky cast a blinding radiance to the landscape, frosty and twinkling. Beyond the garden wall, family tombs and gravestones wore a white veil, and the trees that lined the cemetery bore snow-laden branches.

She stood close to the glass doors, gazing at the view. The outside chill pierced the windows, making her shiver and the glass steamed with her breath.

'Merry Christmas, my darling.' Richard entered the dining room. Annabelle stood unmoved, unaware, concentrating on the landscape. He stood behind her, taking in her scent, conserving to memory how she looked at that very moment.

'Close your eyes,' he asked, folding his arms around hers, holding a red leather box detailed with gold inlay. She closed them tightly as instructed. He placed the box in front of her; his arms encased her whole body; his tall stature towered above her.

'Merry Christmas, Belle, open your eyes.'

Richard lifted the lid.

'Ah, Richard. I don't know what to say; it is beautiful!'

'Nothing can match your beauty, but it is quite lovely,' he kissed her cheek. 'Here, let me put it on you.' He took the silver charm bracelet and fastened it around her petite wrist.

April opened her eyes to concerned faces. She sat motionless, transfixed on her grandmother's eyes for a few seconds, then wiped the tears from her cheeks.

'I'm okay; just a bit overwhelmed, thanks, Nan.' April smiled with rigid falseness.

'Now, who's ready for some dessert? There's raspberry Pavlova, homemade, of course, none of that shop-bought stuff, or sherry trifle,' Sarah rose and gathered the empty plates, casting a knowing wink at April.

'I think I shall have the Pavlova; any more alcohol and I'll be unable to stand up, Mum,' Julia tentatively eased herself up from her chair to help clear the table.

'That sounds delicious; I think I shall have that too,' Michael added, collecting the serving dishes and following into the kitchen.

April remained planted, hoping roots would grow to keep her fixed in one time. The charm bracelet shone in the candlelight. Once again, she had seen the image of Richard, his love and devotion to Annabelle. April closed her eyes, lay back on her chair, and longed to sense him again. Her heartbeat pounded; her body tingled this new but now familiar feeling. She had no choice but to embrace it; she no longer had the strength or desire to resist.

The mood changed. April could no longer hear the clinking of cutlery from the kitchen. A delicate song came from the front room, but the carol was not coming from the stereo. She stood up and noticed the room had changed. It was still festive but lighter; the view through the glass doors was still frosty white, a crystal blanket of snow, but it was bright as day.

She drifted into the front parlour; the familiar tone of Emily's voice filled her ears.

'There you are, dearest Annabelle. Is it not delightful this morning? You were quite right, of course. The snow has such a magical feel.'

Emily stood at the window, her back to the room, her eyes fixed on the snow-covered footpath; her auburn hair shone with flashes of red in the snow-lit space.

'Merry Christmas, my dearest, oh, your charm bracelet, it is lovely. I helped Richard choose it; I knew how much you would love it. Although he did not need my help, Richard knew exactly what to get you. Oh, dearest, do you love it, say you do?' Emily turned to face her, rushed over to grab her hands. 'Of course, you do. I cannot wait until after dinner! Are you coming outside with me? Let us go for a walk in the snow like when we were little,' Emily clasped her sister's hands, pulling them in tight to her heart.

'Of course, darling, just as when we were children,' April felt the words fall from her lips before she understood. It was her voice she heard — then again not — somehow removed.

'I do love you so very much; Merry Christmas, dear sister.' Emily flung her arms around her.

April stood motionless in amazement, not knowing what to do. Then, instinctively, her arms enfolded Emily in return; she squeezed her younger sister tightly. Closing her eyes, her lungs engulfed with the sweet scent of her perfume.

'Annabelle, what is it, dearest, whatever is the matter?' Emily's eyes lingered on her sister's face. 'Oh darling, why are you weeping? It is Christmas; there is absolutely no reason for you to be crying.'

Emily took a white linen handkerchief from a concealed pocket in her velvet dress and gently brushed her sister's cheeks.

'I do love you too,' April said, the words sprang from her mouth automatically. April felt her body drenched in emotion. With no control over her actions, she flung her arms around Emily and held her tight, 'I love you, Emily, my darling.'

CHAPTER TEN

'Oh!' April shouted.

She opened her eyes and jumped out of her chair. 'No, this isn't happening, it can't be real, I'm losing it, I've gone mad!' April trudged the dining room up and down across the patterned carpet.

'What's wrong?' Sarah rushed back into the dining room.

April turned to look at her, ashen-faced and panic-stricken.

'My goodness, you look like a ghost! What on earth's wrong?' Quickly, she rushed over to grab her; Sarah held her arms tightly, fixing her to the spot.

'Nan, I think I've gone mad! I've finally lost it!' April stepped back with a pale face and an expression of sheer confusion.

'I'm sure you've not lost it, and you're not going mad. Just sit down and tell me what the matter is!'

April sat with her head in her hands, her long auburn hair draped over her knees. Her voice was muffled as she tried to explain.

'April! Sit up and tell me properly. Sarah lifted her head straight, swept back her hair.

April took a deep breath, closed her eyes for a moment, took another breath, and looked directly into her grandmother's eyes.

'Nan, I've just seen Emily. But, this time, she wasn't a ghost! This time, I think *I* was the ghost!

'Oh, my dear girl, how can you be a ghost?' Sarah wiped April's tears with a napkin. 'Now, you say you saw Emily again. Was she in here with you?' She gazed around the room.

'No, Nan, she was in the front room; she was singing and watching the snow. I heard her, so I went in there, and she saw me. Oh, Nan, she was so beautiful. I held her in my arms. I could smell her perfume. It was so real.' Again, tears flooded. April sat, arms tightly wrapped around her chest, wishing her heart would stop aching.

'All right, we can figure this out.' Sarah soothed.

'She saw my bracelet. I mean, Annabelle's bracelet! She told me how she'd helped Richard choose it. What's happening? I'm not sure if I'm here or if I'm there. I've spent most of today in another time, another bloody century. Nan, what's happening to me?' April dropped her head back onto her lap, sobbing.

'I think it may be time for a nice pot of tea.'

Tears fell from her chin, resting on her legs. 'What's a cup of tea going to do? How's that going to help?'

'I'm not sure if it will help. But it's easier to think things through over a cuppa. Now, you'd better wipe your face before your parents see you like this.' Sarah passed her the already wet napkin.

April raised her head and wiped her face. She'd forgotten about her mum and dad; they had no idea.

April followed her grandmother into the kitchen, passing her parents in the hallway, her mother with the dessert tray, her father following behind with plates. April kept her eyes down, desperate not to make eye contact with them, and they simply headed into the front room.

'So, April, while we're alone, tell me again. You saw Emily?' Sarah quizzed while filling the kettle.

'Yes, but I was in the dining room still. Nan, I never left the room. But… I *was* in the front room with her... I know

62

this sounds ridiculous; I suppose I dreamt it. Do you understand? I know it sounds mad!' April's voice was strained and tired.

Sarah remained silent for a long while, taking it in, rolling it over in her head. Then she replied, 'I suppose, if you say you were in the front room with Emily, then you were there.'

'What? That's what I've been saying, but it doesn't make any sense. I can't be in two places at the same time,' April said through gritted teeth. 'It wasn't like a dream, not like earlier. This was different. I was *there*, talking to Emily. I was awake. But then, I was still sitting at the dining table. I don't understand it.'

'What I mean is, perhaps you had been there before. You were just reliving or remembering a memory, just as you've remembered all day. I saw the look on your face earlier, when you were drinking your mulled wine,' Sarah smiled. 'Was it Emily you saw?'

April said nothing, just shook her head, very slightly, almost hoping it wasn't noticeable at all. She guessed her grandmother had seen it in her expression. However, Richard hadn't been there; he was only a figment of her imagination. How could she be having these feelings for him? She'd never met him; he'd lived a century ago.

'I think, if we look hard enough, look at all the facts and look at it with a clear mind, I think, we shall find exactly what this all means!' Her grandmother's statement put April slightly on edge. What on earth was she thinking now?

Sarah continued fussing over china cups and saucers, not consciously doing anything. Things were different between them, April was different, and she felt herself getting frustrated with her grandmother, something that had never happened before. Everything was frustrating. Things had changed, strange and inexplicable things.

'We should start at the beginning! Then, look at everything, step by step. What do you think?' Sarah looked directly at April's confused face.

'Well, I suppose so,' April said with a shrug. What was there to lose? She needed to do something, or she would go mad if she hadn't already.

'Well, it started in your attic when I looked through the box of things,' April said, calmer now, taking a rational perspective.

'Yes. Yes, and I felt that too when I found them. So, it started there.' Sarah replied, thinking.

'Nan, you knew something would happen, didn't you? That's why you showed me the case? Where was the box? I can't believe you never knew it was there, that you'd never seen it before.' April questioned; they both stopped what they were doing and looked straight at each other.

'We need to sit down,' Sarah answered calmly.

They both sat at the kitchen table. April traced her finger over the blue and white checked cloth, then dropped her head in her hands.

'Nan, I don't understand what's going on?' she sighed, head still in her hands, her voice tired.

'Look at me,' Sarah lifted April's chin. 'I don't have the answers you want, but I am sure that this…' she shrugged, 'whatever it is, I'm sure it's happening for a reason.'

April was calmer now, bar a confused expression.

'What is it?' Sarah asked.

'There is something else, isn't there? I can see it in your eyes. Nan, what aren't you telling me?'

Sarah sat back and crossed her arms. 'Everything happened so quickly that day in the attic. One moment I was there looking at the photo, the next she was sitting beside me… then darkness.'

April pulled herself upright, her brow creased. 'And?'

'Black with flashes of red, thick and suffocating. And the pain. I suppose I must have been dreaming, but there were no images, not like a dream. This was a feeling,' Sarah paused, taking in her granddaughter's expression. 'As I said, I awoke to find your mother fussing over me. But it was not your mum.'

'What d'you mean, was and wasn't?'

'I found that case weeks ago, back in October. When did you move here?' Sarah nodded. 'It was December. It wasn't your mum.' April didn't say a word. 'I pulled myself together, cleared my head, making a cup of tea. I kept going over the afternoon, what I had done, where I had been, retracing my steps. But I couldn't go back into the attic, not until the next morning. I've never been afraid of the dark, and this is my house; I've lived here all my life; there is nothing here to fear. But… that darkness. And the voice.'

'Emily?'

'I think so. Crying. No, sobbing, a desperate lonely sob.' Sarah's voice cracked as she swallowed the lump in her throat. 'I put the frame on the hall table. I knew you would see it, knew you'd notice it,' she smiled. 'Every day, every single day, I sensed her here. Then it stopped. Nothing, that was the day you moved to Bury.'

'Nan, I've seen her many times, and Annabelle,' April fidgeted in her chair. 'But not like that, not a ghost.'

'Do you want to tell me? You don't have to. When you're ready.'

'No, it's okay, I think I need to, you know, get it off my chest,' April took a deep breath, holding it for a couple of seconds before exhaling, 'I saw her in the attic, just as you did when I held the frame. But then, the oddest thing happened. It felt like a dream as it couldn't be real. Mum said I must have fallen asleep, I don't know, but I was in the garden. It was the day the photos had been taken. It was warm and sunny; the lavender was in bloom. I saw the captain talking to the photographer. Emily was late for her photo, looking for her brooch.'

'Her brooch?'

'The Wedgwood one. Nan, Emily walked straight past me, so close I could smell her. Was I dreaming?'

'I don't know, Little One! I don't know.'

'To be quite honest, after today, I'm not sure what's real and what isn't,' April looked down at the table. The image of Richard had pressed itself onto her mind.

'What is it?' Sarah reached across the table and took her hand, 'Darling, please, what is it?'

'I've seen Richard. Nan, he's tall, his hair is dark, and he has twinkling green eyes, and his smile…' the words had fallen before she could stop them. But she didn't care. She didn't feel embarrassed saying it, not this time. 'This is a new feeling for me. I know it sounds… mad. I'm not feeling like me anymore; does that make any sense?'

The pair of them sat opposite each other, holding hands. The charm bracelet chinked on the table as April rested her hand down.

'I'm not sure if these kinds of feelings ever really make sense. You like him, don't you?' declared Sarah after a few seconds.

'Nan, I've never felt this way about anyone before. I understand how ridiculous it sounds. But…' April hesitated. 'I feel I know him.'

'I'm not sure it does sound ridiculous; it just doesn't sound like you. Maybe, that's what feels different,' Sarah hesitated. 'April, what about Annabelle? Have you seen her?'

'I have, in my dreams…'

'But?' Sarah squeezed her granddaughter's hand.

'It's different with Annabelle; I've dreamt about her. It was awful,' April stopped.

'Go on.'

'With Annabelle, it's a feeling,' April tried to gather up her thoughts. 'I had a dream about her. She was pregnant; they were both so happy, her and Richard. Dr Hickson had told her she had to rest, to be careful. They'd lost her mother giving birth to Emily when Annabelle was four years old. But, Nan, Annabelle lost the baby. I saw her. I felt the pain and sadness — *her* pain. It was an awful thing. I ache every time I think about it.'

April could not help herself, could no longer hold it back and broke down in tears, sobbing into her sleeve, recalling the loss, fear, and not knowing.

'Oh, April, it's okay, I understand.' Sarah pushed her chair back, screeching across the kitchen tiles, and walked around the table.

'Do you; do you understand? Because I don't!'

'Little One,' Sarah paused momentarily, looking at April, then in a gentle voice. 'I think it is obvious and straightforward, maybe hard for you to take on board, but obvious nevertheless.'

'What on earth are you on about, Nan? What's *obvious*?'

Sarah crouched down, looking April in the eyes; they were red and sore. Trails of tear stains patterned her cheeks. She held April's head between her hands.

'Little One, you saw Emily earlier, didn't you?' April was too tired for words; she simply nodded, 'and you held her in your arms, and you smelt her perfume; she saw your bracelet?' Her words were clear, but April could not respond. Although, in April's head, her experiences were real and tangible, spoken aloud, the reality was, these things were impossible and absurd.

'Darling, you *are* Annabelle!' Sarah's words were adamant, direct. 'Do you understand what I'm saying?' She gently kissed April's forehead.

'What?' April's mouth was dry, her head fuzzy. She desperately tried to erase the feelings of loss: of Annabelle's loss lingering inside her entire body.

'I know it's hard, but let's look at this another way. Logically,' Sarah began.

'Logical, there's no logic to any of this.' April stood up sharply. She'd not meant to raise her voice, but this was bizarre.

Sarah simply hugged and kissed her cheek to calm her.

'All right, perhaps *logical* was the wrong word. But I think we can find it if we believe. This is about life, death, love, and family. Our souls come back time and time again. Our souls remain the same, in new bodies, with new lives and new names. Not everyone can remember those memories, past events and past loves. But, and I truly believe this; I believe that we are connected to the same souls, life after life.' Sarah guided April back to her chair, perched herself on the edge of the table, and held April's hand.

The charm bracelet dangled; the silver charms glistened in the stark kitchen light. April said nothing, lost for a reply. Her grandmother's words did have strange reasoning.

'Nan,' April's voice was shaky; she looked deeply at her grandmother, searching. 'What about Emily? Why's she still here? Surely, you can't come back as someone else and be a *ghost,* can you? She was, *is,* a ghost, Nan; I saw her with my own eyes, and so did you!'

'I don't know why she's still here; I don't know why she hasn't moved on to wherever we go when we die. Though, we need to deal with one matter at a time,' she coughed slightly and then continued. 'Answer me this: You saw Emily tonight, and when she spoke to you, she was actually speaking to Annabelle. Yes?' April nodded. There was no point arguing; Nan was right. 'And, with Annabelle, it's more a feeling, her pain, her grief. Am I right so far?' April nodded again.

'Now Richard, you keep seeing him, don't you? You have feelings for him. I can see that, despite the fact he lived over a century ago, and not forgetting he was your great-great-grandfather. But, most importantly, he was Annabelle's husband!' Both sat silent for a few moments, contemplating the strange revelation as the room's mood altered.

April and her grandmother looked at each other but said nothing.

Cold. The kitchen flooded in a bone freezing coldness. Sarah gasped, clutching onto April's shoulder, exhaling a fog of frozen breath before them.

'Nan, what is it?' April's voice shook as she slowly stood.

'I'm not sure.' Sarah rose from the table's edge.

The lights flickered, and then nothing, the room plunged into darkness.

They stood, glued to the tiled floor. A slither of light from the hallway glimmered through the gap in the kitchen door as it rattled slightly, tapping against the doorframe. Through the slit, a light cut the room; a million dust motes danced in the beam. April turned and looked at the window. In the darkness, she could make out its frame, tightly shut and not the reason for the breeze. But the space was heavy, unearthly, a still coldness.

A smell, a sweet perfume wove through the chill. The delicate scent caught April, recognising it as it filled the kitchen, intense but sweet.

Within the shaft of light, a white flicker. Slight, then growing with a blue hue danced through the air. Finally, it dropped to the floor, vanishing.

A silver mist swirled around the table, about their feet, until it filled the space in front of them. A figure formed in the dim light from the hall, draped in a blue glow. It slowly developed into a smoky apparition, gradually becoming a figure.

There she stood. As in the photograph, her auburn hair piled high, dressed in a blue gown, and at her neck was fastened the Wedgewood cameo.

With no awareness, April stepped closer, letting go of her grandmother's grip. Sarah watched in wonder and a little fear, gazed from April to the ghost.

'Emily,' April said softly. 'My dearest.'

The ghost held her arms outstretched, pulling April into an embrace.

'My dearest Annabelle, how I have missed you. I have waited for you for so long.'

~

The kitchen door swung open.

'Have you two finished in here? It's quarter to eleven. I take it you two didn't want dessert. If we're going to the cathedral service, we need to leave in about half-hour,' Michael said, standing in the doorway. 'Why've you got the lights off?' He flicked the light switch off and on again. 'That's better; I'll take a look at that light fitting after Christmas. Don't be long, you two!' He strode back through the hall.

Neither spoke.

Sarah stared wide-eyed. Glare bounced off every surface; she pressed her fingers to her eyes.

The perfume had gone. The figure had evaporated in the stark light. Both stood rooted to the floor tiles. April quickly took hold of her grandmother's hand as she saw her sway.

'Nan?'

Sarah sat down heavily, her elbows on the table.

'Oh, I'm just a little… umm, amazed, that's all.' She started. 'It's not every day you meet your great-aunt.' There was an uneasy pause. 'I saw you both, as if…'

April leant back against the kitchen table. 'I felt her. I could feel her in my arms, warm and real. Nan, everything makes sense. I understand now.' April twiddled with her charm bracelet, her eyes fixed on the space where the ghost had stood. 'I know there's a lot ahead of me. But I can finally put some reason to all these...' April hesitated, unsure whether she should continue. 'These feelings I have for Richard.'

'Darling, those feelings belonged to Annabelle.'

'Yes, I know. I know.'

'And he's dead. He lived over a hundred years ago,' Sarah added.

April looked at her square. 'But I can't just switch them off. It's me; I'm the one who's having these feelings now. Not, Annabelle, she's dead too.'

'It's one thing to embrace your past life, but it would be dangerous to try and relive it,' continued Sarah.

Tears fell down her cheeks as April stared hard at her grandmother. Then, she quickly looked away, down at her bracelet.

'I know all that's true, Nan. All these *feelings*. I know all the facts. I know how odd all this sounds — bloody crazy. But it's here, inside me.' April pressed her hand to her heart; the silver charms jingled. 'Something has been growing, changing, getting stronger since the move. Life was normal before; I did *not* want to move. But I've realised I belong here, Nan; it was you who said maybe it was meant to be.'

'Yes, I did,' Sarah nodded but said nothing more.

'I know I've only seen Richard today, but I've known him for over a century. I don't know how this will work or how I'm going to cope. I can't shut out these feelings I have, not just for him but for Emily. I need to know why there are no photos of her and why you knew nothing about her,' April's voice was calm, her expression eased. 'And, most of all, why she is here now!'

Sarah sat for a while, compiling her thoughts.

'All right, Darling. But let's take this one day at a time,' she reached out and clasped April's hands. 'I'm here for you; you know that. Maybe, don't tell your parents just yet. Although, I think your mum *knows* something isn't right.'

'I'm not sure how Mum will take it, that I was once her great-grandmother! Nan, what if they don't believe me, think I'm mad?' April gave an unsure smile.

'I think we'd better make a move, or we won't be able to get a seat in the church. Go and wash your face, and I'll get our coats. Don't worry; it'll be fine.' Sarah nodded with a hopeful smile.

As April stood and opened the kitchen door, Sarah remained seated for a few more moments, then took a deep breath, her heart still erratic. April turned in the doorway, her hand on the light switch.

'I now understand why I belong here, home with you.'

CHAPTER ELEVEN

They entered the cathedral through the great arched doors.

Row after row of folk wrapped in winter coats and scarves had already gathered, seated on the long pews. The grandeur of the architecture, the decorated arched ceiling, and stained-glass windows blew all clouded thoughts from April's mind, forming a determination to enjoy the evening regardless.

They found an empty pew close to the front, in the glittering light of one of the waterfall chandeliers reflecting off the polished stone tiles. Rows of tall stone pillars reached up to form high arches, crafted centuries before that extended heavenwards to line the long aisle with a canopy of elaborately carved and intricate paintings. April beamed at the pair of Christmas trees that stood either side of the aisle, festoons of metallic ribbons and giant baubles in reds and golds.

The air was cool, fragranced with the subtle scent of pine. April perched at the end closest to the aisle, within full view of the church organ. When the music began, it pierced the atmosphere like an announcement, and all fell still.

Sarah leaned over and spoke in her ear, but as April turned to answer, her grandmother watched the organist contently.

'What was that, Nan?' April nudged her elbow, trying to grab her attention. But her grandmother frowned.

There it was again. A voice. Too distant to decipher the words.

As she gripped the wooden seat on either side of her legs, that familiar numbness began creeping her spine. Turning her head, she pressed her ear against her shoulder to stop the ringing. The church organ bellowed, far too loud in her ears. Instantly, the carol faded as the voice came closer. April inhaled the cool air with her heart thudding loudly in her chest, blood now rushing through her skull.

Deep breath. In. Out. It will be all right. Stay calm.

It filled her lungs, sending a brisk tingle down the length of her spine.

Composed now, April steadied herself on the pew and stretched each finger as she slowly opened her eyelids.

Her clothes had transformed, no longer her dark jeans or black wool coat. Now, a long gathering of green velvet draped her legs. Daringly, she glanced beside her. Long legs covered in dark tailoring and shiny black shoes. She traced his thigh up to the dark suit. Richard. He slid his hand closer; she jumped as he folded his long fingers about hers.

Rigid, her back one with the solid back of the pew, April couldn't take her eyes from his hand. It was warm. Then, with a rapid beat, her heart pounded, restricted by her corset. She squeezed his hand, her fingers entwined with his, unable to distinguish whose was whose. She was trembling.

'What is it, darling? You are shaking. Are you warm enough?' Richard removed his hand, brought it up to touch her face. He brushed her blonde hair from her cheek.

Never had she been so close. She couldn't help herself — the sound of his voice, deep and soft, and caress of his hand. April had no control; her tears welled, then overflowed. Through blurred, wet eyes, April stared at his closeness.

'Oh darling, your father said you were likely to cry; you get so emotional.' Richard leant closer and kissed her cheek. His lips felt hot and genuine, his breath wisping her hair.

She gasped. She didn't want this to end.

74

The church organ began again, a familiar piece, and the congregation stood.

April had not been fully aware of her surroundings, fixed on Richard. Now, as she gazed around, she saw them, an abundance of feathers, glittering hatpins, furs, and top hats.

April rose, taking balance from the solid back of the pew in front of her. A woman in a brimmed hat fixed with a pearl hatpin, mere inches from her. Everyone now turned around. The woman smiled warmly. April felt the deep pang of recognition — she knew this woman — *Anna*.

'Here she comes,' whispered the woman, her hand reaching for hers.

She was there, on her father's arm, her sister.

In time with the organ, Emily paced the aisle dressed in a long lace gown, high neckline and long fitted sleeves, draped in a delicate veil, a winter bouquet in hand.

James stood, refined in his Suffolk Regiment military uniform. His red jacket with gleaming gold buttons, trousers, and shoes like mirrors. He gazed, glassy-eyed, as she reached his side. The Wedding March finished, and silence fell.

Richard turned to his wife, leaned close, kissed her cheek and whispered in her ear.

'I love you, Belle.'

~

April remained silent and motionless for the rest of the Christmas service, almost unaware of the organ or jubilant crowds around her. Richard had cast his spell

The family walked the short journey home. The late hour was crisp; cars and footpaths wore a glittering blanket of fresh snow. April moseyed, arm in arm, with her grandmother, who, from time to time, glanced at April to see the same quiet expression.

'Now, that was truly a treat,' Michael said as he closed the front door behind them, shutting out the chilly night.

'I agree, lovely.' Julia replied, unwrapping her scarf a little, her cheeks flushed in the warm room. 'How about you, Mum? Did you enjoy yourself?'

'Yes, it was lovely,' Sarah had settled herself in her chair, watching April, as she sat opposite on the velvet settee.

'Well, it's late; I think we should be getting home. We'll be back nice and early in the morning. Don't forget; I'm cooking the turkey tomorrow; you could do with a rest. You look absolutely shattered,' Julia remarked, cautiously glancing to April.

'I'm just a little tired, it's been a busy day, what with shopping this morning. I will have a hot chocolate, and then I'm off to bed,' Sarah replied, stifling a yawn.

'Come, April, let's go home, let your Nan get to bed.'

'Mum, do you mind if I stay tonight? If that's ok with you, Nan, can I stay here?'

'I don't mind if your Nan doesn't,' Julia replied, with an exhale of relief, as she ushered Michael back out into the cold. 'See you both in the morning.'

'Nan, I'll make that hot chocolate,' April headed through to the kitchen. As she entered, her eyes roamed the space; only a couple of hours before, she'd seen Emily here. She pondered how it hadn't frightened her.

April filled the milk pan and turned on the hob, and stood, chin in hand and elbows on the work surface, watching the milk as it got hotter and bubbled. Unaware, she hadn't noticed her grandmother behind her. April poured two mugs of hot chocolate, turned to see her sitting at the table. She saw at once how different she looked, how the day had taken its toll.

'Nan, is there anything I can get you?'

'No, darling. As I told your Mum, I'm only tired after the day we've had.' Sarah hugged her warm mug. 'I need a good night's sleep.'

'Well, we'll have this and head off to bed. I love you.' April sat down on the other wooden chair. She lifted her mug to her lips, watched her grandmother over the rim. Sarah's eyes were closed, the mug cradled in her hands. 'Nan, you head on upstairs. I'll lock up.'

'It's all right, I'll wait for you, and then I'll find you a spare nightdress.'

April walked through to the front room, tipped some coal onto the fire, and replaced the empty scuttle on the hearth beside her grandmother's chair.

'All ready! Nan, are you sure there isn't anything I can get you? You aren't looking yourself.'

'Honestly, Little One, please don't worry. I'll feel right as rain in the morning. We're going to have the best Christmas.'

April held her grandmother's arm as they ascended the stairs. They reached the top, and both headed into her grandmother's bedroom. Sarah walked over to a large tallboy close to the window and slowly opened the bottom drawer. Its silky rosewood veneer had a touchable quality, and April ran her fingers over the surface.

'There you go. I'm sure this one will be fine. I know it's not very trendy, but it'll do for tonight and will keep you nice and cosy,' Sarah said, handing her a cotton nightgown with long sleeves and a ribbon tie at the neck. The front yoke was embroidered with pink roses, and the floral theme followed at the cuffs.

'It's sweet; it'll do perfectly.' April took the nightgown and hugged her, not wanting to let her go.

'Darling, what is it?'

'I do love you.'

'Now, off to bed with you, you can sleep in the room at the end of the hall. You'll find a spare toothbrush in the bathroom cupboard. Do you realise it's nearly one o'clock in the morning? Sarah said, yawning.

77

April stood at the long swivel mirror, holding the nightdress to her chest, turning this way and that, the reflection of the four-poster bed behind her. She watched the charm bracelet twinkle in the low lamplight. There was a belonging, an all-encompassing sense of home as she settled into the bedroom untouched by time.

She climbed into bed, resting back against the carved headboard. She could see the garden from here and the churchyard beyond that. Both were crisp and bright, the moon shedding dust twinkles to the snow.

Exhaustion won, April shifted down onto her pillow and turned off the lamp and closed her eyes. But her mind was alive with images, memories of the day. It slotted them together, fashioned some kind of bizarre puzzle.

There is logic to all this if you believe. Nan's words rolled over themselves, time again. Yet each time, they gathered more questions. *Reincarnation? Ghosts?*

CHAPTER TWELVE

A dense blanket of fresh snow covered the garden. Boughs of the large tree hung heavy over the crisp whiteness. It had been a glorious Christmas, now New Year's Eve brought the dawn of a new century.

Captain Warner strode into the parlour and steadily carried a silver tray with crystal punch glasses. He handed one to each of the family and took his place beside the fire. The clock hands were at two minutes to midnight. He raised his glass.

'I would like to make a toast,' he cast his eyes across his family. 'To my dear Emily and my new son-in-law James, I wish you love and happiness. To Annabelle, and Richard, who is like a son to me, may this be a fruitful year for you both.'

'To the family!' they all rejoiced.

'Now, it is almost midnight and a new century dawn; we hope that 1900 will bring us prosperity and peace, with a swift end to the war in South Africa, and of course, the safe return of our local young men serving their country.' They lifted their glasses again as the mantle clock chimed midnight and the family toasted the new century.

~

January; cold and frosty with a renewed crisp covering of snow throughout the long month; as it ended, the approach of February brought more relentless snow, bleak and dismal yet. The panorama remained white; the forgotten grass lay deeply hidden under its thick winter blanket. The sky was grim, drab with its grey, lifeless palate.

James stood, in silent contemplation, with no regard for the miserable weather; it simply dampened his mood further. Richard closed the door behind them, though James made no response to the creaking hinges. They watched the repetitive pattern of falling flakes touching and melting on the glass.

'Have you told her yet?' Richard asked.

James swallowed hard, his mouth dry. 'No,' he replied shortly and brushed an invisible piece of lint from his sleeve. 'She was full of song this morning; I could not ruin it.'

'She needs to know. It is inevitable. You should be making the most of your time together.' Richard placed his hand on James' shoulder. 'You know she will have Annabelle.'

'You are right.'

'You will feel better once you have told her,' Richard sympathised.

James rubbed his hand over the back of his neck in a pointless act to ease his tension. 'I cannot find the words, you know.'

'If you keep leaving it, it will only make things worse.'

James drew himself up, filled his chest, opened the dining-room door and headed for the parlour.

Emily sat at the piano, singing quietly, her fingers effortless over the keys.

At his entrance, she turned to him with a beaming smile. 'My darling.' She closed the lid and headed towards him with a swish of her skirts. 'Whatever is it?'

James closed the door silently behind him, his head low tracing the patterned carpet.

Taking his hand, she rubbed it between hers. 'Your fingers are frozen.' Emily looked straight up into his eyes, but they avoided her.

James guided Emily to the fireside chair. He remained silent; his eyes persistently traced the pattern under his feet. Maybe it was better to say nothing than break such sad tidings without first preparing her. She reluctantly sat as he knelt before her. A log hissed; red sparks flew as he gazed at the glowing embers, pondering, searching for the right words to say.

'James, James, look at me, tell me please? What is wrong?' She pressed her palms to his cheeks, cradling his face in her hands.

'Emily, I love you. You mean the world to me; you know that?'

'Of course. And I, you. Darling, whatever this is, just tell me,' Emily leant forward and planted tiny kisses over his forehead.

'I have to leave next month.' The words stung his tongue but left his chest empty, lighter from the burden. Yet, as he watched Emily's face drop, her eyes swell, he wished he could pull them back, hold on to them.

'Next month? You are leaving next month?' Emily's hands fell from his face; her eyes darted to the fire. She reached over, took a poker from the stand and jabbed at it.

'My Battalion, we are being sent to South Africa. We leave on the eleventh of February,' he said slowly.

Emily flung the poker onto the hearth; it clattered harshly on the tiles. Then straight-backed, she made no sound. Silence.

'Emily, I am leaving for Africa next month.'

'I heard you. I heard what you said.'

'I am sorry. I know it is so soon after —'

'I understand.' Emily sat perfectly still; her hands gripped in her lap.

James pulled back on his heels, sat on the chair opposite and studied her. The short slow breaths, the slightest rise and fall, the careful glance to her hands, then up to his face. Emily stood, her fingers smoothing the creases in her dark blue dress. Then as she faced him directly, he saw it, that look of utter defiance.

'You shall return home to me, do you understand? You shall return home so we can live our perfect life together. Do you understand me, James? If you do not come home, I shall never forgive you.'

He nodded. 'Understood.'

There was no more talk of war. Instead, the family spoke of peace and aspirations for the new century. Annabelle took to holding her sister more often than usual, her arms folding around her in an unspoken acknowledgement.

~

Emily perched at her dressing table, her hands resting in her lap, staring hypnotically into her oval mirror, looking past her reflection, preoccupied with what life lay before them. Slowly, she re-entered her conscious mind with a light tapping at her door.

'Emily, can I come in?' Annabelle called lightly.

'Of course,' she turned on her padded stool.

Annabelle sat on the end of the bed, her arm wrapped around one of the bedposts.

'How are you, dearest?' she asked warmly.

Emily, determined not to show any emotion, shook under pressure, 'I am perfectly fine, as you can see.'

'No matter what may lay before us, I will always be by your side,' Annabelle began hesitantly. 'I am your sister, and I have always been here to look after you. It is no different now you are married.' She felt her lips rise in a smile, though her chest gripped with uncertainty.

'But it is different. I am no longer a child. You should not have to look after me.' Emily pressed her lips together.

'Dearest, that is not exactly how I meant...' Annabelle breathed. 'You know I am here for you.'

'I do. But it is no longer your... responsibility to care for me. I am married, so it is James' responsibility,' she snapped. 'And now that I am his wife, he is leaving me.'

'Oh, my dearest. James will return home. Father says the war cannot last; we shall have our men home soon.' Annabelle soothed.

Emily cast a sideways glance in her mirror and smiled at her sister's reflection. 'You are right. Now, when are you heading back home?'

'I shall stay. Richard can cope without me for a while longer. I can be here as long as you need me, dearest.'

Emily abandoned the dressing stool and sat on the bed next to her sister.

'I appreciate you being here, but your loyalties lie with Richard, at home with him,' Emily squeezed her hand. 'You are his wife; treasure that.' She brought her sister's hand up to her mouth, kissing it. 'Please, promise me you will go home. James will return to me.'

'Richard understands my need to be here with you.'

Annabelle brushed her hand gently across Emily's cheek, 'You look so much like Mother,' Annabelle gulped with the need to hold back tears.

'Do you miss her?' Emily sat, looking at her knees, her face consumed by melancholy

'I remember her still. She is clear in my thoughts, and I still miss her dreadfully. But, I have you to remind me, you look so much like her.'

Annabelle wandered over to the large bay window, resting her hand on the back of the bedroom chair. The pink drapes framed the snowy scene like a stage setting.

'Tell me about her,' Emily silently wandered over, resting her head on her shoulder. 'What was she like?'

'She had hair like yours, rich auburn that shone like amber in the sun; it hung in ringlets to her waist. I would watch her brush it for hours,' Annabelle's face became wistful as her voice trembled. 'The sunlight would shine through the bedroom window and make her face glow. Her skin was as fair as porcelain, and her eyes the deepest brown…' she shivered, 'when she smiled, the room would light up.'

'Please, go on,' Emily said, her head still resting on her sisters.

'As I reached the age of four, Mother was expecting a baby — you. We would lie on her bed, and I would lay with my cheek on her tummy and feel you move and kick. Of course, I did not understand, but I took her word for it, and that was how it was — I would have a brother or sister. For me, it was having someone to play with,' she smiled, resting her hand on Emily's. 'I'm sure that I imagined a baby doll. She would stroke my hair and call me her Little One. She promised me, no matter what, I would always be her Little One.'

Annabelle sobbed as the pain floated back to the surface. The memory flickered in and out of focus until before her eyes, the sight of her dead mother. She gripped her eyes tight, eager to expel the vision.

Emily squeezed her arm, pulling her close and kissing her shoulder, 'I can sometimes imagine her in my mind from all the stories you have told me. How lovely she was and how much she loved us both, even if…' she swallowed hard, '…she died because of me.'

'You cannot say such things. Mother loved you from the very moment she knew you were growing inside her; she loved you,' tears trailed down Annabelle's face. 'Please, do not ever think any different; she loved you, just as I do.'

'I have always loved her, even though I never knew her, I suppose it is the same.'

Annabelle pulled a linen handkerchief from her pocket and wiped her eyes, studying the wet patches darken the embroidered roses, lost in misery.

A lone bird caught her attention; it swooped, soaring daringly close to the window. With an impulse, Annabelle's hand went to the latch, compelled to call to the tiny bird. But the bird fluttered its wings and disappeared into the white sky.

'Annabelle?'

She shuddered slightly; Emily rubbed her arm to warm her as her tone lifted. 'We would sit for hours in the study, me beside her on the settee, the sun streaming through the sash… I would watch the birds while she read. Book after book, hours we would spend. Sometimes, she would create stories about long lost and far off places. And then… and then one day, she was gone.' Annabelle stopped, unable to continue, her voice paralysed.

The vision of their dead mother, white and blood stained, flirted for her attention.

Emily pulled her closer and flung her arms around her. Both stood for a few moments, veiled in sorrow

'But then,' Annabelle continued with a shaky voice, 'but then we had you to look after. Father did his best, and I loved you so much. Every time I looked at you, I saw Mother. As you grew, the more like her you became. Oh, Emily, I am here for you, just as I have always been. No matter what life brings, we shall always have each other.'

'I shall remain strong for James' sake. For us both. He must know that I can cope; I do not want him to worry. It will be terrible enough for him over there.

'Come; let us go downstairs; dinner will soon be ready. You must make the most of the time you have left with James.'

~

The cruel uncertainty dawned with the dark February morning. Brutally early, the sky, a dull grey, hung bloated with snow. Emily halted at the turn of the stairs, faced with the sight of James in full uniform.

He stood tall yet was swamped by his young and boyish features. As all those that had gone before and those who would follow, James stood ready to serve his country, with no knowledge of when he would return home or if, indeed, he ever would.

The callous weather was harsh in a blinding snowstorm. The crowd cheered over a hundred strong, and the railway station wore a coat of uniforms — another wave of British Military to descend upon African shores. Yet, a veil of melancholy and misery hung heavy beneath the cheering — the steam train awaited its departure. Heaps of chests and kit bags lined the icy platform as the snow continued to camouflage them in a guise of white.

Overwhelmed with sheer bewilderment, Emily cast her eyes across the crowd, aware of the same expression on every other woman, the blinding fear of becoming widowed or childless.

A piercing whistle blew, loud above the sound of the bustling crowds. The men began to collect their kit bags and board the train. The blizzard and mass of uniforms made it impossible to distinguish man from man.

Emily threw her arms around his neck; her heart fell into despair. She filled her senses, something to remain with her until his return if indeed she could bear to let him go at all. She gripped him, sinking her nails into his jacket.

'Emily, everything will work out, just you see. I shall be on my way home to you very soon. Please, my darling, you know I love you more than the world. Never forget that.' His words warmed as he whispered and kissed her. 'Always remember that I love you more than anything.'

James eased her sobbing face from him, peeling her hands away, holding them tight in his. She stared, pink and flushed. Then he reached down to retrieve his kit bag. She felt the end coming, running at her like a wild beast with great claws and gnashing jaws.

'I must go. I must go now. Remember that I love you, Emily. Please never forget that, with every beat of my heart, which right now is breaking.'

James took her hand one last time and pressed a small, folded piece of paper into her palm. Emily squeezed her fingers over it.

The loud whistle blew for the second time as the rest of the men boarded the train. Steam billowed across the platform, and the whistle sounded.

'I love you, James. I will always love you and when...'

'No more words. If anything should happen, I want you to read the letter, but only then.'

'I love you, my darling.' Emily shouted over the din as the train began to move.

'Promise me, Emily,' he shouted.

'But...'

'No, promise me. Only read it if anything happens to me, not before.'

'Yes, James, I promise.'

'Only God could keep me from you.'

For the last time, James kissed his wife. For a moment, all was silent; no one else existed. He turned his back and jumped onto the train.

Steam consumed the air as uniformed arms waved frantically from the open windows as an eerie silence fell over the platform. Finally, the train was swallowed into the blizzard.

CHAPTER THIRTEEN

Hours became days, became weeks. Overwhelmed by grief, Emily retreated to her room. Even with an empty heart, she realised she had no choice. It made no difference where she was; James was not there.

The first signs of spring appeared; buds and blossom; warmer days brought brighter mornings and lighter evenings. Some days were easier than others.

Annabelle watched the ritual grow.

Emily would sit in the fireside chair, staring out of the window, waiting for a letter. Warmer days had moved her to the garden, although her frame of mind had not altered. At least the location was a change of scene. However, the letters from James had not yet arrived. There had been no news at all.

Early sunshine soaked through the drapes. Emily lounged on her window chair in the quietness of her room and listened to the voice's downstairs, their cheery tones. She scowled.

Following the sound into the dining room, she was greeted with the breakfast table laden with birthday gifts.

'Happy Birthday! Come, sit down.' Annabelle gestured.

The sun glistened optimistically through the glass doors, flooding the room. Emily sat beside her father, staring out through the open doors at the lavender.

'Would you rather your gifts now or after breakfast?' Annabelle asked.

Emily merely nodded, looked at the heap of gifts, a mass of pink paper and white ribbon, and took the top one and pulled the ribbon. It unfurled in her hand. Inside lay a blue leather box. She lifted the lid.

'Emily, do you like it? Both Richard and I thought it was beautiful. We knew it was perfect,' Annabelle squealed. 'Do you like it, say you do?'

Emily lifted the brooch from the box, filling her palm. Leafy tendrils and a floral frame in silver shone in the morning light, a blue Wedgwood cameo in the centre.

'I love it,' Emily replied, holding back tears. 'I truly do. I do not know what to say.'

'Open this one next,' her father slid a large box over.

Emily opened it, easing off the ribbon and letting the paper fall away. A large wooden box lay on the table before her. Emily ran her fingertips over the mother-of-pearl inlay. On the pink paper lay a tiny key on a thin white cord.

'Open it. There is more.'

Turning the key, the lid clicked and rose slightly. Inside were three silver items. She reached inside, removing them in turn.

'They are lovely.' Tears trickled down her cheeks to her chin as she turned the silver hairbrush in her hand.

'They belonged to your mother,' her father began. 'I thought it was time you had them, knowing you would treasure them. I had them engraved with your initials; your mother would have wanted that.' He reached over and took the hand mirror. In scroll engraving her initials, ERW.

'I don't know what to say. Thank you.' Emily uttered, overwhelmed.

Annabelle watched her meticulously place the silver items back into the box, and then turned to her father and gave him a nod.

'And this one too,' her father said, handing Emily the last gift. 'It arrived this morning.'

Emily's heart leapt from her ribcage and lodged itself in her throat. She took it. An envelope bearing her name in James' distinctive hand sat in her fingers. She carefully placed the unopened letter into the marquetry box along with her other gifts, then pushed the box to one side.

'So many gifts, thank you. Now, what is for breakfast?' Emily asked Mary, who stood beside the dining table wearing her customary beam. It eased her sorrow a little. 'I am hungry this morning.'

The breakfast conversation passed over Emily. She heard the family talk, nodded when it seemed appropriate, but she was not listening. Annabelle spoke of her brooch, asked her thoughts, her face full of pleasure and delight. She had answered, with *I love it*, and *it is beautiful*, but her thoughts sat firmly on James. Though, cruelly, all she could recall was their last moments stood on that frozen platform. How the cold leached into her heart filled her with dread. She wanted to recall happier memories. She needed to escape, all the while her eyes were on the box.

Mary cleared the plates, aided by Annabelle while her father read his newspaper. Excusing herself, Emily left the table, gifts in hand, running back to the sanctuary of her bedroom.

She placed the marquetry box on her dressing table, ran her hand over the smooth surface and eased open the lid. Then, tentatively, she took out the envelope and stared at the handwriting.

This was what she had waited for — had longed for these past months. Yet now it was here; she could not bring herself to open it.

With the sun on her back, she slipped her finger under the seal. On seeing her name, her heart thudded, and warmth spread through her body.

My darling Emily,

It is so tough to sit here in the blistering sun, knowing that you, my love, are there without me. But I promise I will be home very soon. You are my life and being without you is no life at all. I just exist, and barely that.

I am not sure how long this letter will take to get to you. It is your birthday soon, and I hope it will be with you by then, so, Happy Birthday, my love.

How is life there? I hope everyone is well, please give the family my regards. You must not worry about me, the war will soon be over, and I will be...

'You all right there, Corporal,' the gruff voice startled James. He put down his pencil, carefully folding the piece of paper. 'You go ahead, you write to your gal. We don't have much else, do we, other than the thought of those we've at home,' he paused, coughing. 'This damn dusty air, give me some good old wretched English weather any day.'

James nodded a half-hearted smile, 'thank you, sir.'

Dusk fell — the air thick with blistering heat, corrupted by the stench of sweat and fresh blood. Comrades lay bleeding in sodden bandages, muffled, suffering murmurs. The coughing travelled into the distance. James' mind wandered back to Emily. His loneliness was immense, mounting with each dawn. He knew he was not alone, they all had stories of loved ones back home, but it was no consolation.

Emily's embrace, her lips pressed to his, eased his heart a touch. James ran his forefinger around the inside of his collar, releasing the stench of stale sweat, his rough uniform, tinged with blood and ground-in dirt, chafed his sunburned skin.

Unfolding the paper, he licked the dull pencil and continued.

...with you very soon, our lives will be full of happiness. All the boys have been writing to their families. John, he's a good chap, his wife is expecting a baby. He talks of nothing else and how good it will be to be home. He comes from a town by the sea; he tells stories of how lovely the place looks in the summer and how much he misses it. I like hearing him talk of home; I think living by the sea would suit us. What do you think, a little cottage near the beach, and our children playing in the sand? It is thoughts like these that keep me going and the idea of holding you in my arms, my dearest Emily.

I love you always, James.

With her body drenched in sunlight and her heart saturated by James' letter, Emily pressed her fingertips to the words, pulling her love closer, committing every word to memory.

'Emily?' Annabelle called whilst she tapped on the door. 'Yes?'

Annabelle peered around the door. 'May I come in?'

Emily nodded, folding the letter, slipping it back in its envelope, then quickly putting it back in the box, turning the key with a swift click.

'Your brooch looks lovely with your dress. That is just what I had in mind,' Annabelle stood in front of Emily, casting her in shadow. 'Are you ready?' Annabelle asked.

'Oh yes, sorry, ready for what?' Emily said, still preoccupied.

'I hoped we could spend some time together, just us. Mary has packed us a basket.' Annabelle reached to take Emily's hand.

'Oh, like when we were children?'

'We can sit by the river.'

~

There was nothing of worry or sorrow, not now, not today. The park was green, flourishing and lush with a thick grass carpet. Annabelle led them toward the river. The Abbot's Bridge made its way across the water; two stone arches curved above the calm surface, and overhanging boughs of the border trees trailed their branch tips.

Annabelle rested the picnic basket on the bank then shook the chequered blanket. It billowed in and gently came to rest on the grass. They sat, shaded by their parasols. Annabelle opened the basket, unfolding a cloth between them. Emily reached for freshly baked bread and sliced ham and placed them on the cloth.

'Thank you.' Emily, resting her hand on her sister's arm.

'For what? It is your birthday.' Annabelle poured them both some lemonade.

'It is a lovely gesture, and welcome. I know I have not been myself of late,' Emily said. 'Thank you for my brooch too. It's beautiful, truly.' She lay back with a sigh, resting her head on the blanket under the shade.

'I am glad you love it. And, of course, I am happy you received a letter too. Did it take long to get here?' Annabelle asked with caution.

'Yes, he had written it many weeks ago. He assures me everything is good. He says he will be coming home soon,' Emily paused. 'Yes, he said he will be home very soon.'

'It is lovely to see you smile. It has been so long since we have had a day like this,' Annabelle turned to look at her sister and continued in a whisper, 'Darling, I have something to tell you. I can no longer keep it to myself,' Annabelle beamed, her face flushed.

'What is it? Tell me,' Emily replied.

'Richard and I are expecting a baby. It is due to be born in December.'

'Well… Well, now that is wonderful, just wonderful. Oh, I am so pleased for you both,' Emily sat up and leant over, squeezing her sister's arm.

'It is still early.'

'What does Richard think? I should imagine he is thrilled, and Father, have you told him yet?'

'Only Richard knows. I wanted you to know first. I wanted you to know before anyone else. I shall feel complete; to be a mother is the most important thing to me.'

Annabelle laid herself back and closed her eyes.

'Oh Annabelle, be a mother and have a child of your own. I shall love to be a mother one day.' Emily's tone aired a slight unease. Annabelle caught sight of her sister's concerned expression.

'And you shall, I am sure of it. You will be a wonderful mother,' Annabelle clasped her hands. 'Everything is going to be all right; I promise.'

~

The captain sat at the breakfast table. 'What a glorious June morning.' He breathed deeply, taking in the fresh air.

Mary poured them all a cup of tea, and the family sat in conversation as they ate.

'The photographer is arriving at eleven,' the captain stated. 'I expect you both resplendent,' he smiled at Annabelle with a wink.

'Of course, may I enquire, will it be Mr Brown?' Emily rolled her eyes, her tone falsely sweet.

'Yes, it is.' He sat back on his dining chair, inhaling deeply with readiness. 'Before you say a word…'

'Father, how can you tolerate his manner? He is so infuriating.' Emily sat back, discarding the sausage that rolled about her plate.

'I understand he may be a little… eccentric, let us say, but he is a superb photographer. And, as we have always used

Mr Brown's services for years, I see no reason to discontinue our arrangement now.'

'Yes, I agree. The wedding photographs of James and I are lovely. However, they would have taken half the time if he had not insisted we continue to stand, frozen, in the snow. Photographs should be taken in the warm. *We must sacrifice ourselves for art,'* she mimicked.

Annabelle smiled at her father and raised an eyebrow as she looked at her sister. 'Then let us hope we do not have a freak snowstorm this morning,' Annabelle stated, placing her napkin on the table beside her. She sympathised with her sister. Their encounters with Mr Brown had never been desirable, if not always memorable.

When they were children, Emily no more than five, Father had commissioned a collection of photographs. Annabelle recalled the warm breezy day. Mr Brown positioned a large fringed Indian parasol to shade the girls and *add a touch of drama*. They wore pretty dresses and sat on a garden seat beneath the shade.

Exasperated, Mr Brown had huffed loudly, clearly lost in his distress, with the task of setting and resetting the tableau. But disapprovingly, he had no control over the weather as the wind blew up ready for a storm, whipping at the long silk tassels and the lacy frills of their dresses. He instructed the girls *no matter what, you must not move*. The occasion had ended abruptly with Emily in tears, too much lemonade and a soiled dress.

~

Annabelle watched from the top of the garden steps, her lilac gown hung to the floor, with fitted bodice and puff sleeves; around her wrist hung her charm bracelet.

The captain stood at the bottom of the stairs, his hand restless on the newel post. 'The photographer is here,' he called up. 'Do come along, Emily.' She appeared at the turn of the staircase. 'There you are, Mr Brown is waiting,' he continued softer now.

'Then, let him,' she muttered. 'Oh, wait…'

With quick steps, Emily ran back up the stairs; a few moments later, she returned, holding her Wedgwood cameo.

The captain stood with the photographer at the bottom of the garden as he assembled the equipment and positioned a scrolled wicker chair under the vast tree. With his hands balled at his hips, Mr Brown rocked on his heels, his waistcoat buttons threatening to burst.

Emily arrived behind her sister, resting her hand on her shoulder.

'There he is, all five feet of him, the despicable little man.'

'Emily! You should not be so…'

'What truthful?' Emily added quickly. 'This better be over quickly.' Then, Emily followed her sister down into the garden with a painted smile on her face.

'There you are.' Her father waved his arm, beckoning her quickly.

'I could not have the photograph taken without it,' Emily said with a sweet smile.

Despite Emily's considered opinion of Mr Brown, the sitting went smoother than expected — no wind. Instead, the sun shone with not a rain cloud. Annabelle had the foresight to sit first. The frills of her dress had behaved, her hands clasped, her charm bracelet around her wrist. *Delightful*.

Mr Brown bent over the tripod, gazing at the image of Emily through his lens. 'Oh, that is perfect, my dear. That is it, hold still...' He raised his head and the sun glinted on his bald scalp.

Eager not to move, Emily squealed with a suppressed laugh. Mr Brown shot up from his tripod, startled.

'Whatever is it?' he shrieked.

'Oh, I am sorry, Mr Brown, there was a wasp, and it was buzzing near my head. I do apologise. I think it has gone now; please continue.' Emily's voice shook as she curbed her laughter.

'Please do not worry, my dear, we shall have another try. There is no greater sacrifice than for that of our art. Hmm,' he pondered, then continued, 'maybe if you sit facing the other way, yes, I think that would be better. Oh, and lift your chin, my dear, let us show off that cameo, shall we,' bellowed Mr Brown.

Afterwards, the sister sat in the study, watching father see the photographer off.

'Emily, I cannot believe you could be so cruel.' Annabelle chided. 'It only caused to prolonging the ordeal.'

'Oh, I could not help myself.' Emily laughed. 'It was the reflection of his shiny head?' They both chuckled.

Annabelle settled herself and opened her book. The leather-bound volume lay in her lap as she reclined, and her mind wandered from the words on the page. Trying not to alarm Emily, she steadily rose and leaned forward, her hands gripping the edge of the desk.

'Darling, whatever is it?' Guiding her back to her seat, Emily took her hand, looked into her face. 'Annabelle, tell me what is wrong. Is it the baby?' Emily's heart pounded in fear and panic, not knowing what to do.

'Please, get Richard.' Annabelle lay back on the settee and closed her eyes; her body ached, from neck to ankle.

Emily dashed from the room.

'Richard, quick, it's Annabelle! It is the baby!' Emily rushed into the parlour as Richard removed his jacket. She tore back into the study.

Motionless, gritting her teeth, Annabelle lay with her back rigid and her hands clasped in front of her. She did not, dared not, move. Beside her, Richard carefully took her hand, stroking his thumb over her fingers.

'Belle, darling,' his voice was soft. 'Tell me what's wrong.' Richard placed his right hand on her flushed cheek and eased her face to him.

'I think I should lie down.' She took Richard's hand with a reassuring plea. 'Please, do not worry.'

'Your father is fetching the doctor. Come along; I shall help you upstairs.' Richard walked her up to the bedroom.

~

'Ah, Dr Hickson, thank you for coming so quickly.' Richard met the doctor at the bedroom door.

'Richard, you can wait downstairs. I shall be down as soon as I have looked at her.' The doctor closed the door as Richard descended the stairs.

Annabelle slowly opened her eyes.

'Dr Hickson. Just a little discomfort, a little stabbing pain. It passed quickly. I am just exhausted now; I only wish to sleep.' Annabelle began to ease herself into a seated position on the bed, all the while repeating her affirmation.

'You lay still. Let me have a look at you.' He examined her, his eye never making contact with hers. She did not need him to say the words or express her thoughts.

'You need rest, lots of it. And certainly, no excitement.'

He closed the door firmly behind him, and Annabelle heaved a long sigh. She changed into her nightgown and slipped into her crisp sheets, staring out of the window.

Mesmerised by birdsong, she honed in, concentrating on the lone chirp. It was there again, the tiny bird with fluttering wings. The bird swooped down to the sill, its tiny head twitching this way and that as it stared through the glass.

Go away, little bird, she pleaded; as her thoughts fell to her dead mother, the vision of her blurred red with blood.

CHAPTER FOURTEEN

Bright light glistened in a honey glow through the room. Annabelle lay submerged, with the crisp linen of the pillows against her cheek; she lay on her side, one arm about her head, her fingers entwining, wrapping her fair hair tightly, almost stopping all circulation.

It will be all right, she repeated, drumming the words into her head; *it will all be fine*. She could not bear to think of what might be, but her consciousness would not let her think of anything else.

Finally, she rose and dressed.

'Ah, my dear, are you feeling better today? Can I get you anything?' Mary asked as Annabelle reached the bottom stair. 'You're looking better for some rest,' Mary added.

'A glass of water, thank you. I shall be in the study.'

Annabelle placed her hand on the cold, brass knob, twisting it, quickly closing the study door behind her. For a moment, she stood her back to the door, resting her head against the wood. Eyes tightly shut, absorbed the calm, soothing her soul. The door nudged, and she quickly stepped forward to allow Mary to enter, carrying a tea tray.

'There you go, my dear, a nice cup of tea, and I thought you must be hungry, so I've cut you a slice of sponge cake to go with it. I know, I know,' Mary waved her hand, '...but water isn't going to build your strength now, is it.' Mary rested the tray on a side table nearby. 'Oh, it's stuffy in here. Let me open the window. You could do with some fresh air.'

'No,' Annabelle gasped. The thought of the little bird, its knowing gaze, drew the breath from her lungs. 'Sorry, yes, of course.'

Mary flashed her a worried glance, then reached over to the study window and pushed up the sash. 'It's a lovely day,' she soothed. The breeze lifted the lacy drapes as they danced, the afternoon sunshine hitting the depths of the garden.

'Thank you, Mary, the cake looks lovely. What time is it?' Annabelle reached over to her teacup, eager to expel her odd mood. 'How long have I slept?'

'Oh, it's four o'clock, my dear. You needed the rest. I told Emily she wasn't to wake you.' Mary headed back to the door, giving her a usual smile.

Annabelle reached for her book on the mahogany desk, its green binding hot from the sun. She relaxed.

'Darling, do come outside. Some fresh air will do you good.' Richard entered, his face sun blushed.

'In a while. Please, you must not fuss,' Annabelle smiled; while inside, she wanted to scream. Richard returned her gesture and closed the door behind him.

'Annabelle, Annabelle,' Emily called from the garden. Returning her book to the shelf, she strolled to the open sash. The summer wind whipped a golden strand of hair across her cheeks as she saw her family between the drapes.

'I'm coming,' she muttered.

Annabelle closed the book, left her sanctuary and headed for the garden. She halted. Neither in nor out of the house, today the garden seemed so open, vast — unpredictable. She should go back to the study, back to her book, safe.

One step at a time. One step, then the next. No need to rush.

Cautiously Annabelle walked down each stone step, the lavender brushing her gown as she counted her way.

She could do this. Everything was going to be all right. *Just take it carefully, and you must rest.*

Dr Hicksons' words were rolling themselves over one another until nothing made sense anymore. There had been blood. Too much to be *common*, not that she had mentioned that to Richard. He would only worry, and what could he possibly do. Father had not been able to save mother, and he had worried enough for them both. He still did.

Annabelle stepped down onto the lush grass, her low heels sinking. It caught her off guard, caused her to stumble, her left foot stepping uneasily, then the right.

She counted: *eleven, twelve, thirteen*, then put her hand on the back of the garden seat, filling her lungs, and painted a smile in place.

'Your sister has beaten me.' Richard stood, hand on hips, his face incredulous. For the first time in four years, Emily had triumphed; Annabelle could not help but laugh.

Finally, she sat, her body heavy, her mind somewhere else. Annabelle closed her eyes, drifted, her sister's voice growing distant, joined by her fathers. Richard, she could feel him; he held her hand tightly. She would be safe now.

Sand. They were at the beach. Shielding her eyes with her hands, she stared up the dunes. It was all right; father was waving from the top. Sand quelched between her toes, looking down; her legs were thin, wet, as she held her dress scrunched in the young fists.

Another wave, she would jump it — this one she would catch. Anna had already scolded her for getting wet, but she did not care. This was important; she had to do this, *had to...* What? What did she have to do? Save her. Yes, she had to save her. It was coming again, tumbling, foaming, crashing, driving up the beach towards her. She could run, should she? No. No, she had to stand and hold firm. She was a *big girl*. She had to save her; had to protect her, *to protect everyone*.

It was growing wilder, foaming at the mouth and baring its teeth. Annabelle braced, gripping her dress to her belly, holding, pressing it tightly. She would not let go. Never let it go.

But there was the wave. Enormous and growing, all-encompassing. It crashed down, churning the sand at her feet, throwing her up in the air, higher and higher. Then she was falling, falling, falling. Down she came, hard, and the sea crashed over her head in a vast, red wave.

Annabelle gripped Richard's hand, her fingertips white with the pressure. She could not move. The pain. Oh, the pain.

Richard sat up, looked at her pale face, sensed her agony, mirrored her despair. He ran across the garden, leaping up the steps. Within seconds, Emily was by her side with a calm voice of reassurance and comfort. *It will be all right.* Though the words were meaningless.

Richard dashed back, and with a whisk, she was in his arms wrapped in a blanket.

Annabelle lay on her bed.

Gradually, the red wave retreated. It pulled back into the sea, leaving the sand stained and gouged. Leaving her empty as it took part of her with it.

~

Annabelle sat, her face close to the window; the morning warmed the glass, and the trains repetitive motion and regular rhythm snared her senses. She was trapped. The sight of trees and fields unremitting. Annabelle shut her eyes, defeated. The ache in her heart and hollowness in her body left her empty. The only sensation was her hand that rest, detached, in Richard's.

The train clattered on its tracks, minutes turned to hours, with no more change than the repetitive Norfolk landscape. Richard attempted conversation, she recalled the sound of his voice, but she could not decipher any meaning to his words. Nothing had reason now. Annabelle sat in silence.

Finally, the train pulled into the station with its billows of hot steam. Richard stood, grabbed the luggage from the rack, and took her hand. They stepped onto the platform. Closing her eyes, Annabelle lifted her face to the sun, absorbing its rays; her heartache eased slightly with the recollections of her childhood, a time of simplicity and carefree days. Then it rolled in, greeting her, that vast wave.

~

Vivid orange wrapped the horizon as the sunrise climbed to meet the morning. The early hour brought respite from her restless night. Annabelle sat at the bedroom window, watching the gulls fly the dawn sky, swooping low to the glistening surface of the sea then far beyond the gaze.

It was no more than five o'clock.

Annabelle removed her cotton nightgown and stood at her mirror. Her reflection belonged to another; it scarcely resembled the woman she hoped to be. Her body was gaunt, and her limbs, willowy as she folded her arms about her stomach. Skeletal hipbones protruded; her ribs rippled below her breasts. No sign remained; as slight as it had been, it had vanished.

Alone in her grief, Richard had left without a word. Not a single uttered phrase of reassurance or love. Now she felt a stranger inside her skin. She covered her body; the sight turned her stomach; the nauseous sensation reached her throat. Annabelle sank to her knees. It grew more forceful; her mind fell into her familiar abyss. She retched, but her body was empty — had not eaten for three days.

She lay upon the floor, her cheek pressed against the bare wood, wishing it would end. That the red wave would take her too.

CHAPTER FIFTEEN

Sleep was a luxury. Now, Annabelle's days and nights mingled into one continual form of misery. She had never felt so alone, so empty, so superfluous. Even with her mother's death, recalling the confusion and melancholy was nothing to this desolation. This loss brought understanding, yet still, she had no power.

She crept from the cottage a little past five and headed for the dunes. Annabelle escaped to this spot as each day dawned, naming it her own. Under her arm clutched a canvas and easel, a box of paints and brushes in her hand. The sun was already up, and she cursed its abundance, lavishing the seascape with its copious brilliance.

Up here, on the lookout of life, she could exist with the elements, having to hold no regard for their feelings. The last two days had weakened her beyond what could heal; one simple phrase had crumbled the walls of her insular world. She would listen to it no more.

Amongst the long spear-headed grass and bare sand patches, Annabelle pitched her easel. Then, removing her shoes, kicking them in the grass, she stood barefoot. Clusters of mauve heather and violet blooms jewelled the otherwise bland dunes. Holding her dress above her ankles, Annabelle paced, watching her bare feet caress the grass.

She unfolded a blanket, spreading it over the rough land, and unpacked her paints. Squeezed colour onto her palette, shades of blue and green and a daub of stark white amid them. With eyes closed against the world, Annabelle swept her brush. A flood of intense azure blue masked the weave of the canvas.

This was her place, sedated and numb. Annabelle continued to paint as the sun grew high and the slow-growing shadows cast her art.

'How long have you been out here?' Anna called as she trudged the sandy dune, her long gown skimming the grass. 'Belle, what time did you get up?'

Annabelle tore white paint along the shoreline, slitting the foreground in a stark gash.

'Belle, come and have breakfast with me.'

Annabelle said nothing but glanced at Aunt Anna; she stood close, her shoulder touching hers. Still, she said nothing; could not bring herself to open her mouth. Words were stifled, lost somewhere in her misery.

This was her place of solitude. Anna was intruding.

'You need to eat today,' Anna sighed, 'I know you think me harsh, but you will get through this, Belle.'

Anna walked to the dune's edge and looked down; the drop was steep, the untouched sand below. A long stretch of beach smooth, the sea settled on the horizon. She turned to Annabelle, who quickly glanced back at her painting.

'Your mother, she felt the same. I tried my hardest, we both did, your father and me. She locked herself in her room for days on end,' Anna gazed back at sea, then up to the morning sky, 'At least you are out here. I do understand.'

Anna walked back and sat on the blanket; she stretched her legs, neatened her petticoats over her ankles, and faced the sky, eyes closed against the sun.

Annabelle watched. The absurdity of it, she knew what this was. While out here, high upon the dunes overlooking the glistening sea, Anna knew she had her attention, that Annabelle would not walk away from the conversation. Not that it had been a conversation. Aunt Anna had expressed her views, but there had been no reply. Just as now. Stood with sand between her toes, Annabelle had no response to give.

These were her emotions. What did her aunt know of loss and emptiness left by an infant?

'Richard loves you,' Anna hesitated. 'It need not be lost; you can try again. You can still have a family.'

'Lost?' Annabelle spat. Those words again. 'You do not understand, do you? All this time, I thought it was just condolence.' Her paintbrush dropped on the palette; white paint spattered the front of her dress.

'Forgive me,' Anna shook her head. 'But you *can* try again.'

'You speak as if I've lost a handkerchief and could simply fetch another from the drawer.'

'Your mother felt the same. But you must remember, things change.'

'My mother again, yet another loss of mine.' Annabelle's mouth stung; her words left a bitter taste.

'You should listen and stop torturing yourself over things that are God's doing, not yours. And not Richards.'

'Richard left me.'

'No, Belle. He went home.'

Annabelle discarded her palette to the blanket. The painting finished, throbbing, alive with emotion, while its artist was dead and lifeless. She walked to the edge of the dune, sitting with her legs outstretched, her feet over the edge.

'Your mother felt the same. Your poor father had no idea how to get through to her. It was months before she was more her bright self again, although there was always something missing. I could see that.' Anna sat beside her, an arm about her shoulder. 'She thought I never understood, but I did. I do.'

'Slowly, Anna's words seeped through the cracks, her brain understanding. Annabelle's eyes remained on the sea as she spoke.

'What about my mother?'

'He would have been two years older than you if he had survived.'

'He?'

'Your brother. Thomas, she named him. He was born too early; the little mite did not stand a chance. As you can imagine, your mother was devastated — no, more than that. Well, you know,' Anna sighed and took a deep breath. 'A part of her died along with little Thomas,' Anna squeezed her shoulder and gently patted her back. She shuffled a little, easing her skirts and neatening her hem, in deep thought. She gazed at the sky, the sun beaming on her face.

'You see, they had been staying here with me. The doctor suggested the sea air would be good for her. And, well, she loved it, just as you do,' Anna stared back at the easel. 'She didn't have your talent; she wanted to be in the sea, have her feet soaked up to her hem,' she laughed. 'Your father would curse, but she didn't care. You see, it was in her nature. Rose had a carefree lust for life, a wildness that grasped your father as soon as they met. He had never known anyone like her, vulnerable, yet full of passion.'

'Emily.'

'Yes, just like Emily.'

'Thomas? How is it I never knew?'

'It was the saddest day I have ever known,' Anna leaned forward and peered over the dune to the beach below, 'she said she was going for a walk on the beach, probably wading up to her knees in the sea, no doubt, as she did most evenings. Your father was in the cottage; I was in the garden. I shall never forget that evening, as long as I live.' Anna faltered, gripping Annabelle's hand before continuing. 'It was never spoken of after... you know...

after the initial weeks. Then life continued. I'm not saying it got better, but it did change.'

A gull swooped overhead, snatching the moment.

Anna let out a long lament. 'That night, Rose had been on the beach longer than usual. She would wander and paddle on the shore, then head back to the garden. The evening was hotter too, that cloying heat. We were to have supper in the garden. Without knowing why, exactly, your father suddenly rushed into the garden, white-faced, life sucked from his cheeks. And that look on his face. It was as if he knew. They had a kind of connection beyond the realms of nature; do you know what I mean?' she stared at Annabelle.

Yes, Annabelle understood; she felt the same with Richard; words were not necessary; she knew his thoughts, emotions, how he loved her. Though now, she felt blind, his love invisible. No matter how hard she tried, she could not hear his heart.

'I didn't know what was wrong. Your father did not say a word, just dashed past me to the dunes. I ran as quickly as I could. Rose, your mother, she had not made it as far as the beach. He found her on the sandy path. It was not steep, as you know, it's quite a gentle slope, but... I do not exactly know what happened. She may have tripped or stumbled, but she lay there, bruised and bleeding. It was the blood that made me gasp. *The baby*, she kept saying, over and over — *my baby*.

Annabelle gripped her hand, wrapping her fingers around Anna's. 'The baby, Thomas?'

'Your father grabbed her; I remember her dress, a shade of dusky rose, her favourite. Now, it was red and soaked with blood.' Anna took a long pause. They both watched the sky, more gulls now — white darts pierced the cloudless blue.

'I had no idea. I cannot believe this. I just cannot take this in, Anna.'

108

'I can still remember the sound — silence — apart from your mother's tears. By the time the doctor came, she was in full labour, but she had lost a lot of blood. I saw the colour of her dress and the dunes; well, they were drenched red. Your father knew it too. He never looked at me, afraid that he may break down, I figured, but he cried too.'

'My father?'

'Yes, Annabelle, he wasn't always so reserved. Of course, he worries. I know that. But back then, he was tender and gentle, and I knew he would lose that composure if he looked at me that night.

'I have seen that side,' Annabelle stopped, choked. She was not entirely sure she could say the words. 'He was very tender and concerned, just before I lost the baby,' Annabelle lay her head on Anna's shoulder. 'He loved my mother; I know that. I remember when she died, even though I was so young, I saw the pain when he looked at me. That used to haunt my dreams.'

'I know, darling girl, I know. Then he had Emily to care for too. He did his best.'

'He always did his best when it came to Emily. He was different with me. It always was.'

'Belle, he loves you.'

'I understand that, Anna. As a father loves a daughter, he loves me, but there is a special bond, a connection, between Emily and Father. I could see it when she was a baby. He would watch her sleeping; I could see he loved her because she reminded him of Mother.'

'There is no doubt Emily has your mother's… enthusiasm and bounce. But that does not mean he loves you any less, only differently.'

'Perhaps.'

'Anyway,' Anna continued. 'The doctor was with her for no more than another hour before it was time. This was supposed to be the most precious day of their lives. But, instead, it was the beginning of the end. Rose regained her strength within a few days, but the baby,' Anna broke off as Annabelle began crying. 'A boy, she named him Thomas after her father. He was fragile, the tiniest thing I had ever seen. The doctor said he was so weak that he would have been a sickly child even without the fall. He lay in Rose's arms for no more than a few minutes before he passed. His tiny hands...' Anna brushed tears from her cheeks.

'After the funeral, Rose locked herself in the bedroom. Days, she was there. She never ate, and I am not sure if she slept either. Sometimes, I would hear her pace the floor at night, hours on end. It is strange; sometimes, I think I can still hear her. But then again, I know you have done the same. So, I know you are not sleeping and not eating either.'

'I have no appetite; my insides feel dead.'

'I know, I understand. That is what I tried to tell your mother.'

'Anna, I know you want to help.'

'Belle, you need to hear me. It was early in the morning; not even the birds were awake. I heard the creaks, the treads, her usual pacing. So, I quietly dressed and went down to the kitchen to make some warm milk. I thought if I could only get her to drink something.'

Annabelle shifted, uncomfortable. She scratched at the dried splatters of paint on her fingers.

'Your mother sat on the chair by the window; she drank some of the milk, more than I thought she would. But never said a word. She looked dead behind her eyes. I see the same in you and, believe me, I had seen it before that day. I talked, tried to make her understand. I couldn't tell if she could hear me at all, let alone was listening. She had drifted off to another world, somewhere your father was not allowed. Do you understand what I am saying, Belle? Richard, do not shut him out. He loves you, just as your father loved your mother.'

'But he left me, Anna.'

'He didn't leave you at all. He had to go home. You are as lost as your mother but as stubborn as your father.'

'Did she listen to you, my mother? Did she hear you?'

'Eventually, she started to. You see, I know that pain. I know the pain of loss and losing a child all too well. Although, I never had the chance to hold mine in my arms; the same pain as you, Belle. I *know* that pain. It still haunts me and will until the end of my days.'

'Anna?'

'I lost my baby; it wasn't even noticeable; my clothes still fit the same, my corset as tight. But *I* knew.'

Annabelle sat stunned, paralysed, had grown roots beside the wild heather. This was unfathomable. Aunt Anna tightly gripped her hand.

'I was young, you see, far too young and far too naive.'

'The father, who was he? I am finding it hard to gather my thoughts, Anna. Does my father know?'

'No, your father does not know. As for the father, he knew but acted as if he didn't. And, even if he had not, it would have made no difference. It was never meant to be,' Anna sighed; almost a hint of laughter left her lips. 'I was a child, Belle. Nothing more than a child. There was no way I could bring a baby into the world.'

A sudden stab of panic clenched Annabelle. She sat in silence, waiting for Anna to continue, could not speak for the lump in her throat. Why was her family doomed when it came to bearing a child? What could they have done so awful that God would take a child from its mother's womb, leaving gaping darkness?

Anna smoothed a hand over her hair, resting her palm on her chest. 'He was handsome, tall, blond, golden, with bright amber eyes. In the summer, his cheeks would blush rich with freckles. I was so in love. Those who knew said it was ridiculous, naive and stupid, a silly young girl's folly. I

111

knew that I loved him. There is no doubt even now. I have never felt that way since and, as the years pass, I never will again.'

'Who was he, Anna? Why was it so stupid?'

'He was the Master. I was in service, worked in *his* house, Maidwell Hall. Oh, I haven't spoken that name aloud for years.'

'Oh Anna,' Annabelle found no other words. Her mind was whirring.

'My mother had secured me the position through an older cousin of hers. The house was a respectable place, and they needed a scullery maid.' Anna smiled warmly. 'They were a young couple with a new baby, though I barely caught a glimpse of the mistress, hidden away since childbirth. But I was conscientious about my work, which made me favoured by the housekeeper who took me under her wing. She treated me like a daughter.'

'Anna, how long were you there, before...'

'It was just before my seventeenth birthday. I was in the parlour cleaning out the fireplace, the last one of the morning. The master came in. That was not unusual. Then he closed the door and stood behind me. In my romantic heart, I had wished for that moment for months. I never looked for trouble; I knew my place; he was my master. But, as he stood in the same room with no one else present, my heart soared.' Anna cast her head to the sky. 'For months I had watched him, wanted him. I loved him. I know you may find it impossible to understand; he was out of my reach. But at that moment, I knew he wanted me too.'

'I do not find it impossible at all. On the contrary, I understand. You know I do. But Anna, it was in vain, surely?'

'It may not have been right, and every time we kissed, I knew he would never be mine. But Belle, our heart does not choose with any rational thought, any more than love asks permission. I loved him, and that was that. During the months following the birth of their youngest child, his wife had become introverted. I suppose he was lonely.'

Annabelle glared in shock at Anna's matter of fact words. She let Anna's hand slip from hers.

'I see you don't understand, do you? You have determined moral fibre running through you, inherited from your father. But Belle, I shall ask you one thing. If Richard belonged to another woman, would that stop you from loving him? Would that love fade?' Anna rubbed her palms down her thighs. 'Perhaps, we should go in for breakfast or lunch, as the morning seems to have slipped away.'

'What about the baby?'

'It wasn't meant to be. I knew that from the very first moment, but it was mine, a part of him that actually belonged to me.'

'You told him, though? I mean, he could not take advantage like that and not expect consequences.'

'He wasn't like that; none of it was as sordid as it may sound. He loved me in his way. We were both young; they were a young family. His wife was ill, and he found solace and comfort with me.'

'But he did not leave his wife for you, did he?'

'Of course not, why would he? He was Sir Samuel Maidwell of Maidwell Hall. It was a respectable house; I knew that would never happen.'

'So, you told him…'

'We were alone in the garden, it was late summer, and the sun was just setting. The house had an orchard; we would spend our time there. I can still recall the sweetness of the ripe apples. He kissed me, and then it was all over. I never saw him again. I left that night.'

'Why, what did he say? Did he make you go? Anna, what about the baby?'

'The baby was mine, not really his, not in a way that he could acknowledge it. He had his own family; I knew that. He never saw me again,' Anna stopped and stood up, her feet trudged until they reached the easel.

Annabelle followed, enfolding her arms around her aunt. 'I am sorry, Anna.'

'I left the house, but I had nowhere to go. There was no way in this world your grandmother would have understood. I felt alone and betrayed. As the years passed, I understood why his commitment was to his wife and his position. The trouble was, I was a child and wanted my fairy tale. And the baby just was not meant to be. So, I went to stay with my mother's cousin, without, I hasten to add, my mother's knowledge. But, within a few days, it was gone; a mere memory.'

Annabelle sighed, 'I understand how hard it was for you; you lost your love and your baby.'

'You see, Belle, life changes.' She looked into Annabelle's eyes. 'Life always goes on, regardless. A new day breaks every morning. The only thing you can do is live it. Those we lose do not leave; they are just not within our reach. You will never forget your baby, just as I never forgot mine, and your mother never forgot Thomas. But importantly, you must remember to love the living. Your parents, at that moment, felt life was over. But it was not. They had you, then Emily. Your poor father lost your mother; she was the love of his life. But you still have Richard, Belle.'

Anna now stood facing the easel. The sun had baked the oils. It was pure, innocent in its execution, but underlying those brushstrokes was pain. The wildness and unpredictability of Mother Nature mingled with the delicate virtue of the seascape.

CHAPTER SIXTEEN

Thick snow had settled during the night in a rich, dense blanket — the landscape like a scene on a Christmas card. Strong daylight filled the antiquated bedroom; April stirred at the sound of clinking china, then a light tap on the door.

'Merry Christmas, Little One,' Sarah gently eased open the door, carrying two china mugs.

'Happy Christmas, Nan. How did you sleep?' April heaved herself up, puffed the feather pillows, and took her mug. Then watched her grandmother shuffle to the window, draw back the curtains. She then sat on the bedroom chair nestled inside the bay window. The winter sunshine glistened through the frosted windowpanes as she sank back into the deep springy upholstery.

'Your parents shall be over in an hour or so. Your mum phoned to say she was bringing you a change of clothes. How did you sleep?' Sarah said, staring out at the veiled white churchyard beyond the garden.

'Okay, although I did dream a bit.' April felt herself standing on the dunes watching the gull's swoop. 'You look a bit peaky, Nan?' she added.

Sarah continued to stare out through the chilled glass.

'What's the matter?' April put her cup down on the bedside table, pulled back the blankets and dashed across to the window. 'Nan?' April knelt at her feet. 'Are you all right?'

April's concern turned to panic as she saw her grandmother's vacant expression.

For a few seconds, she sat motionless, still gazing out the window. Then, she turned. April slowly took the mug and placed it on the floor. Her grandmother looked old and tired, morning light defining each line that etched her years.

'Oh, Nan, whatever is it? Please, you're scaring me!' April pleaded, rubbing her hands between her own desperate to warm them.

'Little One, don't worry, everything will turn out as it should. But I think it's my time. You're back where you belong,' Sarah smiled.

'Nan, no. Do not say that. You are not going anywhere. You are tired; why don't you go back to bed for a while. Mum's cooking, and I can help her.'

It was an awkward attempt to convince herself it was nothing. When, in truth, April felt the truth of it tumble down around her shoulders. Had she known all along?

'I'll go and put some logs on the fire; the coal is probably all burnt out. Make sure we're all warm and toasty.' Sarah carefully stood, patted April's shoulder and left the room without another word.

April remained knelt beside the chair, with a cold mug of tea and the callous daylight. She folded her arms on the velvet seat and rested her head. As the polished floorboards began to press on her shins. April pushed her weight down harder until her toes tingled with numbness. The sky was clear. It was all she could see and stared up into the icy blue. Her stomach turned as panic swelled. The loud beat of her heart thumped against the edge of the seat: emotions, feelings of loss and emptiness.

~

'Merry Christmas!' April opened the front door to her parents' greeting.

'Mum, can I have a word?' April grabbed Julia's arm, dragging her to the furthest corner of the room.

'Whatever is it?' Julia had barely removed her coat before April had snatched it, clutching it tightly to her chest.

'Your Nan, is she all right? How is she feeling this morning? I knew she wasn't right last night. I shouldn't have left her like that; she'd overdone it, I told her to take it easy, but she never listens to me,' Julia continued to unravel her scarf, keeping her voice low.

'Mum, is there something I should know? Something you need to tell me?' The dreaded realisation finally dropped like a copper coin; spinning on its end, April's heart plummeted. 'Mum, she's…?' April's voice soared above the carols from the stereo beside them, but she could not finish the sentence.

Michael popped his head around the door.

'Everything okay in here? Breakfast is ready.'

'We're fine, love. We'll be there in a moment,' Julia nodded, her tone calm but her eyes wide.

Michael returned without another word.

'I think we should have this discussion after breakfast. You can help me clear the kitchen.' Her mother turned for the door with an expression of not another word, leaving April bemused. Julia stopped in the doorway. 'Don't worry; everything will be all right. I promise,' she added.

'Will everyone stop telling me it's going to be *all right*. Nothing is bloody all right. It's all far from bloody okay,' April spat.

Julia gave a curt nod. 'Please, April, for your Nan's sake then. Come on.'

'Sit down, you two, don't let it get cold.' Michael ushered April to the chair next to her grandmother. It was the same place she had sat the evening before, through the doors, the same crystal white covering. But, this morning, things were not the same. April's heart was heavy as lead and ached so badly she could not think straight. Fear and dread swam in the pit of her stomach. Everything she had seen the past few weeks had been too bizarre to comprehend, but that strain was nothing to the devastation that tugged at her heart.

April picked at her croissant, tearing off small pieces and the pastry flaked on her plate.

'Do you know, I can't remember the last time it snowed on Christmas day,' Michael looked across the table, eager to start some conversation. 'More coffee, anyone?'

April shook her head, fiercer than she had meant, then turned back to the pile of crumbs and half-eaten croissant on top. She brushed her fingers together over her plate and wiped them on the napkin.

'It's just like one of those old-fashioned Victorian Christmas cards,' Julia replied, folding her napkin. Within that moment, April's thoughts went to Annabelle. She had stood at the same glass doors, a Christmas morning much the same over a century before. It came crashing down over her head, the realisation of yesterday's events flooded in. For the first time during breakfast, April turned to look at her grandmother. She reached over to place her hand on top of hers gently. Sarah squeezed it in reassurance.

When I was a girl, I remember Christmas morning after breakfast. I would walk with my grandmother while my mother prepared the turkey. She would bundle me up in my long, red scarf. I only ever remember wearing that scarf on Christmas morning,' Sarah paused for a second, with a glazed expression, then smoothed her long white hair down to the ribbon.

'We would wander through the churchyard, treading through the snow. I would follow behind and walk in her footprints, placing my feet in the imprint made by her boots. There were wrought iron benches under the trees back then, not like the wooden ones there now. She would clear the snow off with her glove, and we would sit there for ages. My feet dangling off the edge. I'd swing them backwards and forwards, with my toes skimming the snow until I had

118

made a channel,' Sarah continued, recalling memories with a content tone.

April sat, mesmerised; she only had recollections of Annabelle as a young woman. But these were stories of her as a grandmother — Nan's memories. April placed her elbow on the table, her face in her palm.

'Nan, what was she like?'

'Annabelle, when I knew her, she was in her fifties. Her hair was silvery then but still tied neatly up. She would let me brush if I were good. She would sit at her dressing table, and I'd shuffle a footstool over and stand behind her, looking into the mirror, my face next to hers,' Sarah paused again and sat back in her chair, resting her weary head on the mahogany.

'Mum, you never told me any of this,' Julia said, leaning forward.

'I was only young when she died. I remember my mum saying I would see her again someday,' Sarah stopped, her eyes glistening in the sunlight.

No one spoke for a moment. Then, April gathered the breakfast plates, Julia swiftly followed her with the cold coffee pot.

April stood at the kitchen sink, staring into the garden, flushed cheeked and tears dripping from her chin into the running water. The day was bright. It made her eyes sting. Julia scraped the remains of breakfast into the kitchen bin, putting the plates on the work surface before turning to April, her hand on her quivering shoulder.

'It will be okay, darling. We all must go some time; it is just the way of things. We all lose people we love, but they are never really gone, you know,' Julia said softly.

There was a tone there, something April couldn't quite put her finger on, but it only encouraged more tears.

'When your grandad died, I felt like someone had ripped out my heart. I may have been a grown woman, but it didn't matter; I felt like a little girl again, and I'd lost my daddy. I locked myself in my room for days, and then…' Julia quickly turned off the tap, soap bubbles sloshing precariously near the top of the sink.

'What was it?' April asked, dipping her hands into the scolding water, wincing, but plunging them back in again.

'Careful, April. Goodness, that hot…' Julia tugged the plug chain and ran the cold tap.

'It's fine,' April began washing the plates, her hands red. 'Go on, what was it, you were saying about Granddad?'

'Yes, well, the strangest thing, you'll laugh because I know how ridiculous it sounds, but… well, he was there with me,' Julia paused. April grabbed the tea towel to dry her hands, pretending not to see how red they were.

'It was late in the evening, and I lay on my bed, looking out of the window,' Julia continued slowly. 'The room filled with a smell, *his* smell, the smell of pipe tobacco. I *knew* it was him. So, I closed my eyes and inhaled, and then I felt the bed move, just slightly, like someone had sat down beside me. I lay there for what seemed hours with my dad sitting next to me.' Tears gently traced her cheeks as she smiled at April.

'I must've fallen asleep because, the next thing I knew, it was morning. I felt better that day, like I understood it. He was with me, no I couldn't see him, but I knew he was there, and that was enough. People never really leave us, darling. Your Nan is going to go; she is ill, it's why we are here, why I had to come home. There's nothing we can do to change it, but she'll always be with you. When you need her, she will be there, just as she is now.'

The words gradually swam through the mire of April's thoughts. She had been drowning in the pain and worry. This was a new side, a part of her mother she never knew; she never mentioned these kinds of feelings — a spiritual side. It consumed April as they finished up. She knew her mother was right, that, if it were possible, her grandmother would always be with her, just as she always had.

'It's half nine. I think I'll make a start on dinner. Why don't you see if your Nan is up for a walk? I think it will do you both the world of good,' she hugged April, holding her close. 'I shall miss her too, you know, she's my mum. But we both know she'll still be here, in this house.'

'Mum, you should have told me.'

'Would it change the matter? It would have only made you more miserable than you've been. Moping around. And to be truthful, she made me promise not to tell you, didn't want you tiptoeing around her, making a fuss. So, you must promise me, April, and I mean this... you must promise not to do that. So, treasure the time you have, don't go dwelling on, well you know...'

April nodded, rolling her shoulders and squeezing her fingers tightly in the tea towel.

'And, while we're here, is there something else on your mind you want to talk about?' Julia hugged her. 'I know I'm not your nan, but I am your mum.'

'Later, mum. It doesn't seem that important now.'

The morning air was fresh and clean. They trudged along the snow-covered footpath beside the churchyard, their boots covered in newly fallen snow. April held her grandmother's arm tightly, giving her support, as well as her need to keep her close. They made footprints in the direction of a wooden bench.

They sat beneath the canopy of naked trees, arched, bare and forlorn over the footpath. Old gravestones tilted, worn by time, with their frosty covering, stood behind them.

'Nan, I love you,' April sat, her hand tightly wrapped around her grandmother's gloved fingers.

'I love you too. I can hear it now. Your mum told you, hasn't she? No, it's okay, don't worry, I was going to anyway. It's my time to go. I shall be with your grandad again; I've missed him so much these past years. But I shall be with you, Little One, whenever you need me.'

'But, Nan, I'll always need you. I don't want to think about life without you.'

'Just as we spoke about last night, we come back again to be reunited with our loved ones. Look at you; you of all people should see that now.'

Her words were true. But this was not a woman from the past, an ancestor. This was her Nan, and this was happening now. It was real, and April felt the pain deep in the pit of her stomach.

'What am I going to do without you?' April shivered as the freezing air seeped through her coat, chilling her aching heart.

'Little One, here I am, sitting on this bench on Christmas morning with my favourite granddaughter, just as I used to each Christmas morning, all those years ago. I know how awful it is to lose someone you love. I lost my grandmother too. I was devastated, heartbroken. But she came back to me. Annabelle didn't go for long, did she?'

The harsh sunshine glared reflectively on the snow. Words, sentiments, memories, and pain circled April's mind as she mulled them over and over.

'What about you, Nan? Do you think you'll come back again? Emily didn't, did she? I still don't know why she's here, or if she's always been here and we didn't know?' April paused, gazing into her grandmother's face before she continued. 'Nan, was that her bedroom I slept in?'

'That has always been a spare room for as long as I can remember. Why?' Sarah asked, rubbing her cold hands together as she watched her feet. She moved her brown leather boot back and forth in the snow beneath the bench until she had carved a channel in the new-laid flurry.

'I dreamt about her last night. Everyone actually, the whole family. I think it was Emily's room. It all *felt* the same.'

April shuffled along the bench, closer to her grandmother, putting her arm about her. Her shoulders seemed smaller than usual, her body thin and fragile.

'I think we should head back now. It's too cold,' April hugged her, rubbing her arm to warm her up.

'I'm fine. After dinner, don't forget, I promised to get the photo albums out. We can sit by the fire like we did when you were small,' Sarah turned to her, frail features cold and shivery in the wintry chill. 'Yes, I think we should head back, see how your mum's getting on with the turkey.'

They passed through the deserted churchyard. The cathedral glistened in the low sunshine; a mantle of crystal snow on its roof; the stained-glass windows lit in ready for the day's service. Slowly, with careful tread, they retraced their footprints home.

April turned the key and guided her grandmother down into the front room, watching her cautiously as she went.

Music filtered the space with festive cheer.

'Oh, this is my favourite song,' Sarah announced as she began to sing along with the crooner.

Julia entered, carrying a tray of warm mince pies, singing at the top of her voice as she rested the silver tray onto the low table. 'You two look frozen solid! Come on, get those coats off and warm up by the fire. I've just put some more logs on.'

April watched as Sarah rested in her favourite chair. The closeness of the blazing fire brought life back to her cheeks; warming her hands, she unzipped her long boots.

'Ah, that's better. I'm starting to defrost now; I don't remember it being so cold when I was a girl.'

Sarah sat back in her seat, her tired eyes staring into the open fire; red sparks spat from the logs inside the brick fireplace, a firework display of darting and dancing flashes. The loud hissing and crackling of the fresh logs, barely audible over the mellow tone of the festive music. April watched her for a while, saving every detail to memory — how her hair glistened like silver, the translucent glow of her skin with a sweep of powder, the perfect shape of her nose and chin, the same as Annabelle's and Emily's.

Until then, April hadn't thought about inherited genes and how all the women had distinctive bone structures and shaped hairlines. Whether blonde or auburn, all were so similar, April included.

She reached for a warm mince pie, the sugary pastry top crumbling as she took a bite, eyeing her grandmother, her weary head resting into the corner of the wingback. April snuggled back on the settee, hugged the gold cushion to her chest, and nestled her chin into the satin. Memories of the past two days crowded in.

The music whipped from the room as a curious warmth spread through her body, lifting her mood. There was a lightness in her chest as she fixed her sight on her grandmother. April concentrated hard, staring in with unblinking eyes. Behind her stood a tall gentleman in a dark grey suit with his large hands resting on the back of the chair.

In impulse, April closed her eyes and inhaled the distinctive aroma of pipe tobacco. She opened her eyes, immobile, as her granddad beamed and placed his hand on her grandmother's shoulder. Sarah smiled and slowly put her hand on his, her eyes still closed. April gasped in both delight and astonishment, and he disappeared as quickly as he had arrived.

CHAPTER SEVENTEEN

'You sit next to me, Little One,' Sarah shuffled her chair closer to the table.

April sat in her usual place next to her, with the view of the garden. The glass doors, steamed with the heat from the cooking, revealed large snowflakes that fell from the icy white sky.

Julia carried the turkey in on a china platter. 'We are such a gloomy bunch today; it's Christmas!' The aroma filled the room, generating reluctant smiles.

The family tucked into their Christmas dinner with renewed enthusiasm. Periodically, Sarah glanced at April, endeavouring to give her some optimism.

Her grandmother's words of reassurance rolled themselves over in her mind, and with her granddad's visit, she understood. *We never really leave.*

However, her heart was heavy and tired from its journeys through the past. April began to appreciate how straightforward life had been, but all that had changed, and in a way she could have never imagined. Here was her new life, filled with memories and feelings, of an old, long-ago existence. Her visions and dreams had captured a forgotten part of history, her own past, like the photographs themselves. What had happened to Emily, and why did no one know anything about her?

'I think it's time to open the presents, don't you?' April said.

Sarah smiled up at her and held out a hand, 'Here, help me up with you; I'm not as young as I once was.'

They all settled down in the front room as the logs hissed and squealed loudly in the fire grate. The afternoon sunlight was dimming, and the twinkle of tree lights filled the room. Meticulously, April distributed the presents and took her seat next to her mother.

'First of all, I think I need to say something,' Sarah perched on the edge of her chair. 'I do not wish to spend my last days with everyone tiptoeing around me. We all know I'm going soon, and it isn't worrying me, not in the slightest. I want to spend my last days happy. I'm old and have had a good life. I'm now ready to go...' she paused a moment, heaved a sigh, 'Now, I'd like to see everyone open their presents with joy, not with these sad faces.'

After most of the presents had been opened, April pottered around the room, gathering up the ripped wrapping paper.

'Nan, open your last one. It's a special one from me.'

'Very well,' Sarah rested the gift carefully on her knees and pulled the ribbon, peeling the wrap free. 'How on earth… How did you get it?' Sarah exclaimed.

'Mum said you couldn't buy it anymore, but you would be amazed what you can find if you know where to look. This came directly from the perfume factory in Grasse,' April beamed, 'it's now a limited edition. They only make a small number each year.'

The tall pink perfume bottle twinkled in the firelight, the glow reflecting in Sarah's face as she ran her fingers over the tassel puffer, a nostalgic smile on her face. 'Thank you, darling, I don't know what to say; this means so much. But now it's your turn, come along.'

April sat on the floor beside the roaring fire, her heart warm. She stared at the last two gifts by her, taking the nearest. The tag read: *To our darling daughter*. April tore the paper off, revealing a book. She ran her hand over the rich green leather, fanning open crisp white pages edged with silver leaf. Then grasped the satin ribbon bookmark beneath the front cover and read the inscription: *For your thoughts and dreams*. She noticed something shine from within the wrapping paper — an ornate pen, with silver scrollwork and wispy tendrils, inlaid with green enamel.

'We thought they might be of some help,' Julia smiled.

'Thanks, Mum, Dad, they are lovely,' April smiled, resting her head on her grandmother's knee.

'And this one...' Sarah nudged.

The last present lay small in April's palm, a black velvet box. Slowly she lifted the lid as the contents twinkled in the soft firelight.

'Nan,' April gasped. 'It's beautiful, but you didn't need to get me anything else.'

Sarah sat back in her chair with a slightly smug smile. 'It's to go on your bracelet, then it will be more yours.'

'Oh, it's my birthstone,' April lifted the silver charm, holding it up to the light as the aquamarine gem twinkled. 'It's beautiful, thank you. I love it.'

April sat with her head on her grandmother's knee, admiring her gift, as her parents clear away the last remnants of wrapping.

'Nan, can I stay here with you again tonight?' April gazed into the glowing fire.

'Of course, you can. You don't need to ask.'

'I saw Grandad earlier,' she remained unmoved, simply staring into the red embers. Her statement seemed ordinary, not alarming, as it once would have been.

'I know. He's waiting for me... but I'm not going quite yet,' Sarah gently stroked April's cheek, 'Not quite yet, Little One.'

Late afternoon light had diminished fast, leaving only the luminosity of the freshly fallen snow. Twinkling tree lights cast a multicoloured allure to its greenery. The late festive evening brought a cosy comfort, with the warmth from the crackling logs, the hot mince pies and an iced cake that sat on the polished table.

Sarah patted April's shoulder and wandered from the room.

April twiddled with her bracelet as it hung perfectly in place, the heavy silver links draping her wrist. She inspected every charm in turn for the first time, her task illuminated by the chandelier above her head — over a dozen silver adornments and a heavy lock and safety chain. Counting each charm as she went, she came to a delicate oval inset with mother-of-pearl. April unfastened the bracelet laying it out, carefully taking the charm between her fingers, tugged, releasing what was, in fact, a locket. Silence hummed, numbing her ear, while down her spine, excited tingles, her heart warm and cheeks flushed, April stared deep into the photograph. There he was, nestle inside the locket aperture gazed back, Richard Hardwick.

'Here we go, I'd nearly forgotten,' Sarah returned, carrying a pile of leather-bound albums.

'Oh, the photos, Nan,' April quickly stood up, grabbed them, helping her grandmother to the settee, the charm bracelet still clutched between her fingers.

'Careful, they're quite heavy,' Sarah said.

'I always remember them being so huge when I was small. They used to look like the size of the tabletop,' April remarked as she sat with three albums comfortably fitted on her lap.

'Here we go, a nice pot of tea,' Julia entered the cosy space, holding the silver tea tray.

'How does the bracelet fit, April?'

'Perfect.' April quickly retrieved the bracelet from under the albums. Then, swiftly closing the locket, she refastened it around her wrist.

'Oh, Mum, your albums, I haven't seen them for years,' Julia sat down with enthusiasm, reaching out to take one from her mother; Michael entered and sat down beside his wife.

Five leather-bound albums, each brimming with scores of black and white memories, between the pages were sheets of translucent tissue to protect them.

April sat close to the fire, warming on her cheeks. The red album was warm on her lap as she carefully opened it. So many years since she had last held it, her heart soared as if it were the first time, the supple leather moulding under the shape of her fingers.

'Oh,' she gasped. An old wedding photograph: April traced her eyes across the congregation; gentlemen dressed in smart suits, women elegant in draped dresses, skimming their hips and ankles. She recognised no one until she came to one lady wearing a heavily beaded gown. The woman was in her forties with fair hair stood close to the bride and groom, along with an elegant tall gentleman, his hair and beard also fair.

'It's Annabelle, isn't it, Nan!' April's excitement shone on her face, 'I can't believe all the times I've looked at this photograph…'

'But it's never meant as much to you as it does now, has it?'

April lifted her head, only to find her mother gazing back at her, not her grandmother.

'Mum?'

'Annabelle, she's important, isn't she? As I said, when we go, we never really leave. And if we do, we don't go for long.' Julia turned back to the album she was flicking through, a smile quietly hinting at the corner of her mouth.

'I suppose not.' April studied her mum as she carefully turned each stiff page, her eyes scanning each memory.

Did she know? How could she? But why say such a peculiar thing?

April looked back at the photo, her heart pounding. But, once again, her thoughts were on Annabelle, her dress, her hair, her bracelet. April's bracelet, there, fastened around her wrist, right where it always belonged. The bride, pretty with dark bobbed hair, stood elegant in the centre, her new husband proudly beside her, young and fine-looking.

'Nan, whose wedding is this?'

'Well, let's see, that's my mum and dad, and that, of course, is my grandmother. And there's that lovely ruby and diamond bracelet; you know, the one in my jewellery case.'

For many long minutes, April scrutinised the photo, carefully studying each member of the wedding party, their clothes, hair and smiles. Annabelle's face beamed back at her, an expression of happiness and pride. Hours passed, April traced her eyes over the albums, photo after photo, but none of Emily or young Annabelle, and none of Richard.

'Nan, I'll pop home and get some things. It's okay to stay again tonight, isn't it?'

'Of course, you know this is where I like to have you, close to me, back where you belong.'

April glanced at her mother, who nodded and smiled.

The evening sky was bright with snow clouds; the lamp posts enlightened the short but cold walk home. April grabbed a holdall and began gathering a few essentials. After a moment, she perched on the edge of her bed, clutching her silver and mother-of-pearl frame.

'Emily, why can't I find you? And where's your brooch?' she whispered. Her eyes scanned the photos yet again, searching for some hidden clue. Abruptly, she turned. There was the box. Her thoughts fell upon its hidden contents. She placed it on top of her clothes, zipped the holdall shut, and headed back.

The rest of the evening passed with the usual festive activities, cake, mulled wine and a singsong of some favourite carols. When it came to bedtime, April kissed her parent's goodnight at the front door, Julia giving her a nod and a *look after your Nan* kind of look.

'What a lovely day we've had, apart from everyone's gloomy faces to start. It's been one of the best Christmases we've ever had.'

'Yes, Nan, I suppose it has. Can I ask you something? I know this is not the normal sort of thing I should ask, but I need to know,' April sat on the edge of the settee facing her grandmother, the last few red embers casting a flush over Sarah's cheeks.

'You can ask me anything you want. If I have the answer, I shall give it to you,' Sarah shuffled back in her chair, laying her old head on the velvet.

'Nan, yesterday when we got back from shopping, I saw Annabelle. Do you know what I mean by saw? I mean, I felt I was her; I felt her emotions and thoughts.'

'Yes, I know you did, and I do understand.'

'Annabelle lost a baby; a miscarriage. I felt the pain deep inside me, the hurt and torment inside my head.' Her face contorted in remembrance; her body slumped forward. Slowly she continued, 'Nan, did you ever lose a baby?'

Sarah watched the expression on her face; April's eyes were full of truth and trust. Sarah turned to the fire; slowly, she raised herself and wandered over to the scuttle; calmly, she shovelled some coal on the gradually diminishing fire.

'That's better; that'll keep us warm for the night,' she sat back in her chair and relaxed her hand over the carved wooden ends.

'Once, a long, long time ago, when I was a young woman, something very awful happened. It was devastating for everyone. First, I lost a little boy, and later, two lovely little girls.'

'Nan, I'm so sorry. I'm so sorry. I should never have asked; please forgive me.'

'Oh, my darling, if you never ask things, you'll never know. And, sometimes, we forget to say what's important; you must never forget that, always to say what's in your heart. The truth is always there. And now, I think it's time for bed. I think you need some sleep.'

'I really do love you, Nan.'

'I know you do; I know, I love you too.'

~

The bedroom was cosy, the pink glow softening the harsh wintry night outside. April sat up in bed; pillow puffed behind her, the marquetry box in her lap. The lock sat empty, waiting for its key. Where was the key? How can we have a box with no key?

You hold the key. You have the key.

'I hold the key? I don't understand.' April answered without a thought, the voice repeated in her head.

You hold the key, Annabelle.

Annabelle? Annabelle, she held the key?

She gazed about the room for a clue, for a sudden spark of inspiration. I hold the key? Idly, she fiddled with the silver charms — of course, the key!

Smoothly, April unfastened the silver charm bracelet and laid it on the crisp white sheet. The silver shone in the pink light. The gems twinkled and glistened. She eliminated each charm in turn until she reached it — an ornate *key*. April clasped the key firmly between her thumb and forefinger and eased it into the lock. With a careful twist, the lock clicked, and the lid released.

The contents were covered by a linen handkerchief, like the one that wrapped the silver dressing table set and embroidered with the same three initials. Underneath, a bundle of letters tied with a ribbon. April flicked her thumb along the edges, examining the pile, each handwritten envelope in elegant black ink. April placed them to one side as she continued to explore the box. From the bottom, she lifted out a black leather book, bound in the softest hide, with gold embossed scrolls at the corners — an album. The front held an oval, gold-rimmed frame, complete with photograph.

April stared in disbelief. The one thing she'd been searching for had been at her fingertips, the key she'd been wearing. She leant towards the bedside lamp, holding the album beneath its light. Before April's sleepy eyes lay Emily and James' wedding photograph, its sepia quality flawless, unaltered by time.

CHAPTER EIGHTEEN

Liquid sunshine warmed the dining room; golden rays gradually seeped into every corner. Emily stood at the glass doors, watching the birds on the lawn, pecking at the moist, dewy grass, eager to grab an unsuspecting worm. They danced between the blades of grass, darting at the ground.

'Poor, poor Annabelle,' she sighed, 'It is what she desires, more so than anything.'

'I know.'

'Richard, I am so sorry, will you please forgive me. I know it is as hard for you. It is just that I know she was so thrilled and complete when she told me about the baby.'

'I understand. I know what it means to Belle and what this means to us,' he paused. 'She hardly said a word.'

'I am sure it is merely the terrible shock. But, you know what the doctor said, it affects the mind, not just the body.'

'Yes, perhaps you are right… I know you are. Everything will be fine when Annabelle returns home,' Richard sighed.

'How long do you think she will stay at Anna's? I thought you were going to stay with her for a few weeks?'

Richard paused a long silent moment where he, too, watched the early morning birds devour their breakfast. The elegant long case clock chimed the hour: eight o'clock.

'No. I thought it was better if I came back.'

'There is no one better to care for her than Aunt Anna. She will be back home before you know it.'

'Mmm, I am sure you are right, Emily. I am sure you are.'

~

'This just came for young Emily.' Mary hovered in the doorway. 'But, as the captain is away…' she continued as her fingers trembled, worrying over the item she held.

'Whatever is the matter, Mary?'

'Look, I think you should give it to her,' her palm lay open. 'I wish Annabelle were here. I think...' she could not finish the sentence but found the words in Richard's eyes — anxiety and apprehension.

'Yes, we all do,' Richard spoke quietly, his words silently mouthed. He took the item, carefully inspecting its source. 'Where is she, Mary?'

'In the garden; the dear girl's been there since after breakfast.'

'Mary, let us not jump to any conclusions,' Richard urged, a sharp stab of dread in his throat. He looked out the glass doors; Emily sat, peaceful and calm.

Richard slowly stepped outside, standing steadily on the top step, his feet motionless, anxiously fixed to the spot. The paper was sharp in his hand.

'Ah, Richard, what do you say to a game of chess? Let us see if I can beat you again.'

Emily watched as Richard cautiously descended the steps, one by one, pausing each time to gain his bearings, daring to take another, wanting to retreat. The trees large leafy boughs dabbled the sun from her eyes, but Richard squinted as if it stung. Then, without a word, he moved the wooden stool, placed it in front of her and sat, his eyes level with hers.

'Emily,' he swallowed. 'Emily, this came for you,' Richard held the piece of paper close to his chest, tight in his grip.

'For me, is it a letter from James?' Emily clasped the corner. Reluctant to release it, Richard gripped, without conscious mind, staring into her eyes as Emily tugged at the corner with increasing force.

'Richard?' Releasing it, he closed his eyes. 'Ah, it is not from James... it... it is a telegram.'

A cold silence overwhelmed the garden. The warm air lingered, thick and suffocating, fingers of fear clawed at the flora, tainting the atmosphere with the stench of dread. Birds hushed. Yet, the sun's unrelenting rays continued to scorch.

'Emily?' Richard's voice fell, crashing loudly into his lap, his eyes boring into his hands, 'Emily?' he pleaded as he lifted his gaze to her ashen face.

She remained silent while her hands shook. She stood, swaying, dizzy, and nauseous.

'Emily, sit down.'

'No. No. No.' Her words were weak and broken. Her feet trudged the silent garden, navigating their way to the house, her mind spinning somewhere in her head, somewhere in her cheated, harsh reality.

~

With the unnoticed passing of the growing hours, her heart lay heavy, her body immersed in this sudden cold emptiness, swallowed by grief. Then, a gentle knock echoed through the door; the brass knob twisted.

'Emily? Emily, I'm worried about you. It's been hours. Do you want to talk about it? Please, I promised your sister that I'd take care of you while she was away,' with the door ajar, Richard remained behind it, his voice seeping through the crack. 'Emily, can I get you anything?'

'No, but you can come in, if you wish,' she replied, devoid of emotion.

Richard gently pushed the door open into the dusky space. A few steps into the room, he could see her outline on the bed, her motionless silhouette like death itself. He lit the lamp beside her, and the light spread through the darkening room, then quietly stood at the open window, the muggy night seeping stickily into the room.

'When is my sister coming home?'

'She did not say,' he paused.

'I cannot continue without her,' she announced, the tone of a child, 'Do you think me selfish and cruel?'

'Cruel?'

'I must be cruel; otherwise, why would this be happening? I do not understand, Richard. Do you?'

'You are not cruel in any way, Emily. *This* is life, it is cruel, but this is war. You have done nothing to deserve this; it is nothing that you have done. It is not your fault, and I wish I could take away this pain.'

'I need Annabelle. That makes me selfish; I need her after all she has suffered. I am here thinking of nothing but my stupid, selfish agony when she has lost someone too.'

'She will understand and want to be home with you. I sent a telegram this afternoon, letting her know.'

'She is not well enough to come home just yet.'

'Have you ever known her to put you anywhere but first? I am sure she will be home soon.'

'But she is not here now, is she?' her slow words floated on the humid evening air. The pink blush of the room cast false colour to her pasty cheeks. 'Richard, my heart has died. I shall never be alive again; it has been snatched away. I had everything once, and now, I have nothing.'

Richard sat silently, listening to her shattered thoughts. Emily's words were his wife's unspoken thoughts. Finally, he turned to face her. 'Is there anything I can get you?'

'No.'

'Then I should leave you; it is late. You should sleep.'

'No. Please, do not leave me. I cannot face this alone,' her voice trembled. 'I am so cold. Can you hold me as my sister would?'

For long agonising moments, Richard stared at Emily, the bed, then out into the night, the delicate drapes lapping at his face.

'Richard?

Gradually, he paced the rug over to the bed. Emily lay unmoved, her dress pale like her skin, her hair tousled across her pillow. Without a sound, Richard lay down next to her, their bodies still and silent as the house.

'I'm so cold. I am sure I shall die tonight.'

Richard eased his arm under her neck, cradling, as her face lay close to his, her breath warm and sweet. The dense darkness veiled the room. Emily raised her hand to his face; her forefinger tenderly traced the outline of his features, his cheekbones, down to his lips. She set her palm on his cheek, turned his face to meet hers.

His lips quivered with hesitance, and he laid his large hand on hers, moving his fingers between hers, entwining them together. He led their hands down to his open shirt collar, pushing their fingers between the buttons. As Emily's fingers touched his chest, Richard pressed her hand over his heart.

'Annabelle lives here,' he gentle uttered, his breath on her face.

'And James in mine,' she breathed.

CHAPTER NINETEEN

Sudden anxiety in the hollow of her stomach wrenched her body forward. Dark and silent. Her eyes were open, but there was nothing but dense blackness.

Her thoughts were on the box and the key.

Within the soft light of the bedside lamp, April sat, with the box in her lap, as the doorknob twisted.

'Hey, you awake already?'

'Nan, sorry, I didn't mean to wake you. What time is it?'

'Oh, I was already awake; I haven't been sleeping much lately.' Sarah entered, closing the door behind her, 'it's about half seven.' She wandered over to the bed and perched on the side next to the lamp. 'Ah, I see you found the key, then.'

'Yes, last night. It was so late, I didn't want to wake you,' April pointed to the bracelet on the bedside table. 'You'll never guess where the key was!'

'Ah, Annabelle's bracelet.'

'Nan, you don't look very shocked. This means I've been wearing it all the time, and you'll never guess what I found inside.'

'Move over, and we can have a good look.'

'Are you ready for this?' April placed the box between them, very gently lifted the lid. Nestling inside was the leather album. April lifted it and handed it to her.

'Ah, Emily, and I presume, this is her husband.'

'That's Lance Corporal James Wright. He was in the Suffolk Regiment.'

'James?'

'Yes, they got married at Christmas. I think it was the turn of the century. He went to fight in Africa, but...' April stopped, had no words to add.

'Ah, the Boer War...' Sarah said, bringing the album up closer to see. 'She was beautiful, and James was handsome.'

'Yes, I suppose so,' April said, lost in thought.

'But not as handsome as our Richard, is he? Although I only have stories of him to go by, my mother would tell me how handsome her father had been, but there are no photos of him,' Sarah leant towards her granddaughter, nudging her slightly with her elbow.

'Yes, Nan. I know you think I'm nuts, don't you?' The dream crept its way back into her thoughts, bombarding her mind with its cruelty. April sat with her face in her hands, desperately trying to drive her nightmare from her brain.

'Do you want to talk about it; I know something is bothering you this morning? What is it?'

'Nan, I had the most terrible night, full of nightmares, but the difference with these is that I know they are real. Well, they were real once, 'she pondered where to begin, re-tracing back to the start. 'Annabelle, she lost the baby. So, she went to stay with her aunt.'

'Aunt?'

'Anna, she lived on the coast, somewhere in Norfolk. I hadn't thought of it before, but that's where I've lived all my life. I could have lived in the same town, walked along the same beach.' April smiled, awkward, not so much of a happy thought, but a sudden realisation that everything was linked — history in a full circle.

'I'm not sure if I've heard of Aunt Anna but continue.'

'Richard took her up there but came home again, I think, after a couple of days. I feel he wanted to stay with her, but for some reason, well, when he got home...' April laid her head back on the headboard, her spine nestling into the feather pillow. 'Emily was at home. She missed Annabelle so much. Then, in the garden, Richard brought her a letter or something, but it wasn't from James. Oh Nan, he died, killed in the war, away from everyone, away from Emily.' Tears fell down her cheeks as she rested her head on her grandmother's shoulder. 'This room was Emily's

'My darling, you feel all this because you are so sensitive and perceptive. You have these thoughts and memories for a reason. Emily herself gives you these for a purpose; we just need to find out what it is. But you must remember, these are things that have been. You cannot change them, no matter how terrible they were and how sad they make you feel. Do you understand?'

April nodded, wiping her tears with the corner of her bedsheet, 'course, but it doesn't make me feel any better.'

'Now, let's have a good look through this box, shall we?'

Sarah held the leather album in her palms and gently opened the gilt clasp. Inside were several pages of framed photographs, family portraits, holidays and celebrations.

'My goodness, another wedding photo.'

'Nan, it's Annabelle and Richard!'

'He was lovely. No wonder my grandmother married him.'

'I know, he was…' April placed a hand over her mouth, keeping the words to herself.

Sarah watched her expression filled with joy, but there was anxiety and sadness deep inside her eyes. April quickly closed the album, putting it down beside her, tucked away like a treasured possession.

'Now, what do we have here? Letters, and nothing else, somehow, I'd imagined a whole menagerie of treasures and jewellery, but…' Sarah said, picking up the box, inspecting it further. 'I could be wrong, but I know that sometimes, these types of boxes have, yes, here, do you see?' She tipped the box back; inside the lid was a pin, with a quick flick from her fingernail — another compartment, with just enough depth to hide some possessions. April held out her hand with anticipation; into it fell a dark green, leather-bound book.

'And to think, you've been wearing the key.'

The green leather book sat tightly within her hands, reluctant to release it. She closed her weary eyes tightly; the book nestled flat against her breast.

'I know what this is. It's my diary,' The words were not hers, but Annabelle's. 'I remember writing in it, not what I wrote, but I'm holding a pen, and there's my inkwell, I'm sitting by a window with the sun bright on the white page, it makes my eyes sore, my whole body aches, my heartaches — I miss Richard.'

'It's all right. You keep it to yourself. You can read it when you're ready. It belongs to you, no one else,' Sarah pressed her hand against April's, still gripping her diary. 'Would you like me to leave you?'

'No.' April eased her eyes open. 'No, course not. I'll have a look later.' She carefully tucked the diary under her pillow.

'It's getting light outside; I think I'm going to get up now anyway. I'll check the fire and put the kettle on for a morning cuppa. You want one?'

April merely nodded. Putting the letters back into the box, she replaced the silver key, her bracelet dangling from the charm. With a sturdy twist, locked, its secrets carefully guarded.

~

The day drifted; long hours mingled together. April wandered the house with no comprehension of time, unaware of the day. The family left her to it, neither asking nor questioning the cause for her state of mind. Sarah, from time to time, would nod and smile. Julia and Michael simply organised the festive activities, lunch, music and games.

With the customary ritual on Boxing Day afternoon, the polished coffee table was set with Monopoly. The board was tatty and worn at the corners, some of the counters replaced over the years — festive cake decorations and the like; a plastic robin and an angel with frayed net wings.

'It's your turn, darling? Here, April, the dice.'

'Hmm?'

'The game, it is your turn?'

'Oh, sorry,' April tossed the dice across the table; it landed in Julia's lap.

'I think that is a three, yes, definitely a three.'

April idly moved her counter, a silver plastic hand mirror that had once belonged to her Sindy doll, long since forgotten.

'It's no good, Little One; why don't you have a hot bath and a nice early night? I know it was early morning. You didn't get much sleep, did you?' Sarah took the silver mirror counter from April's fingers and nodded.

'That's a good idea, darling; you don't look yourself today. I'm not surprised you look exhausted; you've been through a lot lately.'

April gawped at her mother, the first expression of consciousness that had occupied her face the entire day. However, her curiosity soon faded, with the refreshed reflection of the diary tucked away in its safe place.

Hot, soapy bubbles soothed her weary body; it ached with the lingering anxiety from the previous night.

As her cotton nightgown and the crisp sheets touched her cleansed skin, they carried her off, mind and soul, to the place she longed to be. The few hours since she had sat with her diary had seemed an eternity — a lifetime. At last, it lay in her hands. The green leather was supple and creased along the spine; its leaves brimmed with feelings and recollections she could no longer suppress. Her fingers flicked the edges of the old paper as it fell open at a particular date and a photograph.

The eyes smiled back at April, the dark lustrous hair, the smartly tailored suit, the handsome features. Her fingers traced the outline of his face, as she felt she had done countless times before.

June 16th, 1900

Oh diary, how can I continue with this pain, this pain that is in my heart and my soul?

My body is mending, although the doctor says it is too soon to know if I will ever be able to conceive again. Inside, I feel broken, ripped apart, unable to heal. I have lost someone very dear to me, who will go forever unknown, but they are still real. My longing is so intense that I cannot see my life without it. I have no place, no purpose in this world, if not as a mother.

Richard tries so hard; I know he does. Why can he not see what this means? If there is no child, there is no us, and then what can I give him? If not an heir, then there is nothing. He continues to pretend this does not matter, but I know it does.

I cannot find the words to tell him what is here in my heart. I do not want him to think me weak.

He pretends to be resilient, to cope enough for both of us. But I know he longs to tell me, but I fear he will never bear his raw soul. I love him with every beat of my heart. I long for his touch, the softness of his skin, the tenderness of his lips, that I no longer deserve if I cannot give him what he needs.

June 19th, 1900

The journey passed. I was unaware of the scenery and other passengers. I know Richard, dear Richard held my weary hand for the whole trip, and his was warm and full of love, while mine was cold and lifeless.

Why can I not find the words to reply to his devotion? I am afraid of the words that would seep from my lips. Words to make him afraid of me, worried that I have changed and am no longer the woman he fell in love with.

When I look back to those days, when motherhood was a thing of the future, I feel another woman wearing my skin, walking my path. I cannot remember how my mind thought without this soul-wrenching pain, which now consumes my whole body.

June 22nd, 1900

Richard left today. He left me. I am alone.

He went back home, and I am left here without him. I could not find the words to tell him to stay. I so longed to put my hands on his face, kiss his waiting lips, but they left, untouched by mine, his arms left without my embrace.

So, I am here, cold and torn.

I try to busy my time. I have taken to painting again, after so long. It soothes a little while the summer sun drenches my body but never warms my heart.

I am now filled with nothing but the pang of tremendous guilt. I have pushed my Richard away. But what can I say to him?

June 26th, 1900

My poor darling Emily, my poor, poor sister.

I am leaving for home in the morning. I received the worst news today; James, poor James, is missing in action, presumed dead. The telegram came from Richard, and I must return to look after my sister.

I have let myself relish in my self-pity, wallow in my sorrow. I cannot. I will not let my dearest sister endure this alone. I always have, I shall always be there to look after her, and if not now, when she is at her most vulnerable, then, when should I be there to take care of her?

April closed the diary, the green leather guarding her secrets. She could take no more. The words had burned, recalling the past conjured the deepest feelings.

CHAPTER TWENTY

Annabelle stepped through the front door and down into the room, the sun illuminating a halo behind her hair. Richard stood in the hall doorway, wanting to speak but not knowing what to say. She placed her large bag on the carpet, her hand still clutching its leather handle, unwilling to release it and acknowledge her arrival.

'I had no idea when you would arrive home. If I had known, I would have received you at the station,' Richard announced, polite and unfamiliar as he clutched the doorframe with white fingertips.

'Where is she? How is she?' Annabelle removed her gloves and laid them on her luggage.

'Emily? She is in her room. She has been there since...' Richard cut off, adjusting his cuff. '...the telegram. She needs you.'

'And I am here now. I am home.'

'So, it would seem,' he snapped. 'She will be relieved; she has missed you.'

Tentatively, she inched towards him, her arms nervously by her side but eager to touch, to embrace him. Richard moved aside, letting her pass.

Making her way to the staircase, Annabelle turned on her heels to face him. The warmth of his body was palpable as her lungs consumed his scent, 'I am home, Richard, I am here, where I belong.'

Annabelle eased up the hemline of her dress as she climbed the stairs, leaving her husband alone at the bottom.

Richard stood, wanting to speak. Finally, the words left his lips in the merest of whispers. 'I love you, Belle.'

~

Alone in her thoughts, Emily lounged on the pink bedroom chair, blindly gazed through the windowpane at the garden below, but it was unwilling to partake in her sorrow. Instead, it burst with joyous birdsong, aglow with sunshine and bountiful with sweetly fragrant roses.

'Darling?' Annabelle called as she entered and closed the door behind her. 'Emily, I'm home, darling.'

'James? James?'

'Darling, it's me, Annabelle.' She gripped Emily's hand. It was cold, clammy and lay heavy and lifeless in hers. The blackness of her dress made her skin appear sallow; her hair lay lank and dull about her shoulders and nothing but blankness in her eyes.

'Emily, please, darling, it's me.'

A spark of life glimmered somewhere behind their gaze, a distant flicker of acknowledgement. 'Annabelle? Is that you? Is it you?' her strained voice was low and hushed. 'Oh, my James, he has left me, oh Annabelle, oh, poor Annabelle, I am so sorry.' Tears fell from her tormented eyes as she covered her face, her hands shaking in spasms with her gasps of breath. 'I am so sorry, Annabelle.'

'Emily, please. Do not be sorry for me.' Annabelle gritted her teeth with the pain of her statement, took a deep breath and continued, 'I am mending, and we can try for another baby soon, I'm sure of it. However, it is you that needs care now, and I am home to look after you, as I always have.'

'James, my James, he is gone; he left me. Left me, Annabelle, he promised he would come home. He said no man was strong enough to take him from me. Only God, only God could take him from me,' Emily dropped her eyes, her limp hair matted over her face, then she began to shake.

Her body moved with spasms as she lost control. 'Why has God taken him from me? Why, what terrible deed have I done to deserve this?' she sobbed. 'Oh Annabelle, oh no, Annabelle.' Then, a gush of tears began to flood, 'how did this happen to us?'

'You clearly need some rest.' Annabelle guided her to the bed, removing her silk slippers. 'There, now please try and sleep; no more of this talk. You look like you have been awake for days.' Annabelle smoothed the sheet, tucked it in tightly under the mattress.

'I cannot sleep; nightmares torment me.'

'Hush darling, I shall call for the doctor to give you something to help.'

Annabelle closed the drapes, muting the midday sun. She eased the brass knob around and, with a gentle click, closed the door behind her.

~

'I have given Emily a mild sleeping draught, just to help her rest; she needs sleep and plenty of it. It is a terrible thing, this war, my sister lost her youngest last month,' the doctor sighed, the weight of a thousand worries on his shoulders. 'I'm afraid when you get to my age, you encounter death so often, in so many ways. But,' he continued, 'to lose young men in their prime and see their wives left behind, it breaks your heart.'

Dr Hickson turned to leave, 'I shall return tomorrow; other than that, I'm afraid there isn't anything more I can do for her. She needs to grieve in own her way. Sleep is the most important thing. The body can cope better when it's rested.' He saw himself to the front door.

Annabelle and Richard sat quietly in the dining room, the air thick and choking between them.

'Poor Emily, she hardly knew I was there, and when she did, it was so awful. She seems to be punishing herself for what happened as if she could have helped it, the poor darling. Whatever can we do?'

Richard paced the room, from the door to the clock and back. His long strides, uneasy, out of character, his hands wringing behind his back, his lips longing to say what was on his mind and in his tormented heart. Finally, after several long moments, he found his voice, although unsteady and low.

'I *was* there for you, Annabelle; I have *always* been there for you,' Richard blasted.

'There for me? *This* is not about me, Richard — we are not important. Our thoughts should be on Emily, and what a terrible ordeal she has had to endure.' Annabelle stood, stunned by his proclamation.

'This *is* about us. There has been far too much loss in this family,' Richard spat as he continued to pace. 'I was always there for you. Even though your heart shut me out, mine was still open. One word, just one word of acknowledgement, of love, and I would have done anything, anything for you. But, instead, you closed off and forgot about me.' Again, his words were gruff but, this time, he bellowed.

'There were *no* words, Richard, no words that I could find worth saying,' she retorted, trying to defend herself.

'Not worth saying?' Richard stopped mid-step. 'Not worth saying? You could have said, *I love you*.' Richard sat down hard on his chair, his eyes still on the carpet.

'That has never changed, never! I have always loved you and always will. I was grieving; I am *still* grieving. My body may be healed, but my heart is not.'

'So, you think mine is? Did you stop to think? Think of anyone but yourself... that I had also lost someone dear to me? Grief is not something you own, Annabelle. It was not only you who was grieving who felt the pain of loss. While you were lying in your silent grief, did you not think of me?

Did you not think of how I was to cope with the grief of losing our baby — of losing my wife?' Richard abandoned the chair, pacing the floor once more.

'Losing your wife? You have not lost me,' she said, then paused to gain her composure, desperate not to cry. 'I am here for you.'

'You are here now, but you came back to be with Emily. You did not come home for my benefit. For us.'

'I was sent away, to Aunt Anna's, remember, you sent me there, Richard. You sent me away and left me there, alone. I needed you, but you left. I did not go to escape you. You came home without me. You abandoned me.' She could feel his eyes boring a hole deep into her heart.

'Annabelle, you had left me long before I came home. You shut me out without a word. Not one word to me passed your lips. Not one word of love, or future, or of grief did you utter; just cold and harsh silence.'

The realisation of the situation drenched Annabelle with a downpour of agony. Richard's feet came to rest at her chair; he bent down, one knee resting on the floor. He lifted his hand to her face, raising her chin, their faces close.

'I do love you; I have always loved you. I am so sorry, Richard,' she whispered, her eyes closed. She could not bear to look.

For a few ticks of the clock, Richard's eyes absorbed her face. Every detail of her delicate but uncharacteristically pained features.

'It is not you who needs to be sorry. I am so sorry for what I have done to you,' Richard reassured as his heart sank.

Her weary eyes met his.

'I am so sorry for losing your baby, for failing at my purpose,' Annabelle's eyes dropped to her lap.

'Your purpose?'

'My role as a wife, I am meant to give you an heir, and I have failed.'

'I think the pain is the loss of what you feel you need to be. But, Belle, you are my wife, and if you never become a mother, so be it. I could have lost you, Belle, and then I would have nothing.'

'We shall never know, but the truth is I may never have a child, I may never give you an heir; if not for that, then what purpose does my life hold?'

'I do not need an heir as much as I need a wife, as much as I need you.'

June 27th, 1900

I arrived home this morning. I needed to get home to Emily. My poor, dearest, Emily, is overwhelmed, but I cannot help her.

What can I do? I cannot bring James back, and I fear that that is the only thing that would soothe.

She is inconsolable.

We fetched Dr Hickson, but there is no cure for a broken heart. She wanders her room, aimlessly searching, but what is she to find? There is nothing that will take away this pain. If I ask, she cannot answer me; her words are full of sorrow and anguish. They make no sense. They are just a muddle of jumbled nonsense.

Today was the first time Richard and I had spoken about what had happened. I feel more guilt now than ever before. I know that in punishing myself, I have punished him.

My darling Richard, I do love him so. I hope our life will return to what it once was, but I know that none of our lives will ever be the same with the tragic loss of James.

August 7th, 1900

Oh, diary, several weeks have passed, my life is as it was, still the devastating mess of turmoil. There are no words of joy and happiness. Instead, the house has become a place of mourning, a deep sorrowful state of blackness.

Father returned from a business matter the day following my return; Richard had sent him a telegram. Father tries his best to keep some normality in the house, but he fails.

Richard is distant. He tells me he loves me but does not show it as he once did. His touch is not as calm and pure as it once was; something keeps him from it, some invisible restraint. I have watched him when he thinks I do not. He is plagued by misery.

I so long for Richard to hold me in his arms, to kiss my lips and to touch my skin. The pain of the past few months has become tangible. It scars us all.

I see Emily, sometimes, while she is not looking. She will search every corner of the house, opening every drawer and cupboard. In her bedroom, she will repeatedly open her marquetry box, each time removing its contents and laying everything out on her bed. Then, meticulously, count each item and place them back in the box in the same order as before. But each time she is never satisfied, she will wander her room searching for her missing belongings, and I cannot help but think, she has not lost anything but James, and the pain of it, the emptiness inside, keeps her searching.

I understand that emptiness.

My heart remains as it was, with a missing piece. I have seen Dr Hickson; he is optimistic we shall conceive another child. We would be able to try again if only Richard would let me near him. But, unfortunately, things are not the same. He is trying; he looks at me with longing in his eyes. However, there is a force greater than his desire, and he cannot stand to touch me in the way he once did.

This family has lost greatly.

I did go home for a few weeks, back to North House, but our bed feels tainted by loss, loss of our relationship, as well as our baby. So, I remain here with Father and Emily.

My place now is with Emily; I know she needs me more than she needs anyone.

Emily's hand silently slid the length of the polished rail as she carefully descended the staircase, heavy bag clutched in her firm hand. When she reached the bottom, she placed the bag on the rug and fastened the buttons of her travelling gloves. Her foot finally stepped onto the firm surface of the hall floor. Securing her hat with a jet pin, her fingers teased any stray hairs neatly beneath it. She then stared wildly at her reflection; the gilt mirror hung, defenceless at her unnatural guise.

Annabelle paused in the doorway, eyes dazed with disbelief at the unexpected sight of her sister's dress. It was not so much her travelling clothes of sombre black or her veiled mourning hat that distorted her face, but the solemnity of her expression, the coldness of her eyes.

'Emily?'

'I am going to stay with Aunt Anna,' she retorted, with not a glance towards her sister. Instead, she numbly stared at her hands, inspecting her gloves, meticulously smoothing the leather between each of her fingers.

'What do you mean?'

'Aunt Anna's, by train.'

'Emily, I do not understand. Why are you leaving?' Annabelle pleaded as panic rose, her thumping heart leaping to her throat.

'I think the sea air will do me good.' She turned to look at her sister.

'I should come with you. Let us talk about it; we can go together, a holiday, together, just you and I,' Annabelle swayed on the spot, her legs starting to buckle. 'Please?'

Emily stood with a blank and distant expression. Cold, indifferent as a passing stranger. 'I shall be going alone.'

'But you cannot, Emily, you cannot go alone. I agree that a holiday and scenery change will be good for you, but you cannot leave now. Does Father know?'

'Yes, he knows.'

'He knows, and he is letting you go? You are not fit for travelling.'

'Not fit? I am not ill.'

Annabelle's mind was full of thoughts — abandonment, incomprehension that her father knew and yet felt fit to let her leave at such a time of need.

'Let me look after you. What will you do, alone?' Annabelle pleaded.

'I will have Anna there. I will not be alone, will I?' Emily adjusted her veil, her eyes closed. 'Annabelle... I know I have lost James; he will never return to me. Everywhere I look, there are reminders of him. Every chair in which I sit, every door I open, every breath I take in this house is suffocating me, covering me in the memory of James.'

'I understand that really I do. It is just that... I shall miss you.' Annabelle took her sister's hand, the kid leather cool to the touch, the touch of an impostor.

Emily eased her hand away, her fingers guarded and concealed. Annabelle's body shivered, and her hand lay open and empty.

'I must leave now.'

'Are you well enough to be travelling?'

'I am well enough. My body is not ill. It is my heart that is broken. The scenery will be a pleasant change.'

Emily's words were distant, rehearsed, but from somewhere deep inside came a flicker of sentiment. Annabelle gripped her hand again, this time reluctant to let go. Emily pulled, tugged herself away and fastened her coat buttons.

'I made you come home before you were well enough. You needed more time to heal, both of you,' Emily announced with blank eyes, but her voice quaked. 'It is my fault.'

'Darling, of course, it is not your fault. None of this is,' Annabelle beseeched.

'If I had not needed you, you would never have left Aunt Anna's so early before you had properly recovered.'

'I am perfectly recovered now. It was not only for you that I came home.'

'Precisely,' Emily snapped. 'You came home to be with Richard. So, you should be alone.'

'Richard? I am not sure I understand. Emily, please?'

'I have written to Anna, telling her of my arrival. My train leaves this afternoon.'

Emily occupied her hands, smoothing her jacket.

'Emily, you need to explain this to me. I am confused. I do not understand what this is about. Why Emily? Please explain why you are leaving,' Annabelle ordered, the questions exploding from her mouth, demanding an explanation. 'You need to be here; you need to be looked after...'

'No. Annabelle, I do not need to stay for my benefit.'

Annabelle stared, her brain trying to understand the words and their meaning. 'This cannot be happening.'

'You need me; *you* need me here. You need to look after me.'

'I need to look after you? But, of course, I do. You are grieving. You do not know what you are saying.'

With a calm glide, Emily left the hallway and her sister. Then, with her back to the room, she watched the outside pass; gathered clouds daubed in tones of grey moved in a funeral procession. And taking a silent breath, inhaling, filling her tightly restricted chest, she slowly turned, her eyes slightly calmer.

'You cannot ignore your relationship any longer.'

Annabelle stood numb.

'Richard needs your full attention. Instead, I have it. Annabelle, I am your sister. I shall always be your sister. However, some things are more important. I no longer wish to be the wedge between you.'

'But... you are not a wedge between us.'

Emily's eyes bored into her sister's panic-stricken features. 'Annabelle, I shall never know what it is to be a wife. My married life was so short. I do not wish to deprive you of yours. I would not wish you, my fate. I must go. My carriage is waiting.'

'No, Emily. You cannot leave.'

'You need me here for *you*, for *your* benefit, not for mine. Annabelle...' Emily left her sentence unfinished.

'What? You know that is not true. You know how much I love you, how much love to look after you, and now, now of all times, you need me; you are grieving.'

'I am not your child. I do not need to be *looked after*; it is you that *needs* Annabelle. I am not the one who needs your attention.'

The sound of hoofs and wheels seeped in from outside.

'My carriage is here. I have to go,' Emily added as she placed her hand on the doorknob. Her fingers gripped hard until pain seized her wrist, and tears stung her eyes, yet still, she refused to look at her sister.

'Emily,' Annabelle wept.' I love you.'

'The pain is too much to take,' she answered. 'I love you.'

The heavy door slammed shut with a deafening thud. Annabelle's head felt fit to split in two with the pain of the parting. She stared at the door, waiting for it to open, for Emily to be standing there, having second thoughts.

~

'I cannot believe that you let her go.' Annabelle sat on the dining chair, her face in her hands, as her mind continued to spin with a deep, sickly sensation.

'Did you try to stop her; did it make the slightest difference?' her father asked as Annabelle lifted her face to look at his. She saw the same expression, a look of misery. 'I tried, just as you did. Emily had made up her mind. There was no changing it.'

'But she... she needs...' Annabelle could not bring herself to say it.

'She needs *you*, is that what you feel, that she needs to be cared for?'

'Yes.'

'Darling, she is a woman now, not the child. Grief has gripped this family with both hands. I know and understand. I remember, far too vividly, the pain of losing someone you love.'

'We are all feeling that loss, Father. But I do not see that hiding away at the coast will help, and how she can need that more than...'

'More than being here with you? Perhaps, Annabelle, it is you that needs her. Leave her to grieve and to mend while you do the same. Then, this family can return to a state of peace.' The captain rose and left the room.

~

Acid tears stung Emily's eyes.

The rain clouds began to bleed, weeping bitter tears, crying puddles, bleak rivers of hopelessness. Even more potent by the monotonous view of the field after field that dazed across her eyes. The gentle motion of the train lulled her mind, numbing it to sleep.

Hidden beneath the leafy boughs of the vast tree, they lay.

She could still taste the cool lemonade on her tongue; hear the sweet morning song of the birds. His hand on her skin tenderly touched her cheek. Her eyes closed; she could feel the sun through her eyelids, warm and pink. Her mouth opened with her lips eager to speak his name.

'Hush, my darling, we need no words.'

Her cheeks blushed; her skin tingled as his tender fingers traced the line of her chin, her neck, down to her breast. Her hand moved up his back. Through his shirt, she could feel his shape, the clarity of each defined muscle. Then, over his shoulder, she reached his bare skin, his neck warm and fragrant. Her forefinger came to rest on his lower lip, his mouth open, the warmth of his rapid breath moist on her fingertip.

His face cast a shadow over her eyelids; she heard his heartbeat pounding fast in time with hers.

Gently, he slid himself closer, pressing his body hard and heavy on hers. Just the delicate layers of fabric between them, preventing them. Every inch of her overlaid by his body, blood pumping fast through his veins, pulsating with hers.

He laid his hands on her face, easing her tousled hair from her flushed cheeks, smoothing it away to see her features glowing and radiant. His face lowered — pressed his lips to hers. Warmth spread through their flesh, their breath mingled, becoming one.

With a bumping motion and a loud whistle, the train came to a stop. Emily's eyes blinked open. Her cheeks flushed, her hands hot and clammy within her leather gloves.

August 10th, 1900

Oh, Diary. Emily left today. It was such a shock. I am sure I have not recovered from it. Still, it was not my sister who stood before me; I am sure it was an impostor. There was no sign of love in her eyes, only some distant light of grief. She had not spoken before of going to Aunt Anna's. Still, I understand that the sea air and change of scenery will be a welcome holiday to the routine, daily grieving that continues relentlessly in this house.

I cannot believe or understand her words. I love her; she is my sister, my life. Maybe this is a sign that I should go home to Richard. There is nothing to keep me here now. Emily has gone.

Why does my poor grieving sister feel that she is the cause of our marital strife? The loss of James has hit us all extremely hard, harder than anyone could have imagined.

However, her grieving and need for care cannot have hindered my relationship with Richard. I am her sister; Richard would never question my loyalty or need to care for my sister. My poor dear Emily, the loss she feels has taken away her ability to see things as they are; she blames herself for everything. This is her way of dealing with the loss of James.

I would like to write that my loss is easing slowly. I would like to be able to write this and mean it. Then going home to Richard, we can ease this loss and try again.

I know I belong with him. I do miss him so. I still yearn for his tender touch, the warmth of his skin, touching mine. I love him.

CHAPTER TWENTY-ONE

Cool tiles underfoot were a welcome respite to the muggy heat. Yet, the atmosphere was thick with unease and awaiting the anticipated thunderstorm. Richard went in ahead, turned on the new electric lights, and space exploded with a bright radiance.

She was home.

For the first time in so long, she felt as easy. Annabelle exhaled, unsure of how long she had been holding that breathe, perhaps months, as now her heart eased. The pain had reduced enough to allow her to feel she belonged in this house.

She no longer felt a visitor.

Instead, she delighted in the modern decoration, its newly papered walls of bold leaves and birds, the bold new floor tiles, the polish on the recently turned bannister and newel post. Home, this was their home.

'I think I shall retire to bed,' Annabelle announced, unbuttoning her gloves.

Richard smiled in reply, 'you look tired.'

For the first time in weeks, his expression was calm, without the undertone of sadness or apprehension. He stepped closer, taking her bag, his eyes fixed on hers.

'I shall take this up for you.'

Annabelle followed a few steps behind. Her eyes on his body as he walked, the taut roundness of his buttocks, the shape of his forearm as he ran his hand along the smooth rail. Then, reaching the landing, Richard turned. Her eyes followed the length of his body to his face as his foot left the last step.

'It is good to have you home. I have missed you,' he spoke shakily, a hint of embarrassment at his confession. 'North House is not the same without you. Are you happy with the new decoration?'

'It feels good to be here,' she smiled. 'Yes, it looks lovely,' she glanced back down the stairs to the grand entrance hall. 'It is perfect, a William Morris design?'

'As requested,' Richard smiled in earnest. She noticed the small lines of delight around his eyes.

'Annabelle?'

'Yes?'

Richard waited a moment while his eyes traced her features. 'It is good to have you here.'

He placed his hand on the brass door handle, turned hard, pushed, and stepped aside to let her through. He switched on the lamp; the coloured glass filled the area with blues and violets from the dragonflies and flowers formed within the leaded glass shade.

Richard rested the bag on the dressing table stool as he caught her reflection in the mirror. Her hair gathered up in an ornate butterfly clip, and Richard watched as she moved, the fit of her dress, the slimness of her waist, the fairness of her skin, but it was the bareness of her neck that teased and tempted till his body ached.

'This room, the house, it...' she began, gliding her fingers over the coloured glass lampshade. 'Home.' There was surprise in her words. She turned as their faces met within the reflection of the mirror.

'It is your room, just how you wanted it.'

'I know. I have just come to realise how much I love it,' Annabelle smiled into the mirror.

'I shall leave you to unpack.'

'Richard?' There was desperation in her tone. Finally, he turned to face her directly.

She took a step closer, and they stood within touching distance, their hands awkwardly beside them.

'What is it?' Richard stretched his fingers; he placed his warm palms on his trouser legs, the heat burning through his skin.

'Richard, it is good to be home.'

She caught the glint in his eye as he smiled and left the room.

~

In long sweeping strokes, Annabelle swept the brush through her fair hair. Then, gathering it over one shoulder as she teased the ends with her ivory comb, she continued meticulously; her mind lost to other thoughts.

The handle twisted with a low knock, and Richard stood in the doorway.

'Richard?'

'I'm sorry to disturb you. I was wondering if I could get you anything, a nightcap?' He hesitated on the threshold, his eagerness apparent.

'Richard, darling. No nightcap for me, but please, if you wish one. Maybe...' she paused, sighed deeply. 'Will you come in?'

His entrance was slow with measured steps across the threshold.

'Do shut the door. There seems to be draught; we shall have that thunderstorm; humidity is in the air. Do you feel it?' Richards's eyes were on her as she spoke.

'I do. I feel it too.'

Richard walked, stood behind her, watching how she brushed her hair in the mirror. He placed his hand on it, sweeping it away. His touch made her jump.

'I have missed...' Annabelle watched his reflection as he stroked her hair; his eyes glittered. 'I have missed this.'

He rested his knee on the stool behind her, his thigh touching her side. Then laid his hands on her shoulders. Her bare skin tingled. She rested her head back against his body, exposing the contours of her neck.

Tenderly, Richard ran his forefinger around the edge of her neckline, the tips of his fingers teased open the ribbon ties of her nightgown, leaving her breast exposed as the cotton fell aside. Raising her hands, she pulled it down so it lay about her arms and rested on the curve of her breast.

Richard's heart thumped against her head. She could sense the beating increase, galloping. With her eyes closed, she lay absorbed in his touch as his fingertip teased her nipples.

Richard stood back. Annabelle opened her eyes, met his smile. Then, in one silent movement, he slid his arm under the curve of her knees, sweeping her up into his arms. He remained standing in front of the mirror, their breaths heating the air between them. Annabelle lay vulnerable in his arms.

Without a sound, Richard strode to the bed and laid her down. She watched as he removed his shirt, the powerful movement of his shoulders; she could almost trace each muscle through his skin.

'Belle, I...'

'No, Richard, please no words.'

She held up her hand and traced her finger along the subtle line of hair that travelled down to his navel. Richard clasped his fingers around hers as she reached for the waistband of his trousers. He rested his knee on the bed and bent to kiss her. Eagerly, she gripped the band and pulled him beside her, her fingers manipulating the buttons.

Desperately, Annabelle pressed her body against his, her breath rapid and hot on his skin. With their bodies intertwined, Richard ran his hand up her thigh and at last entered her. A feeling they had not felt for an eternity.

CHAPTER TWENTY-TWO

Sarah laid her head back against her pillow.

'Nan, the doctor said you aren't well enough to be at home now.'

'April, you know as well as I do, if I go into hospital, I'll never leave it. Not how I'd like to, anyway.'

'Oh, Nan.'

'We all know my time is nearly here. I want to spend it in my own bed, with my belongings.'

'I know. I know you're right. I'd want the same.'

April took her grandmother's hand and placed it very gently in hers. Its frailness made her heart miss a beat. The lively, vivacious lady she once knew now lay as weak.

'Grandad's here, isn't he?' April lay beside her, her head resting on the pillow, her hand still clutching her grandmother's.

'Yes, he's waiting, very patiently,' Sarah took a deep sigh and closed her eyes, 'I miss him so much. It's been such a long time.'

'It must be so awful to lose someone you love so much. Someone you planned to spend the rest of your life with.'

'We had many long years together, lots of wonderful memories. The memories always stay. You never lose them; at least you never lose *them*.'

'I can't imagine feeling that way,' April said, but in truth, she did know.

'You'll find someone someday. And when you do, you'll know straight away that he's the one, the one you were meant to be with,' Sarah smiled.

'I do know; I do know what that feels like.'

'Oh, Little One.'

'I don't want anyone else,' April said adamantly. Finally, she closed her eyes in stubborn defiance. 'No one else.'

'I know, I know.' Sarah squeezed her hand.

'Nan, when it comes to Richard, my thoughts and memories as Annabelle are as real as my own. Do you understand that? Do you know what I mean?'

'Yes, darling, I do. But, Richard, he was my grandfather. Richard belonged to Annabelle.'

There was a heavy thick pause. The dresser clock ticked, creating waves of rhythm across the room.

'Yes, he did, but I feel Annabelle's love for him as if it's my own. Do you see? I love him, Nan. I love him with all my heart. My heart loves him, and I know I'll never be able to love any other man, only Richard.'

April opened her eyes, cast them towards the window. The midday light was muted and dull. Snow had begun to melt, and rain through the night had left slushy puddles amongst the dirty white mounds of old snow.

Gently, so as not to disturb her dozing grandmother, she manoeuvred herself off the bed and wandered to the window.

The magnificent tree stood naked and vulnerable at the bottom of the garden. Its boughs no longer wore white sleeves but wept with the last drops of melting snow. April longed to see it, abundant with its emerald leaves, rustling in the summer breeze. It had seen so much life that tree, standing its ground for generations, unspoken scenes of life, love, and loss.

'Poor Emily,' she sighed; the glass pane warmed with her breath, misting her view, absorbing her words. 'Poor darling, Emily.'

Annabelle, oh, Annabelle.

Swinging around, April scanned the room. It was still, almost lifeless.

'Emily, Emily. Are you here?'

Only the short, rapid breaths of her grandmother pierced the atmosphere. No other sound found her ears. She paced the floor, her senses alive. Her feet led to the dressing table, its large oval mirror, the upholstered stool, both familiar to her touch. She gently eased the seat out and sat. With her reflection was central in the mirror, the room behind her lay timeless. April closed her eyes, listening, her body waiting, her heart wishing.

Her grandmother's rhythmic breathing melted into the back of April's consciousness, allowing her ears to fall prey to a beat. It grew stronger. April let her body relax into its pulse. Her own heart rapid in harmony as her skin tingled with a sensation of touch — exhilarating. The stool moved, and she felt a touch by her side and heat to her back. She sensed warm, soothing hands on her skin, touching, gliding, and loving.

'Oh!' In an impulsive reaction, April opened her eyes, her cheeks flushed and hot. The familiar sound of her grandmother's breathing returned to her ears.

'Oh,' she whispered and watched her flushed reflection.

Annabelle. Again, the voice came soft and sighed. *Annabelle.*

'Emily? Where are you?'

Find it, Annabelle, find it for me.

'Emily, find what? I don't understand.'

With a sudden thud, April's senses fell back into reality. She turned on the stool, as her grandmother as she stirred.

'April, are you still here?'

'I'm here, Nan. I'm still here.'

'Ah, there you are.'

'I was just... um; I was just sitting at your dressing table. It's lovely. I think I recognise it.'

'Oh darling, of course, you do. It was my grandmother's. It came out of her house in Northgate Street, hers and Richard's.'

April lay next to her on the bed, their heads touching.

'I remember when you were tiny. I would sit at my dressing table, and you on the end of the bed, and I'd let you brush my hair for what seemed like hours. You would love to brush my hair, oh so very gently until you said it shone like glass.'

'Nan, I don't...'

'Yes, many hours. I would sit, and my Little One would brush my hair.'

'Nan, you go back to sleep.'

'It's all right, I remember.'

September 17th, 1900

Diary, I have had no word from Emily. Each week I write to her, and with each passing week, I have no reply. I cannot help but think that her melancholy has changed her, and she no longer wishes to see me. I have had some letters from Aunt Anna, though she writes regularly, they seem oddly vague. However, she is quite adamant that Emily shall return home soon when she is ready.

I feel so helpless in this matter. No words I write can change her mind. What can I do?

I am home with Richard. I love him so. We are as we once were; his touch is gentle and tender. His love is as strong as his touch. When his hands glide over my skin, I tremble, as when we first met; his kisses are as if they were our first.

It is early, too soon to be certain, but I hope we may be expecting another baby. I have not mentioned this to Richard. I know that it is too soon to know, but my heart desires and skips with happiness at the very prospect.

I wish dear Emily were here. I should be telling her my thoughts and secrets. But, instead, I must continue to confide in the pages of this diary.

'Will you get that, please, Lizzy?' Annabelle sat in the front parlour. The afternoon light was fading fast; she positioned herself next to the large lamp, its elaborate shade bright over her book. The heavy glazed front door opened, and she heard faint, whispered words, hurried and breathless. Curiously, Annabelle rose and walked into the entrance hall.

'It's Mr Hardwick Senior, Madam.'

'I can see that, Lizzy. Let him in,' Annabelle walked towards the door, 'Father, an unexpected visit, what do I owe this pleasure?' Annabelle gestured towards the parlour door, 'please, come in and sit down.'

'Annabelle, my dear.'

'Yes, please come through.'

Mr Hardwick stood tall inside the front door, his feet firmly planted on the coloured tiles. He ran a shaking hand over his large moustache. Cautiously he followed Annabelle though into the parlour.

'Some refreshment?' Annabelle enquired.

'Annabelle, my dear, I think you should sit down.' Mr Hardwick sat opposite, perched on Richard's green leather armchair. 'My dear, it is Richard.'

'Richard? What is the matter, what is it?' Annabelle fidgeted to the front of her seat, her hands worrying in her lap. 'Please, you are concerning me. Whatever is it?'

'My dear. You must not panic. However, there has been an accident.'

'Richard!' At the words panic and accident, the worst scenarios flooded her. 'Please, tell me, please!'

'My dear, Richard, he has suffered some injuries.'

'Injuries? How? I need to see him, now! Please take me to him, this instant.' Annabelle stood by the door, eagerly fretting with the charm bracelet. 'Now, if you please.'

'Yes, yes, of course. My carriage is outside.'

~

The cold, metal bed frame and starched sheets were too perplexing for Annabelle to understand; she hovered as if out of her time — rootless.

Richard lay in the unfamiliar bed, his face bruised, swollen and congealed with dark blood above his right eyebrow, a vertical split to his lower lip and a gash to his chin. The nurse fussed over his hand, tightly bandaging his wrist.

'Do not worry, my dear,' her father-in-law patted her arm, enticing her into the room.

But Annabelle could not reply if she had even heard the words. Her body remained rigid, static; however, her thoughts scattered in fragments across the cold tiled floor.

'The doctor has assured me he will make a good recovery and be well enough to come home in a few weeks,' he continued, guiding her through the doorway.

Annabelle was mute. How could she string together any words for this impossible situation? *I will never know what it is to be a wife; I do not wish you, my fate.* Emily's words rolled in summersaults.

She pressed her hands to her ears. No more.

'He will not die, will he? I cannot lose him too. He cannot die.' Erratic, uncontrollable questions dashed from her lips.

'No, my dear...' Mr Hardwick placed his arm on her shoulder and guided her more forcefully towards a hard, wooden chair. 'The doctors have assured me; just a broken wrist, a few cuts and a couple of broken ribs, nothing more. So he shall, as I said, be home soon.'

Annabelle sat, dazed, the atmosphere strange, the room foreign. How could this be happening?

Mr Hardwick sat on a chair beside her. 'We were out riding on the estate. Richard was helping me check the fencing along the far side, near the river. Something startled the horses. I am not sure what it was. Mine was a little uneasy, but Richard's bolted and threw him clean off,' he took her hand, gently rubbing the top of it with his fingers. 'It was just an accident. Richard has ridden that horse many times, and that track many, many times, as you know. It was simply a terrible accident.'

Richard stirred.

'I shall leave you two alone. I will be outside.' Mr Hardwick left the room, closing the door behind him.

'Oh Richard,' Annabelle wept, perched beside him on the bed, then tenderly placed her hand on his.

'Belle. What a day I have had.'

'I cannot believe this has happened.'

'You know how it is; just one of those things, I suppose. It was no one's fault,' he wheezed. 'You were preoccupied this morning. I watched you in the mirror.'

'Richard, I am fine,' she replied quickly, avoiding his gaze. His green eyes were duller, weaker than usual, and the matter sent a dark shiver through her bones.

'I have seen that look,' Richard countered, moving slightly to look at her directly, then gulped and coughed hard, 'I know that look in those eyes, Belle.' The pain in his ribs was sharp. 'Say you are, please. Is it true?'

'Oh, Richard,' Annabelle gripped his hand at the comforting thought. 'Maybe, but it is too soon to be certain. I do hope so.'

'My Belle, you look the most beautiful I have ever seen you!' Richard uneasily edged himself across the bed. 'Here, let me hold you?'

Annabelle lay close, her eyes closed, wishing they were at home. She could not bear to look at the stark white walls. She lay wrapped in his arm, her head carefully on his shoulder, as he kissed her hair.

It took a moment for her wandering thoughts to register Richard's stillness. She sat up quickly, laying her hand on his cheek., but his vacant eyes stared past her, immobilised by pain.

'Richard?'

His large chest spasmed with the deep, harsh coughs.

'Richard?' Now panicked, 'Doctor!' she shouted.

The metal bed, so cold and unfamiliar, now held them fast — suspended, with no way of escape. The white walls closed in, drawing the air from the room.

'Hold on,' she urged.

Richard's eyes dulled. They no longer appeared green, merely the cold embers of something she had loved.

'Stay with me,' she pleaded.

The doctor, closely followed by a nurse, dashed past Annabelle.

Coughs turned to gasps, to choking. Dark blood filled his mouth and splattered the white sheets with each desperate exhalation.

'Richard! Richard!'

'Please, my dear, let the doctor do his job.' Mr Hardwick held her firmly by her shoulders; as she writhed within his grasp, tormented at her distance.

'No!'

The room was dense with panic — the pandemonium, relentless for what seemed millennia. Annabelle observed as a tormented spectator.

Then, all fell silent.

Paralysed, Annabelle's body felt numb. Her legs buckled beneath her. She lay crumpled on the floor with her knees on the cold tiles as silent cries left her body. She quaked. She brought her hands up to her face, noting small spatters of blood, as at last, her words broke free.

'Richard! Richard! Richard!'

She staggered, her numb feet barely able, her dress tangled about her legs, she stumbled her way to the iron bed. At that moment, no one else existed. Her hands grasped at the soaked sheets as she reached his side, his hand open to meet hers.

'Richard?'

Richard's mouth moved in faint motions, eager to talk, but his body was unable.

'Don't say anything. Richard, I love you.'

'Look... after my ba-by.' His last rasping breath left his broken body and touched her face. She watched as the light left his green eyes. She took his hand, eased herself under his arm, and lay in Richard's lifeless embrace.

The door ajar, she could see the bed. The room was full of dusky light. It had been all day. Only wisps of sunlight had peeped past the drawn curtains. Aching fingers gripped the doorframe, unable to resist, she pressed hard, her fingertips white and numb. Pain, that's all she felt; agonising, ripping, tearing pain.

A hand touched April's shoulder, then a whisper.

'The doctor will be finished in a moment. Then, why don't you go in, sit with her?'

With a choking lump in her throat, her reply was no more than mumbling nonsense. 'Can't do it, not meant to... Why? Not now, too much to say! This isn't happening,' she wiped her face on her sleeve.

The doctor turned and headed to the bedroom door. 'You can go in now. She's comfortable,' he nodded and walked down the stairs.

April slipped through the gap; the door creaked with her movement; Sarah lifted her head, her eyes on April's wet face.

'Oh, please, don't look so sad. You know this is what I want. It's my time to go, and I'll be so happy to see your grandad.'

'I know, Nan,' she replied, with a gentle sigh and the tiniest hint of a smile.

'You know what that feels like, don't you?' Sarah nodded. 'It's time I was with him finally.'

'I know, Nan, I know.' April forced a smile and sat on the bed next to her and held her hand, examining the transparency of her delicate skin, memorising each blemish, every crease and wrinkle.

'So, my Little One, what have you been up to the past couple of days? I'm sorry, I haven't been particularly good company, have I?'

April responded in the same vein. 'Oh, not much,' she lied, desperate to confide in her.

'I think you must have been up to something; what about the box?' Sarah asked with her usual perception.

'I've been reading the diary... and *so* many dreams, too awful.' April's face dropped, her stomach churning with the intense emotions.

'It's okay, I know,' Sarah sighed.

'You know?'

'Yes. Richard?

'Hmm, it was so awful, no, worse than that. He's...' April couldn't bring forward the words; the pain of it was still too raw.

'I know, darling.' Sarah patted her hand as April squirmed at the sight of her paper-like skin. How quickly she had deteriorated. 'The accident?' whispered Sarah.

'You know? You knew?'

'Yes, not in detail. But yes, I knew about the accident.'

'But Nan, you never said. All this time, and you never once said.'

'My darling, how could I have told you? You love him, don't you? So, how could I have told you that? It was something you had to find out, to remember for yourself, just like everything else. I knew, when the time was right, you would find out. It just had to be like that.' Sarah flinched.

'Nan, shall I get the doctor?'

'No, no.'

'I know how you must feel.' April's voice was lighter.

'Little One?'

'The longing to be with Grandad. To have him hold you in his arms and say I love you.' Silent tears trickled down April's cheeks and dropped in sequence onto the bedsheet.

'You will be with him again, one day,' Sarah replied.

'When I'm dead!' April retorted, instantly regretting it. 'Oh Nan, I'm so sorry, I didn't mean...' April sobbed.

'Hey, come on now. I know I'm dying, and I'm not scared or sad about it. I'm old. There have been some hard and sad times. But I've also had some wonderful times, especially with you, lots of lovely memories of being with you,' Sarah gripped April's hand with strength, despite the brittleness of her fingers.

'You have to remember all the lovely times we've spent together, we've had twenty years together, haven't we, and my goodness, to think you are now almost twenty-one.'

A rasping breath took hold of her chest. Then, with a deep inhale, she rested for a moment, her head back against her pillow as she waited to let it pass.

'I feel blessed to have finally seen you grow up into a fantastic woman, determined but compassionate, gentle. I didn't miss it; I saw you grow up this time.' Another long choking breath and she lay still, her eyes closed.

'Nan, you should rest now.'

'No, not yet.' Sarah opened her eyes and reached under her pillow. 'This is for you.'

'What is it?'

'For you, after I'm gone. It's something that belonged to you. It used to be mine, but it truly belongs to you now.' She handed April an envelope. 'No, don't open it yet. But, sometime soon, you'll know when. When you do, you'll understand.

'Nan, what is it?'

'No, you're not ready yet. So, one thing at a time, there's no need to hurry, we have all the time in the world, and you must always remember that. Time is nothing but a tick of a clock; it continues to pass, regardless, just as we do.'

April placed the envelope on the bed and examined it. A regular white envelope with the words: *Little One.*

'Nan, it's all going to be all right, isn't it, in the end?'

'Oh, my darling,' Sarah lifted her arm. 'Come here, lay by me, just like when you were so small.' April lay next to her grandmother; her fingers patted her upper arm. 'Everything will sort itself out. It always does.'

'But Emily? I still don't understand?'

'I know you don't. But you are clever, and you will work it out. And, when the time is right, you'll meet a nice young man and settle down.'

'No. No man, no one will ever be Richard,' April said.

'Yes, I know, only Richard. Just promise me one thing?'

April turned her head on the pillow. 'What is it? I'll promise you anything; you know that.'

'Promise not to push every man aside. One day, you'll find the one. Don't lose him because you're too blinkered to see.'

How could she promise to love another man when in her heart, the memory of Richard was so vivid, so intense, so painful?

'Promise me!'

'I promise, Nan; I promise not to let myself be blinkered. I'm not sure I can promise to be able to love anyone else.'

'Now, that's all I can ask of you. That's all you can ever ask of yourself.' Sarah heaved her body with the repressed pain that shot through her chest.

'Nan, I think you should rest now. Can I get you anything, some water?'

'No, I don't think I need anything,' she paused, closed her eyes. 'I think I'm going to go soon. He's close. I can feel him.'

'Yes, Nan. I know he is.' April lifted herself from the pillow, her eyes constantly on her grandmother.

April stood facing the bed. She sensed a presence behind her and glanced at the door; it was as she'd left it, slightly ajar. Gently, creeping through the atmosphere was the distinct aroma of pipe tobacco. April's grandfather placed his large hand tenderly on his wife's forehead, and light illuminated Sarah's face — tranquil. April paced back to the door, leaving her grandparents to their long-awaited reunion.

CHAPTER TWENTY-THREE

North House, Bury St Edmunds
December 2ⁿᵈ, 1900

Dear Aunt Anna

I have no words to express what is in my heart. Richard is gone. An accident, they keep telling me. Yet, how can this be? How can it be just a sad accident to take my Richard? What is just about it?

I need Emily. It has been so many months since I have seen her and even more since we have spoken. Each week, I write to her and never have I had a reply, surely now, if never before, she can find a place in her heart for me. I must have pushed her away, pushed her aside with my grief.

I feel so cruel. How could I have done such a thing when she, herself, was grieving for James, her darling, James.

And now I sit here and find that fate has cruelly dealt me this same hand. I am so alone in this world, only having Emily.

Please, please, try to make her see how much she means to me and how much I need her.

The funeral is soon, and I fear it so. I cannot say goodbye to him.

Yours truly, Annabelle

North House, Bury St Edmunds
December 2nd, 1900

My dearest Emily

My heart is hollow and empty as I write these words. I have lost Richard. A tragic riding accident, just an accident, they keep telling me. It happened so suddenly that I still pour his nightcap and call his name. How can I continue without him? I have nothing left in this world.

We had hoped, for a very brief time, that we might be blessed with the chance of another baby. But sadly, my hopes were too soon. It was a premature thought and was not meant to be.

I do hope you read this letter. Unfortunately, we have drifted so far apart that I am no longer sure of our relationship.

Grief has captured this family firmly in its grasp, and it is reluctant to let go. We are all that is left. Please say that you will see me. It has been so long since we have spoken; my heart is desperate for your love. I remember our parting words. You said you would never know what it is to be a wife and hoped I would never suffer your fate. Unfortunately, fate has a cruel way, as I am here suffering, with every breath of my lungs and every thud of my heart.

I beg you, Emily, my dearest sister, please read this letter and reply.

There is so much for us to say.
I love you.

Always, your sister

Beach Cottage, Winterton-on-Sea
December 8ᵗʰ, 1900

Darling Annabelle

My heart is with you, my darling girl. You are strong, and although fate has indeed dealt you a cruel hand, you will overcome it and continue. I know you will; you must, for Richard's sake and your own.

I urge Emily each week with the arrival of your letters that she must reply, she must see you. I am afraid my words are ignored. She speaks little, has spent these months gazing into nothingness. You must see her. You have many words to say to each other. Too long has passed, I am afraid I have let it continue for far too long, and now, with the tragic loss of Richard, maybe too long, for some resolve.

Nevertheless, you must be strong, and so must she. For, if nothing else, Emily is your sister, she is your flesh and blood. You shall always have each other if nothing or no one else.

I fear I cannot leave her at this time, I have no choice, yet my heart will be with you on that day. Please say you will come and see us afterwards. Let me know as soon as you can.

I have written to your father expressing my sympathies. My brother is tough, but remember that he has suffered, as you do now. You must take his words as a consolation; they are from his heart.

All my love, my darling, Aunt Anna

December 9th, 1900

He is gone.

No longer my husband in flesh and blood, no longer will he walk up to our bedroom, no longer will he hold my hands in his. He is dead, and so is my heart.

The carriage arrived, the horses with their black flouncing feathers, the pomp of the ceremony. I sat, as a dutiful wife should, beneath the protection of my veil. My face, my numb, dead face, sheathed in black. Father sat beside me, with pain, a familiar pang of losing a soul mate. Words of peace left his well-meaning lips but not enough to soothe. I am sure no words can relieve this pain, the aching that consumes me beyond all hope.

The journey was endless, endless to the destination. My body was frozen and numb as we sat, as cold to the core as my heart, the heart that thrived with the love we shared. Without that love, I am but a shell, empty and broken.

Continually, our carriage followed in the wake of Richard's hearse, his empty body encased in a wooden casket. My thoughts wandered to his poor body, cold in the winter's chill and alone, so alone. I wanted to break it open, split it with my bare hands, scratch at the wood that covered him like a shell, hold him in my arms until I too died. Still, I sat and watched, and I gazed upon it, a continued reminder of my fate, the callousness that has been bestowed upon me.

An eternity, I had to bear the service, the tears and the silence. Tears from the mourners, mourning a man that many hardly knew.

How dare they cry my tears, tears that I cannot. How dare they miss his smile, a smile that was meant for me? How dare they speak of his qualities, his qualities that only I knew? Only I, only I, as his wife, knew his love. Only I knew the tenderness of his touch, the softness of his kiss, the strength of his body.

I watched, with scornful eyes, their faces, awash with salty tears and sorrow. The words that were spoken went unheard by my ears, words of Richard's abilities and triumphs, his loyalties and loves, all these he shared with me, and now I have nothing. I cannot continue and have nothing to triumph; my loyalty was to my love, my Richard.

Today, I put my husband in the ground beneath the cold, hard earth. His empty body will lie there, alone and dark. My body lays here, in our bed, alone, and I will forever be in the dark.

Therefore diary, I have no words of consolation. I have received none to console my dead heart.

CHAPTER TWENTY-FOUR

Annabelle hovered in the doorway.

'Darling, darling girl, did you get my letter? I am so sorry about Richard. I wanted to come, but I couldn't. There was just no way in the world that I could leave your sister.'

'Hello, Anna, where is she?'

'Emily, she is in the garden. Would you like some tea?'

'No. Thank you, I just want to see my sister.'

'It is so cold out there; see if you can persuade her to come inside? She insists on sitting out there all day. Even if she sat closer to the cottage with some protection from the wind.'

Annabelle paced the floor, slow and measured until she stood at the back door. Then, with her eyes on her boots, she headed down two stone steps and into the garden.

The white painted fence around the garden was low, purposely, to not distract from the incredible view. The cottage sat high; the garden backed the dunes, then the sea with a gate that led down a winding footpath to the sand. The beach was deserted, private, and peaceful at this time of year, a local or two walking their dogs. Only the sound of crashing waves and lapping shoreline filled the salty sea air.

'Emily? Emily, it is me, Annabelle.'

The garden was empty, the bench vacant. Again, and again she called each time with no reply. Gusty wind thrashed the long grass, whipping the sand into a storm as her feet trudged the first dune. Above the sea, the colourless sky wrapped the vista, touching the violent waves. From here, the world appeared abandoned, but for a lone figure standing against the wind.

'Emily?' Annabelle struggled to be heard over the wind. It blasted her face, numbing her lips and choking her. Then, carefully, pushing against the blustery weather, shoulders forward, head down, she staggered over the dunes. Emily remained, frozen and unmoved, even by the wind.

'Emily, I have so missed you. My goodness, it is freezing out here.'

Emily's eyes remained fixed on the rough waves, her once silky hair now equally wild like the North Sea — a tangled, knotted mass down her back.

She stood wrapped in a large patchwork quilt, made from oddments of squares, floral, brocades, and silks. Annabelle recognised this, a favourite of Aunt Anna's, meticulously crafted over many of her younger years. As children, Anna would put this on their bed when they were sick. Annabelle instantly thought of James and how Emily must be suffering, devastated, eaten by her grief and loss to be swathed in the quilt. Then, her own terrible loss throbbed at her temples — all too raw. No matter how the time drifted, it was no healer; it devoured her ability to function. She longed to be wrapped in love again, to feel secure and safe, to taste happiness. As a child, she had lost herself in the warmth of the patchwork; it soothed with its reassuring comfort.

The frigid wind crashed over the waves and lashed at Annabelle's face. Icy, bitter and cruel, her feet came to rest behind her sister. Still, Emily remained silent.

'Emily, I really need to talk to you.'

'Annabelle?'

'Yes, it is me. I am here. I am so sorry I have not been here sooner. Oh, it is so awful of me to have waited so long.' The overwhelming sense of guilt churned in Annabelle's stomach, and acid bile crept to her throat. The choking lump made it nigh impossible to speak.

'I am sorry, Annabelle, I am so sorry.'

'I know, darling, I am too. I am so sorry about James, and I have not seen you until now,' Annabelle leant towards her. 'Please, say you forgive me.' Emily remained closed tight, no limbs visible, only the wrapped folds of the patchwork, from neck to feet. 'I have tried to be a good sister, but I have pushed you away.'

Silence battled with the deafening wind for the capture of their ears. Emily did not answer. Annabelle stood lost.

'Richard. I am sorry,' Emily finally murmured, 'I am so sorry for Richard.'

Emily's sentiments carried in the chilly air. Annabelle was desperate to answer but was unable to unearth the words. They were buried somewhere beneath the hard, frozen earth. His name brought memories of his touch, aroma, and green eyes. Then, the remembrance of the last light, as it snuffed out, like a spent candle.

'We need to head back. We cannot stay out here.' Trying to find Emily's arm, Annabelle grasped the quilt and guided her away from the sea. Turning around, Annabelle cast her eyes over the dunes, scanning the beach below. A sharp intake of freezing air stung her lungs. Shaken, she gasped at how close to the edge she stood, how Emily had remained static against the thrashing elements, mere feet from the sheer plummet to the shore.

Emily's feet trekked the dune, but her mind was oblivious to her direction, and Annabelle eagerly clasped the quilt to keep her close.

'Girls, come on in now. I have made soup. It is far too cold today.' Anna stood on the back step. The girls walked through the gate; Emily dropped to the garden bench as her legs collapsed beneath her.

'Come on, Emily, we must go in. You know Anna, heaven forbid, you do not do as she asks,' Annabelle placed her gloved hand on her sister's shoulder. 'Emily, please. It is freezing.'

'I do not deserve to be warm.' Her words dropped, emotionless and monotone.

'You do not deserve? What on earth are you talking about?'

'I do not deserve to be anything but cold. I am cold.'

'Darling, you must be frozen to the bone by now. How long have you been out here?'

'I deserve it. I deserve it all and more. Annabelle. I am so sorry for Richard.'

'But Richard's death is nothing for you to be sorry about. It was awful...' she paused, desperate to remain composed, '...it was terrible, but it was an accident, a tragic accident. It was no one's fault; least of all yours, darling.' Annabelle wrapped her arm around her shoulders, quilted folds between them, her fingers clutching to hold on, desperate for some warmth.

'Richard, it was not his fault. It was mine. He loves you so much, and I love James and miss him. Annabelle, I do not deserve to miss him; it was my fault.' There was a silent pause, only the sound of the sea. 'He will never forgive me.'

'Richard? James? Emily, you are confused, so very confused. Come along, darling, we shall have some nice warm soup. You can cosy up by the fire.'

Annabelle stood in front of her, placing her hands on her shoulders. Emily's eyes were dull, her body stiff. Annabelle tried to lift her, entice her to stand, drag her off the bench if necessary.

'Please, darling, *please*, you are worrying me.' Annabelle shook her sister gently at first, then harder and more forcefully. 'Look at me, Emily. Look at my face,' she wept. 'Do as I say. God damn it, Emily, will you listen to me!'

Defeated, Annabelle slumped on the bench beside her unresponsive sister.

Emily bowed her head, faced the hard ground where the blanket hid her feet, matted strands of untamed hair strayed across her face in a webbed mourning veil.

'Emily, Emily, please,' she pleaded between sobs. 'This is my fault. I have always looked after you, the one time you needed me the most, and I let you down.' Annabelle knelt before her, the hard ground firm and cold on her legs. She hunted for Emily's arms amongst the vastness of the patchwork quilt. 'Please look at me; I never meant to let you down. As God is my witness, I swear I shall never fail you again,' Annabelle wept, deep gasps of sorrow and laid her head on her sister lap.

Slowly, Emily raised her head, showing her dark sunken eyes, and placed her hand on Annabelle's frozen cheek.

'Please, darling.'

Finally, Emily stood; the large patchwork quilt fell from her grip. It tumbled onto the bench, and great folds draped over Annabelle's lap. Emily looked down, her eyes met Annabelle's astonished dumb expression, but she remained still.

The brutal northerly wind persisted as her long hair lashed her pale skin. Annabelle sat on the cold ground, tangled in the patchwork. Wiping her face, she scrambled to stand and took a step. Her eyes left her sisters. It was impossible to think.

Emily was longer herself, no longer petite and slim. She stood before her, expectant, carrying a child, clearly close to being born.

Annabelle clasped her hand to her mouth, pressing back the lump in her throat. That great wave rose above her head, ready to swallow her whole, this time, it was black.

~

'Please, Annabelle. Do not leave like this,' Anna pleaded. 'This must be resolved. You must stay, or you will regret it.'

'Resolved?' she snapped. 'What on God's earth do you expect me to do?'

'The baby, think of the baby. Emily cannot, will not.'

'Oh, I see, it is down to me to think of the baby. But, of course, Emily cannot, look at her, not even thinking of herself. How long has she been out there?'

'Annabelle, please darling, the baby.'

'Baby, how dare you even use that word on me, as if it will make a difference?' she yelled.

Annabelle sat down hard on a kitchen chair, looking out of the back door. Emily remained seated on the garden bench. Seconds grew to minutes with no words, no sound but the harsh beat of her heart in her ears. Finally, Annabelle spoke, softer this time.

'So many happy times, Anna, so many times we have spent in that garden, playing as children,' she strode to the window. 'But now, all I can see is dread, death and pain.'

Her gloved hands covered her eyes, blocking out the cold that stung them like darning needles.

'You will have happier times again.'

'What happened to us, how did this happen, my sister and my husband — *my* husband!'

'Annabelle, I can imagine how this makes you feel, especially now, with Richard gone.'

'Do you know, Anna? Do you really? How can you imagine how this makes me feel? It was a sacred vow, exchanged in the presence of the Lord, and now, what is left? How am I supposed to feel?'

'I am sorry, but the truth of the matter is, that baby will be here in a matter of weeks. Then, there will be no time to grieve. You will need to think about the baby.'

'Baby! How can I think about the baby? That baby, when I think of how it was conceived?' she spat as she walked back to the table and sat, weary. Anna sat beside her and clasped her hand.

'*You* must be the one to think of this baby. Emily will not. I have tried to reason with her and convince her that she must start thinking of this new life.' Anna's voice was tender but to the point. 'Think about it, Annabelle. Emily wants to give it away. But she will regret it. You both will.'

'What can I do about it?'

'You need to make her listen. I know how angry you are, but you both need to listen. Find a way through this, Belle.' Anna walked to the back door, watching Emily.

'Please, *please*, Anna, do not call me that. No one, but Richard, can call me that.'

'He's gone, Annabelle,' Anna retorted. 'Forgive me.'

'I am sick to death of those words. My brain is saturated with *sorry*. It means nothing anymore. Nothing has changed, and it has made no difference to how my heart feels. It no longer has any meaning to me.'

'Look at her. Look at her, Annabelle; she is a child herself. This did not happen out of malice or deceit. This happened through grief and her need to be loved; you know that. Now, the task lies with you. You are the only one left to love her. If she does not have you, she will have no one. Neither of you will. Who else do you have? Other than each other, you only have the baby, do not let this baby go.'

Annabelle stood, grabbed her bag from the tiled floor and walked out of the kitchen.

'Annabelle?' Anna quickly followed her to the hallway.

'Richard is gone. He was my husband, mine.' She spoke to the floor, her eyes examining the old terracotta.

'I know, I know. But Emily is your sister.'

'Yes, she is. My sister and my husband.' Annabelle took another couple of steps towards the front door, then turned to face her aunt. Reaching out, she gripped the newel post, her fingernails gouging at the old wood. 'My husband!'

'Annabelle, do not walk away.'

'Whatever I do will not change the facts.'

'Annabelle?'

'I shall go and unpack.' Annabelle stepped to the foot of the staircase, placed her leather boot on the bottom stair with apprehension.

'Good girl.'

'I am not doing this for thanks; I am not doing it for you. And I am certainly not doing it for Emily,' she sighed. 'I do this for that baby. A baby with no choice, and neither... *neither*, it seems have *I*.'

Her weary legs trudged the staircase.

With particular care and attention to detail, Annabelle unpacked. Meticulously, folding and unfolding each item in turn, as the task absorbed all her power and thought.

The last of the afternoon light diminished, leaving her room dark. Her energy spent, she wilted onto the bed, her head heavy on the pillow, her blood barely pumping through her veins. With no more care for this torturous day, her eyelids dropped, and darkness covered them.

Lightly, a hand glided up her arm. The tingling sensation travelled her spine as his hand reached her breast. Tenderly, smoothly, it caressed and teased the silky skin of her bosom, the long fingers tantalising her aroused nipple. The neckline of her dress, cut low in the summer heat, enticed his eyes. His longing was evident, his breath hot and moist on her skin; with each glide of his fingertips, her body ached with desire.

She turned her face to him, the midday sun reflecting behind his dark hair; his face glowed with intensity. She could see her reflection, deep inside the green pools of his eyes. She sat on the edge of the bed. His hand reached out, touched her back.

'Lay here beside me; let me feel you close.' She turned and laid back, her legs barely on the mattress. He grasped her around the

waist, pulling her close, closer to his body. His arms were hot through the thin cloth of her nightgown.

His body lay bare and glistening with life. The sheet about his waist allowed her eyes to trace every line and curve, each defined shape of his tense muscles, the sheen on his skin.

His long fingers clutched hers, encased them tightly in his firm grip. Then, with one swift but gentle movement, he pulled her delicate body upon his. She lay pressed against his hot skin, only the cool cotton of the gown between them. His passion pressed against her body, longing for her. She put her lips to his, plundering his mouth. His warm breath mixed with hers, caressing, taking her mouth with hunger.

Within moments, the heat was intense, her nightgown hot and moist. With his long arms, he reached down and clasped the hem, easing it up her body. With one last manoeuvre, he pulled the gown up over her arms and head, their bodies hot and naked.

CHAPTER TWENTY-FIVE

Aunt Anna removed the hot bread from the oven; with folded cloths in each hand, she guided it onto a wooden board.

'There you go. Come on, both of you. I will not have this any longer; let us eat breakfast. Annabelle, can you please pass the jam pot?' Anna sat at the table; Emily, between them. 'How did you both sleep?' Annabelle remained silent, although the question had clearly been aimed at her.

'Annabelle?' Still, she said nothing; her eyes met her aunt's and said it all. 'It is a cold, windy day — no sitting outside, Emily. You need to be by the fire. Annabelle will sit with you. Annabelle? I need to go into the village, to the butchers, so I shall leave you two to catch up.'

Annabelle shot her a look of panic.

'I shall not take no for an answer. You are both adults, and you are sisters, flesh and blood. Best you both start remembering that. There are some demanding times ahead, and you will need each other more than you realise.' Anna got to her feet and paced to the kitchen door. 'Emily?' Anna looked directly at her, but Emily remained unmoved. 'Emily, my girl, you need to talk to your sister. You best make a start while I am out.'

~

Annabelle put another log on the fire; it crackled and hissed as the heat warmed the damp wood. Emily sat on the large tapestry settee, her legs outstretched and covered by the comfort of the patchwork quilt.

'I remember one Christmas when you were poorly, Anna tucked you up in that quilt, and you slept so soundly that night,' Annabelle said as she sat on the chair opposite. Just looking at her face, the pain was so immense it hurt her eyes and made her head pound.

'It is nearly Christmas?' Emily muttered.

'Yes, very nearly.'

'I do not want it this year. Nothing is the same. I have no James.'

'It will come, nevertheless, if you wish it or not.'

'I do not deserve any happiness; I have no James.'

'No, Emily... No, you have no James, and I have no Richard; Richard, who was my husband, he was mine, and now he has gone!' Her words hit, cruel and harsh, but her heart ached too much to care. 'My husband, you have no husband, and neither do I,' she spat in a wave of unleashed anger.

'We are both alone.' Emily's words were untouched by the harshness. 'We have nothing left, no one and nothing.'

'My goodness Emily, what has happened to you? If only you would open your eyes and look, look at me. You have me. Despite how I feel inside, you have me. I am your sister. You must stop this; stop this wallowing and let us get on with life. We are all we have; we have lost everything else.'

'I do not deserve anything or anyone. I am guilty. It is my fault, and I am paying for my sin.'

'Emily, no matter how this happened or who was to blame, it did happen, and we have to deal with it. But, despite it all, I am your sister, and you are mine.' The pain of her own words stung her lips, but her head overruled her heart. 'I am here to look after you.'

Emily's voice lowered to a whispered with words that at last had a conscious thought. For the first time in months, she looked at Annabelle with emotion. 'I do not deserve you. What kind of mother will I be?'

Annabelle could not remove her eyes, despite the suffering it caused them. Emily continued, with misery consuming each.

'I was to be a mother someday and a wife. James and I were to have a baby, which is the baby I should be carrying. That is the baby I want, not this one.'

'No, Emily. It is my baby, *mine*. The baby I was meant to have, mine and Richard's!' she spat, spiteful, like the hissing logs.

Annabelle stood up sharply, paced to the fire and reached for the long iron poker. She plunged the metal into the depths of the hot smouldering logs; repeatedly stabbed and thrust. Red burning sparks spat and leapt with each jab. She stood, facing the chimney breast, the large oval mirror reflecting her tormented image. Its angle, reflecting her sister, her face buried in her hands.

'That is my baby, Emily. I will not let you part with it. It is not yours to give away.'

~

Emily sat beside the fire, the patchwork quilt over her body, her pregnant bump rising like a mountain beneath the coloured fabric squares. A wooden box rested upon a table in front of her. She rummaged, selecting items, placing them regimentally in order.

'How about this red one next, right there, at the top, near the star?' She picked up the fragile glass bauble, holding it out in front of her.

Annabelle took it. 'About here?' she asked as she reached to the top of the tree, the ornament dangling in her fingers.

'A little to your left… yes there.' Emily leant slightly over the chair's arm to get a better look.

Annabelle hung the bauble from a spiky branch, twinkling with the reflection of the blazing fire.

'Can I have a blue one now? I shall put it just here.' Annabelle gestured to another branch just below.

'Oh no, we will need a green one there; you have a blue one behind your arm.' Emily sat in her chair, supervising from her spot.

'Where?' Annabelle stepped back from the tree to get a better overall view. She sighed. 'Now, dearest sister of mine, perhaps you should finish it yourself,' Annabelle smiled, taking a green decoration from Emily's fingers, hanging it on the branch. 'Yes, that looks better.'

'I know, I have a better eye for these things,' Emily said.

Annabelle paced backwards across the room, studying the impressive tree. It stood in the corner of the room, as tall as the ceiling and wide enough to touch the far wall and the wood of the nearby fire surround. Standing behind the fireside chair, she leaned over the back, placed her arms about Emily's shoulders, laid her head on hers. Their hair mingled, strands of golden ribbon and wisps of brown hair, lacklustre. Emily ran her frail hands over Annabelle's arm.

'It will all be perfect; you see,' Annabelle kissed her hair. 'Just perfect.'

'Yes,' Emily laid her weary head on her sister's arm. 'Maybe I should rest a little.'

'Do you want me to help you upstairs?'

'No, I think I shall stay here beside the fire and just look at the tree.

'I shall go and start dinner; call if you need me.'

'When will they be back?' Emily asked.

'Soon, they only went into the village to collect the goose.'

'I do love Christmas. It will just be different this year. Annabelle. Do you think James will be waiting for me?' Emily's voice had a childlike innocence.

'Waiting for you?

'When I go? Annabelle, you have to promise me something.'

Annabelle remained behind her. She could not bear to see her sister's face, to look into her tired eyes.

'Annabelle, please, I need you to promise me something. It is essential,' Emily begged.

Annabelle walked around the chair. She removed the wooden box and sat on the table in front of her. 'Now darling, what is all this about?' Annabelle's voice quivered.

'I know things are not what they should be. I am frightened I am too weak,' she heaved a sigh. 'Mother died to give me life. I am going to die, just as mother did.' Her words were thoughtful and direct. Annabelle lowered her head, not listening. 'I am weak, and the doctor has said that there is a risk.'

'Emily, everything is going to be perfect. You wait and see. You will have a beautiful baby and...' her words drifted.

Emily took her hand and held it tightly. 'I need you to be there for the baby.' Emily rested her head back. 'Remember how you looked after me when I was young? You were always there for me, even when I have been so cruel.' Emily closed her eyes. She sat motionless for a moment. 'I have been very cruel and have done something I am being punished for. But it is how it needs to be. So, you need to promise that you will look after the baby, *your baby*. This has always been your baby. It does not belong to me.'

Emily took a deep breath and gazed into the crackling fire. 'James, do you think he will be waiting for me, or do you think that I will be alone? I betrayed him, and I do not deserve to be happy in death any more than here.' Emily pondered her sister's concerned features. 'I love you. I am sorrier than I could ever find words to express.'

Annabelle patted her hand. 'I know you love me, and I love you too. Now, you must stop worrying about all this; it will make you ill. I promise to help you look after the baby. I will stay here with you both for a while. When you are fitter, then I shall return home.'

'I shall never return home. I belong here. There is nothing for me back there. I could never show my face there again;

everyone will know.' She gripped Annabelle's hand. 'If I stay here, then you can take the baby back home with you as your own. It is your baby after all,' she paused, 'I like it here, I like the sea air... watching the waves, how the wind blows my hair and how the sun warms my skin.'

'You want me to take the baby back home with me?'

'Yes, of course. You will be a wonderful mother. It is there in your heart; it is your purpose in life, remember? You told me you wanted nothing more in the world than to be a mother.' Emily rested a moment before she continued.

Annabelle sat speechless, desperate to hold back the black wave as it edged forward.

'This is the only thing I have left to give you, the only thing in my power to try to make amends. I know I can never bring Richard back to you, but I can give you the one thing that is part of him. I am so sorry, Annabelle. I never meant for any of this to happen. I love James.'

'I know, I know.'

'Do you think he will be waiting for me, Annabelle?'

Annabelle reached over and kissed her cheek. 'Of course, he will be waiting for you, darling. James loved you very much; I am sure he is waiting for you right now. But you are not ready to go just yet, so he will have to wait. We can all stay here if you wish. We can sit on the sand in the summertime, build castles, and paddle our feet in the water. Remember how we used to run through the shoreline when we were children, and our hems would be drenched with salty seawater, and how Anna used to chase us around the bedroom so she could wash our dresses?'

Annabelle's voice turned into a whisper as Emily closed her eyes and drifted off to sleep.

CHAPTER TWENTY-SIX

February 11ᵗʰ, 1901

Christmas passed quickly. Father spent the days here with us. I watched him over lunch; he could barely bring himself to look at her, our dear Emily.

She is his daughter. How can he cast her aside?

As a family, we have no choice but to continue as best we can. It has been difficult, the most difficult decision I have ever made, but there was only one answer. I am to bring this baby up as my own. So we shall remain here for a while. Emily, however, is unsure whether she shall return home. She always did prefer the sea air to that of the town. I know and understand that everything reminds her of James. She is grieving so terribly.

Today brings an added reminder of her loneliness, as it marks the anniversary of James' departure to Africa. Emily stayed in her bedroom for the entire day. I took her meals and stayed with her while picking at her food, but she ate little and said nothing. I am not sure whether she cried or not. Her face was so numb with grief.

Oh, my poor dear Emily, I am lost for answers. The weeks are ticking past, and the baby is due in a matter of days. Our concerns are growing. She is so tiny and frail these days; the doctor says she is grieving herself into her grave. I cannot bear to think

*of it. I am sure she will make it through. She must.
But I am haunted by thoughts of our mother. I
cannot lose Emily too.*

*My love and concern for my dear grieving sister
have erased any hurt I may have felt. I know that it
was not only Emily who was grieving so, but that
Richard also felt the loss of our baby and, indeed, the
loss of me. I pushed him away, so he had nowhere to
turn; I pushed him into the arms of my sister. The
fact still agonises my heart, but it is an agony of my
own doing. I am to blame for this turmoil.*

'You will love it like your own, won't you?'

'Of course, I shall. I love you so very much; how could I
not love this baby?'

'I am so deeply sorry, Annabelle. You do know that?' Her
words hung in the air. 'Every day that passes, my only
thoughts are of how sorry I am for everything that has
happened,' she stated. 'It should have never happened,
Annabelle, I am so sorry, but that will never be enough, will
it?' she sighed. 'I wish I could turn back time.'

'Emily, look at me. What is done is done, and no amount
of wishing and sorrow can alter it. You only have one thing
to concentrate on, keeping your strength for later.'

Emily dropped her head back against the pile of pillows;
only a few moments slipped by before another contraction
gripped her. Annabelle rinsed and wrung out the cloth, put
it to Emily's head, smoothing her brow as it subsided.

'I do not know if I can do this. I am afraid, so very, very
afraid.'

'You are going to do fine; it will all be over soon. I shall
get some clean water and another drink; you need your
strength.' Emily lay; her eyes uneasily closed as her anxiety
twitched her eyelids and tortured her face. Annabelle
quickly left.

'Anna, the doctor?'

'Yes, my dear, he's on his way.'

'I am afraid,' Annabelle's voice broke and shook with tears. 'She is so weak, what if…'

'I know… Oh, there he is.'

Anna opened the front door. The doctor quickly crossed the threshold; beads of moisture sat on the shoulders of his long, grey overcoat; his brown bag hung from his hand.

'Well, let me see her. How has she been doing then, Anna? The last time I was here, she had not had much sleep. Any better?'

'She has not slept and is very weak,' Annabelle quickly answered before her aunt had the chance to close the front door. 'I am so afraid. What if…'

'Ah, Annabelle, my dear, why don't you go and boil some water?'

Annabelle headed to the kitchen as Dr Williamson led her aunt to the foot of the staircase. 'So, Anna?'

'She is frail, but they are quite far apart. We have a few hours yet, which worries me somewhat.'

The doctor trudged the stairs, gently opened the bedroom door to see Emily lying very still in the large bed, the patchwork quilt over the sheets, her hands gripping its edge. He placed his bag on the floor and took out his stethoscope and a glass thermometer.

'Emily, well, how are we today? Let me pop this under your tongue. Now, I am going to check your own and the baby's heart.' Emily lay motionless, in dread, with the onset of another ripping contraction; and tried with all her might not to flinch.

The daylight hours dwindled into dim dusk; a pink hue flowed through the cottage. Anna bought the brass carriage clock from the parlour and placed it on Emily's dressing table. The minutes ticked. The contractions grew.

Hour after hour, the hands of the clock swept its painted face.

'Quickly, doctor, she needs you,' Annabelle called and ran to the door.

'You wait out here, Annabelle, let the doctor...'

'Oh Anna,' she wept. 'I am not sure she is strong enough.'

'Then it is just as well she has you for a sister. But all we can do now is pray.'

Annabelle sank to the carpet and pressed her back against the dark wood of the balustrade facing the bedroom. The only light was the lamp on a table in the front hall. Low light shone in rays through the cracks in the bedroom door. The air was thick, dense with anxiety, deep-rooted fear and dread as Emily's muffled cry seeped through. Annabelle turned from the door, pressing her cheek hard against the bannister; her knuckles whitened as she gripped. She gazed, tracing the veins on the back of her hand.

Anna stepped toward the door, placing her ear to its dark wood. Cries and sobs came from within for several minutes, then a loud, piercing scream.

Annabelle leapt to her feet. 'No! I must go in. She cannot do this without me. Not by herself, Anna,' she wailed, rushing through the door, almost sending it off its hinges, it came back with a slam.

Dr Williamson looked at Annabelle. Silently he shook his head.

Emily was barely conscious.

'I am afraid it isn't good. The baby is in some distress,' the doctor paused for a second to regain his composure. 'Emily is very weak. It is as if she has given up. We will have to hope for the best and, as I say, pray for them both. I shall call when you can come in.'

Annabelle nodded; there were no words in her dry mouth. Her heart sank to the floor, her body paralysed by shock, as her head began to spin. She sat back on the carpet;

her spine pressed hard against the spindles, elbows on her knees and her head heavy, filled with dread.

She waited, the time unbearable — lonely. She could hear Anna soothing her sister, not deciphering the words but low and tender. Her thoughts went to when they were children, how Anna could mend any awful drama with a few words and a cuddle, how everything was better, tucked up within the folds of the patchwork quilt. How much she loved her sister.

'Please God, please do not take them away. They are all I have; you have taken everything else.' Her muffled words repeated as the silence from the bedroom seeped through the door crack.

The silence grew louder, louder, as it deafened her.

Annabelle took a deep breath, her palm pressed to her chest. She heard a sound; it penetrated the thick silence. It was a cry. The baby. Her heart leapt, but she sat, paralysed, and waited.

She waited, and she waited.

She could hear the baby; its sound caressed her ears. The moments increased to minutes, the intense ticking of time as it leaked loudly through the crack in the door. The door handle lowered, and it creaked open. Anna stood a small bundle in her arms.

'It's a girl,' she said. The words should have been sung from the top of her lungs, joyous, but they came in a tearful sigh.

'Emily?'

'I think you should come and sit with her.'

Annabelle fell mute. She raised herself on shaky legs and entered the bedroom. Her sister lay perfectly still, auburn hair tousled on her pillow, her skin pale against its colour.

'Oh, Annabelle is the baby...?' Emily uttered through slow breaths.

'It is a girl, darling, a beautiful girl.'

Streams of tears fell. One by one, they dropped into a puddle on the bedsheet, then Annabelle looked up at the doctor.

'I shall leave you two alone,' he said softly.

'Annabelle...' she took a deep breath, 'I am sorry.'

'Oh, Emily, no more words of sorry.'

'But I have to leave you, just like everyone else.' Emily closed her eyes as she drifted in and out of consciousness.

'No, it is all going to be perfect. You just need to sleep a while.' Annabelle took the wet cloth and wiped it over her sister's forehead. 'You have a sleep, darling, and when you feel better, you can see your baby.'

Emily opened her eyes, 'No, she does not belong to me.' She closed her eyes once more, eased her head to one side. 'I think I shall go now,' her dull eyes gently closed. 'I cannot see him, Annabelle; I cannot see James. Will he come, take me with him?'

'James will always be waiting for you, but not now because you are not going to leave me, are you?'

'James, I cannot see him. Annabelle, He is not here. I betrayed him just as I betrayed you?'

'Do not be ridiculous. James will always love you; you were grieving; I know that now.'

Annabelle eased herself onto the bed beside her sister, cradling her in her arms, rocking her gently, her baby sister. 'No, Emily, you are not going to leave me; whatever will I do without you here? I need you! No, Emily! Do not dare leave me, NO.'

Emily's cheek sunk onto her sister's damp sleeves, her eyelids tightly closed, and her last warm breath seeped into the night air.

'Annabelle, remember to love me.'

CHAPTER TWENTY-SEVEN

September 2nd, 1901

I cannot believe she has gone.

Time has passed, but the pain is still severe. It eats away at my already broken heart. She was my sister, my flesh and blood, and she has gone, like everyone I care for.

They all leave me. All I have now is Rose.

Oh, Rose, she has Emily's hair and fair skin. As the months have gone by and she has grown, I have watched her. Sometimes I cannot take my eyes from hers. Her blue eyes are changing colour; they are turning green, like her father's.

She lays in my arms, warm and content. But it is when she looks at me, it rips at my heart. She has a look of Emily, her expressions and smile. It unnerves me. I must look away, I can only see my sister, and I miss her too much for words.

I stand on the beach, hear Emily's voice echoing through the waves. I feel the touch as the wild wind brushes my cheeks. I see her every time I close my eyes.

I am haunted.

I cannot help but think she stands beside me.

September 4th, 1901

We are leaving for home tomorrow. Part of me wishes we could stay here forever, but I know where I belong. My home is with Father, and that will be Rose's home. The town will be the perfect place; she will attend the girls' school, just as we did and our mother before us. She will become a wonderful, educated woman. The future seems so far off, but Father has already begun to make plans.

Poor Father, he spent most of the summer here with us. For hours I watched him. He gazes upon Rose, a fine jewel. He even played with her on the beach. However, his poor heart is still aching. He cannot talk about Emily. The mere mention of her name sends darts of agony through his eyes, and he swiftly changes the subject. I am worried about him. He will not speak of his sorrow. I fear he wants to forget her, to help erase the horror of these past months.

Her birthday was full of anguish. Father spent hours by her graveside, talking and wishing. He misses her so much, to lose the precious child that you lost your dear wife to... But, of course, I know all these emotions and pains, to lose my baby, then Richard, to lose my dearest Emily as well.

All we have is Rose. She is now my life, my reason for living. I am so fortunate to have her. We could very easily have lost her too. The pain of the circumstances has eased, and I now understand how ill Emily had become and missed James so very much. I cannot blame her for what happened. After losing the baby, I closed myself off to everyone who loved me and was there for me. My Richard, my dearest darling Richard, I shut him out of my heart.

Time passes, and with each new day comes a new memory, a memory of my sweet Rose. I add these memories to my cherished thoughts of Richard and Emily. Therefore, Diary, this will be my last entry. I shall lock this diary away with so many other things, so I shall not be reminded of the past and can always look to our future. Rose and I have a new life ahead of us. The past will remain in the deepest corners of my mind and pockets of my heart.

'Are you sure you are ready? That it is not too soon?'

'If I do not go now, Anna, I may never return. It is my home. It is where I belong. And it shall be Rose's home too.'

'What about your father?'

'I know he is still very hurt, but surely, he cannot lock her memory away forever?'

'Annabelle, he only does it because he loved her so very much. He misses her, just as you do.'

'Will you look after Rose for a little while? I need to do something, to say goodbye.'

'Of course,' Anna smiled.

Annabelle squeezed Rose's cheek and closed the front door, and headed out into the humid air. She would miss the village, but this was the right thing to do. Annabelle reached the church, pushed on the gate and wandered across the grass. She stood in silence, her slender figure casting its long afternoon shadow as she stared at the carved words.

'This is all wrong, Emily,' she wept.

I am always with you. I will never leave your side.

Emily's hand slipped into hers, tender and warm.

Annabelle closed her eyes, savouring the silent moment.

'I shall always remember to love you,' she whispered.

CHAPTER TWENTY-EIGHT

Bitter air nipped at the early Christmas Eve crowd. The market square was full of the usual festive traders. The hot aroma of the roast chestnuts surrounded Annabelle as she strolled past, pushing the baby carriage through the market, relishing the sight of Rose in her knitted bonnet and coat, snug amongst the folds of the patchwork quilt, gnawing on the ivory of her teething rattle.

'Mr Sedgwick,' Annabelle declared and smiled at the aged shopkeeper. He stood on the footpath outside his premises, *Sedgwick & Sons Fresh Green Grocery and Produce.* Behind him, a display of trees and holly wreaths obscured the windows of fruit and vegetables.

'I am looking for a Christmas tree, Mr Sedgwick.'

'Of course, Mrs Hardwick, I have just the one for you. I put it aside especially. I had hoped to see you.' Mr Sedgwick wandered to the side of his shop, near the alleyway. He returned heaving a colossal tree; its needle-laden branches poked and prodded at his jacket sleeve. 'It is nice and full as you like it.'

Annabelle studied the tree's branches, her gloved fingers teasing at a pine needle.

'Thank you, Mr Sedgwick; it looks perfect, as usual.'

'It's been quite some time since you last visited us, Mrs Hardwick,' he paused a moment, switching his gaze to the carriage. 'We were very saddened when we heard the terrible news of Mr Hardwick. Such a kind young man.'

There was an awkward silence. The sudden apparent din of the rambling crowds crashed at Annabelle's cold ears as the shopkeeper's words repeated in her mind, over and over: *such a kind young man.*

Once again, Mr Sedgwick looked at the baby. 'She has her father's eyes.'

Annabelle battled to regain her composure; she looked down as Rose bounced with the rhythm of the tinkling silver charms as she frantically waved her rattle. Her large eyes glowed with contentment.

'Yes,' Annabelle smiled at her daughter, 'Yes, she does.'

'It must be nice to be home, Mrs Hardwick, especially at Christmas. It's a time for the children, don't you think?'

'Yes, Mr Sedgwick.' Annabelle could not remove her eyes from Rose. The frigid air nipped at the infant's cheeks, flushing them as pink as a sun-ripened apple.

'And, of course, your dear sister. Mrs Sedgwick was taken -back at the news. A sudden fever, was it?'

'The Christmas tree, Mr Sedgwick?' she asserted, looking back at the tree.

'Of course, forgive me. You have our condolences.' He bowed his head. 'Shall I have it delivered as usual?'

'Yes, please. And that holly wreath too if you would.'

'Of course, after midday, if that is convenient?'

'Thank you, and Merry Christmas to you.'

'Thank you, Mrs Hardwick, and to you.' His words fell into the icy air as Annabelle, with eagerness, disappeared into the bustling hordes.

Dodging between the shoppers, she headed home through the market. A group of carol singers stood within the glow of lantern light on the hill. She rested for a few moments, listening, remembering. Finally, her eyes fell upon Rose waving her rattle, who handed it to her mother and grinned with two tiny bottom teeth.

'For Mama? Thank you, Rose.' Annabelle took the rattle and shook the silver trinkets before giving it back. Rose continued to shake the jingling charms to the music.

The towns familiar faces shopped for gifts and wandered the streets. The hill gathered with dozens of local townsfolk as the carollers sang. Annabelle watched and sang, her gaze travelling the crowd.

Something caught her eye — unexpected. Yet, before her mind had time to register, it was gone. Within a blink, the moment had passed. She scanned the crowd, face after face.

'Just a dream Rose; just a sweet dream,' Annabelle gazed at her daughter, her flushed cheeks and red nose. 'It's time to go home, my darling.'

At the front door, she paused. Her thoughts again went to the crowds on the hill. She could not help but wonder. How cruel her imagination could be, how wicked to let her think she had seen…

'You look cold to the bone.' Mary took Annabelle's gloves and hat and placed them on the hall table.

'I am fine, Mary, just a little dazed.'

'It must be the cold. I told you not to be out so long. I think we shall have snow later. Did you get a tree?'

'Yes, it will be here around midday.'

'Perfect. We can decorate it this afternoon. Rose will love that. You and Emily always loved seeing the tree delivered.'

'I know, her favourite time of year. This time last year we...' Annabelle swiftly turned towards the fireplace, removing her face from Mary's sight.

'Has my father arrived home yet?'

'Early afternoon, my dear.'

'It will be good to spend the season as a family.'

'I understand, my dear. Rose will bring some young life back into this house. Some much-needed joy into our lives.'

'Yes, but it will never be the same. We have lost so many.'

'You sit by the fire for a while. I have just made it up. I'll take care of Rose.' Mary turned to the jingling rattle. 'There you are, Rosie Posy, are you Mary's little angel?'

The infant waved her arms as Mary lifted her out of the carriage. Annabelle lay her head back in the fireside chair, her fingers numb with the stiffness of icicles, her nose frozen and pink against her cheeks. She rested her elbows on her knees as she leaned closer to the fire. Vivid red and amber flames danced along with the crackles and hisses from the damp logs.

Annabelle splayed her fingers towards the fire, slowly regaining their mobility; she stretched them in turn. The thin band of gold glistened. Then, mindlessly, she spun the ring against her cold taut skin with her thumb and forefinger. Lost in dreams of what had once been, she gazed upon the ring, remembering the moment it was placed on her finger. Annabelle lay back in the chair, her weary head against the velvet, melancholic, she drifted.

Annabelle, my beautiful sister.

'Emily? Where are you?'

I am here, darling.

'Emily, I cannot find you; where are you?'

I shall always be here with you.

'I do not think I have the strength to go on.'

My sister, you are far stronger than I could ever have been. You must; you have Rose.

'Sweet Rose. But Emily, you should be here.'

You need to be strong. You are her mother; Rose was never mine. She is my gift to you.

~

Suddenly, Annabelle's body jerked. She awoke with a start.

'I'm on my way,' Mary called. Her voice grew louder as she entered the room. 'The Christmas tree is early.'

'What?' Annabelle sat perfectly still, her back to Mary, startled, trying to gain her bearings.

210

'The front door. Did you not hear the knocking? If they knock any louder, they'll come crashing through it!'

'Oh, the door, the knocking…Yes.'

Annabelle leant forward, studying the crackling fire; the logs now burning fully spat bolts of crimson sparks. Mary stepped up to the front door, unbolted the lock, easing the door open.

'My goodness!' Mary stepped backwards, hand to her mouth. 'Good heavens!'

'Mary, whatever is it? It is the same size we normally have; I am sure it will fit…'

'Annabelle, my dear, it's not… the tree, dear.'

'Not? Then what is it?'

'My dear, I think you should come here.'

Annabelle stood, straightened her dress. She continued to adjust the cuffs. 'Oh, Mary, whatever is the matter?'

'There is someone here to see you,' Mary declared incredulously.

Annabelle turned on her heels, gazed toward the open door. Then, with precise steps, her feet slowly carried her to the front door.

'Hello, Annabelle, may I come in?' He paused with a smile that shone through his eyes, but he was different, worn, and distressed. This young face now wore a mask of age, far too old for his years. 'It is about to snow,' he continued.

Annabelle stood, her feet planted, her body rigid, as her head spun with the velocity of her daughter's spinning top.

She stepped closer as her mouth gradually found the word her mind kept repeating.

'James?'

CHAPTER TWENTY-NINE

Crisp snow lay thick and dense. For weeks, it had melted away into slushy puddles only to be covered by a new layer whiter than the last.

April stood inside the bay window, her left knee on the pink bedroom chair. The view beyond was her favourite: the pathway and grass, camouflaged beneath the new white blanket, the old gravestones wearing snowy jackets, tall skeletal trees in regimental rows with their brittle branches weighted with snow. The freezing air pierced the windowpane, chilling her face. She leant closer, so her warm breath formed misty patches on the glass.

A movement caught her eye. Beyond the graves, between the bare trees, an elderly lady brushed the powdery snow from a bench before she carefully sat. Her dark green coat vibrant against the white setting. Her long silvery hair was tied back with smooth strands over her shoulders; her face was peaceful. April watched, paralysed. Then, the lady looked at April. Though her eyes were so far away, she could feel them — love and contentment. She smiled, and April returned with a nod. The lady then rose, brushed down her coat, strode along the footpath and disappeared.

April lost grip; her knee slipped, and she fell on the chair. 'It was,' she whispered, 'I know it was.' There was no point in rational reasoning. April now knew that there was more to life than was tangible. She held all of Annabelle's memories and loves; they were embedded into her soul. Even a new body could not erase them.

Her eyes, oblivious, stared into the grey sky. Fluffy snowflakes drifted, gently falling on the cold glass. Her eyes gradually focused on the snowfall, tracing each new flake as it rested and then melted to nothing.

'More snow,' she whispered. 'More snow, Nan.'

April filled her lungs, holding her breath a moment until it stung, then stepped to the bed. Her outfit lay ready, the dark trouser suit and long wool coat. She ran her fingertips over the black fabric.

'You'd like these, Nan, really smart, but I hate the colour. Dad said it was appropriate, but I can't help thinking you'd have liked something a bit brighter.'

~

'Mum, do you think Nan would mind if I borrowed her amethyst brooch and earrings for today?' April sat watching her mother wash the breakfast plates.

'Of course not. I think that's a lovely idea.'

'Mum, I don't think I want to go home.'

'Home?'

'I mean, I feel happier here, in this house, Nan's house,' she paused, watching her mother, expecting her reaction. 'She's here, you know. Nan's here with us. I know she is.' April sat back in the chair.

'What makes you say that?' Julia sat down opposite, drying her hands on the towel.

'This morning, I saw her outside on the bench in the snow, just as we did on Christmas morning. I could see the peace in her eyes; she was letting me know she was all right.'

'I know, sweetheart. She was with me this morning. I awoke to smell her perfume; before I opened my eyes, I knew it was her. I knew she was standing there because I could smell her,' Julia reached for April's hand.

'But...' sighed April. She clutched her mum's hand and rested her cheek on it, trying to ease her anxiety.

'Today will be all right; you will get through it... It won't be *her* we put in the ground, just an old shell she doesn't need anymore. Her young and vibrant soul will always be with us,' Julia smiled. 'You don't have to come home yet if you don't want to. Dad and I will be going home tonight. But, if you feel you want to be here, that's perfectly okay with us?' She kissed April's hair, resting her lips there as the moment lingered.

'I'll be okay, Mum. You're only across the road if I need you,' she replied, lifting her head. 'I need to be here; you know, I can get my head around things if I'm here.' April had an awkward expression, somewhere between a smile and a frown.

'Things will get better. You know you can talk to me. I don't want you to think you must do this all by yourself.'

'Mum, there is something,' April said cautiously.

'Emily?' Julia smiled knowingly.

April could feel her stomach turn with confusion, how could she know? 'How did you know?'

'The two young women in the photo frame? You don't need to say anymore,' Julia squeezed her hand, 'But I think I need to tell you a story.

'Mum?'

'One day, when I was about seven, I was playing in the garden,' Julia began, 'right at the bottom, under the tree. That was where I always played; the sun always seemed brighter, you know, warmer, at the bottom of the garden. It was summer and so warm. The sort of heat that warms you right to the heart.' Julia sat back on her chair and closed her eyes a moment. Then, opening her eyes, she looked at April, who returned with a smile.

'Well, I'd laid out a blanket, had sat all morning playing with my teddies. I had loads, I loved them, and everyone knew it — most birthdays I got a new one, but I still had my favourite,' Julia nodded. 'I remember, I had a china tea set.

It was white painted with pink roses and ribbons. It's quite fragile, now thinking about it, but I was so careful with it. I felt like my mum with her best china,' she sighed, paused again with a nostalgic smile.

'We had a teddy bears' picnic, my furry friends and me. I'd read them stories of fairies, princesses, and unicorns. I had a whole library of books full of tales of fantasy adventures. That was my favourite game in the summer, and I loved being in the garden. I felt safe and protected, right there under that tree, guarded by the high walls. That tree held some sort of magic, do you know what I mean?' she gazed at April, not expecting an answer. 'Silly, I know, but I still feel like that, even now.'

'Mum, I know what you mean,' April replied, as a smooth grin grew on her face.

'The garden was silent, well as silent it could be with birds and grasshoppers, even the odd bee around the flower borders. I felt protected under my tree, peaceful, with no other noise other than nature itself.

Julia rose and headed to the kitchen cupboard, fetched two coffee mugs. April noticed a new softness in her step.

'Fancy a cuppa?' she nodded in question. 'Coffee?'

April nodded and waited, knowing she would continue in her own time. The kettle seemed to boil quickly. Julia finished with a swirl of the coffee spoon, lightly tapping it on the side of her mug and placing it in the sink.

They both sat hugging their mugs.

'Where was I... yes, Mum stood just inside the glass doors, calling me for tea. I'd been out the entire day. *Come on, Julia, your tea is ready*, she called. I said I'd be there in a minute. So, I continued to fuss with the tea set, pretending to pour it into Fred's cup; he was the oldest bear and my favourite. I'd had him since I was born, a present I don't know who from. Anyway, Fred always had his tea first. Then, I heard her. I didn't take much notice at first, and then... *Go on, Julia, we can play again tomorrow.* The voice was sweet, and a flowery perfume filled the space around me. I will never forget how I felt. I felt *loved.*

'Now, I know no one else in the garden with me that day; well, no one I could see. But I heard her with these very ears, and I will never forget the sound of her voice. After that, I knew I was never alone in that garden.'

'Did you ever tell Nan?'

'No, I was only a child. I thought this was *my* friend. I didn't want to share her with anyone. There was no thought on whether Mum and Dad would believe me. I didn't think that she was a ghost or anything like that. I was a child, only seven. Why should I question my senses? I'm sure we only do so when we become adults.'

Julia took a breather and smiled at April, her head to one side, examining her daughter's thoughts.

'Mum, was that the only time you...'

'Oh no,' Julia quickly interrupted. 'That was our favourite game, teddy bears' picnic. I'd set her a place for tea next to Fred. I called her Princess, she always smelt so lovely, and I thought that was how a princess would smell, like flowers.'

'Did you ever see her?' April was curious. It was so unexpected.

'Not when we played, I knew she was there; there was never any doubt about that, I could sense and feel her. Odd, now I think about it, but then, it was simple. She was my Princess.' Julia took a gulp of coffee. 'I didn't need to see her. I knew she was there. I could see her in my mind's eye, although not with my physical eyes. Does that make sense?'

April nodded, 'That makes perfect sense.'

'That winter, about November, I think, I was sick with glandular fever. Looking back, I understand just how ill I was. My whole body ached. I couldn't get out of bed for days and days; it may have been weeks. I slept by day but lay awake at night. One afternoon, I lay in bed, cuddled up

216

to Fred. He was lovely; he was light brown mohair and glass stud eyes. He was a Stieff, not that I would have appreciated that then, even if I'd known,' she smiled warmly.

'Anyway, it was getting dark outside, and Mum said I needed to see if I could eat something, so she went to make me some tomato soup. I snuggled up to Fred and then smelt her perfume. I didn't open my eyes at first, just lay there. I can remember smiling, feeling peaceful, and having a hand on my forehead. It stroked my hair. Her skin felt like silk, not like any hand I'd ever felt before. Then, I heard her voice as she sang. I can't remember what the words were, only that it was beautiful.

'After a few moments, she moved her hand and sat beside me on the bed. The bedclothes pull tighter over my body. Then, I opened my eyes and saw her. Her dress was light and lacy. Her hair was long and dark, and she was much prettier than anyone I'd ever seen. She really was my Princess.'

'Mum... that was Emily.'

'I know, darling, I know.'

April sighed, closing her eyes.

'I never saw her again. That was the only time. I started to get better the next day, and within a week, I was back to school. But every so often, when I played in the garden, she would be there. Then, as I grew older, it gradually became less often, and without really noticing it, I stopped playing with my teddies and started going out with my friends. Before I knew it, I was grown up.'

'Mum, she's still here in this house. I don't think she's ever left it.'

'I wonder what happened to Emily, you know, in life.'

'I know what happened to her.'

'It can wait, darling, when you are ready. You have me, you know,' Julia clutched April's hand and looked at the kitchen wall clock. 'Come on; Nan will be waiting for us.'

217

CHAPTER THIRTY

Michael held out his hand. 'The cars are here, you ready?'

'Yes, let's get this done.' Julia buttoned her black coat. 'Ready, darling?'

April nodded from beneath her hat. Outside, parked on the snowy road, were two black limousines. The lead car was laden with flowers — a wintry floral spray lay atop the coffin. A tall gentleman in a sombre suit opened the door of the second car.

Nan would like that, very swish, April thought.

The cars headed east out of the town.

'Almost there,' Michael repeated periodically as the car turned left or right.

Finally, they pulled around a corner to see the village church with its freshly laid white carpet leading to the door.

'It looks more appealing in the summer,' Michael said, peering out of the steamed window.

'I think Nan would approve. She loved the snow,' April replied as the sombre gentleman opened the car door for her. She nodded her thanks and headed toward the gateway.

Was this the worst moment of the day? She thought, *or will it be in the church, or maybe when we're back, knowing it's all over?* Her mind drifted like the windblown snow.

Lost in her thoughts, April came to with her mother's hand on her shoulder. 'Ready?'

It was time. They followed along the forlorn pathway in a procession, the fresh snow crunching beneath their feet.

They trailed in Sarah's wake into the church. Once inside, the coffin was sat centrally on a stand. April traced her mother and father's steps into the front pew, the rest of the congregation filed in after. April dared not turn to see who was there, who had come to grieve; she was barely holding back the tears — one well-meaning smile, she would lose it.

Concentrate on something.

Her eyes wandered to a carved marble plaque on a side wall, a scroll with fancy gold inlay words. As to what it said, she couldn't see, but her eyes travelled the outline of its profile, each rolling curve of the carved scroll.

Stifled sniffs and muffled weeps echoed through the heights of the ancient church, bouncing off the stone walls: sobs, sympathies and the rustling of tissues.

The service progressed, not fast enough.

Nan, where are you? You're always with me when things are hard; where are you?

A hand slipped into April's. She did not look at the empty spot beside her, but she knew whose hand it was.

I'm here, never fear. I'm always here when you need me.

Julia leant towards her daughter, a strange expression on her face. 'Can you smell that, April?'

'Yes, Mum, I can smell it.'

'She's here, isn't she?'

The service passed in a blur, an hour of bewilderment and emptiness.

Julia nudged April. 'Time to go, darling,' she nodded to the centre of the church.

April waited beside the pew with her parents to follow the coffin out into the snowy coldness; the wind blew the falling snow in great sweeps of white blindness.

April kept her gaze on the back of her mother's coat; her boots trudged the snow until everyone stopped. The churchyard fell under a new spell of silence. All bar the thud of her rapid heart. She could not look. She knew it was there — the hole.

'It's all right, love.' Michael cradled April in his arms.

'They can't put her in there, Dad.' April lost the battle as her tears burst free.

She turned, her face whipping around the churchyard, how dingy and gloomy it was, how winter had hung a murky cloud: no light, no colour, no solace. The snow no longer looked magical; it now spoke of loneliness.

'No!' she cried,

'Hey, come on, darling,' Michael soothed.

'Not in that cold hole. That's my Nan.'

April, April, listen to me. You're much stronger than you realise. You must see this through. Do you hear me?

April raised her head from her father's arm.

Do you understand me? It's just a hole, some dirt, that's all — no big fuss. Now, come on, Little One. I'll stand here with you.

April looked at her father's face as he stood watching the graveside, turned to her mother, a handkerchief pressed to her eyes. Neither heard nor had noticed anything. April pulled away from her father and stood beside her grandmother. Her emerald brooch glistened, and her coat untouched by the falling snow. Her face was more youthful than April remembered, her smile sweeter, and her eyes full of life.

'Nan, I miss you.'

I know, Little One. But I haven't left you.

The vicar spoke his last few words of prayer and comfort. Then, gradually, the subdued voices of the mourners silenced, and the crowd dispersed. Cars pulled away on the crunchy gravel drive. The coffin lay deep within the hole; thick snow now lay on the polished wood, gradually covering it altogether.

'Come on, April, we must get going. The car is waiting.'

'Can I have a minute, Dad? Please,' April implored. 'There's something I need to do.'

April rambled through the maze of old headstones. She was being pulled.

I think this will help. Sarah stood by a large stone tomb. She pointed to the far side, beckoning April to follow her.

Here, Little One. Here it is.

April traced her grandmother's invisible steps and looked where she pointed — an expanse of grey stonework, the top covered in deep snow. Each side of the tomb was engraved with the names of the *Hardwick* family. April wiped her gloved fingers over the surface, dusting away the fresh snow. Carefully, her forefinger traced the carved letters that still sat deep inside the slab while her lips silently mouthed the words. Her tongue became numb and useless, and a nauseous lump began building in her throat. Woozy; she pulled off her gloves and tugged at her coat buttons.

Inexplicably warm, April looked at her grandmother.

You need to see this. Then, you can lay these things to rest.

Once again, April's eyes fell to the inscription.

Here lies the body of Annabelle Jane Hardwick
Devoted Wife, Mother, and Grandmother
b. 27th March 1876, d. 8th September 1934

There it was, her last resting place. She was stunned at seeing her name, her life engraved in stone, *her life*, but then not. It was her name, but a different body, an old body.

Overwhelmed, she stepped back.

After a few moments, the thought dawned on her. What lay in front of her was the Hardwick family tomb. With quick, hurried strokes, she brushed her hands over the stonework, her arms flying in large sweeps to clear away the snow. She found it.

Here lies the body of Richard John Henry Hardwick
Beloved Son and Husband
b. 10th July 1873, d. 1st December 1900

Underlining both their names, the words:

Where immortal spirits reign, there we shall meet again.

The reality, enormity of the harshness was just too much for today, for her heavy heart to take, today of all days.

'No.' April's cry carried across the empty graveyard. Her legs buckled, her limbs frozen and numb. She knelt, huddled against the rough stone, her face resting over his name. 'Richard,' she sobbed as tears stung her cheeks.

'Why do I lose everyone?' she whispered, between inhaled spasms. 'Why are they taken from me?' A vast torrent of tears fell from her eyes, her face sodden, glistening and sore.

Gently, she opened her eyes and re-read the engraving.
Where immortal spirits reign, there we shall meet again.

Over and over, her numb fingertips traced his name.

'Is he there waiting for me? Why didn't I stay there with him? Why did I come back, only to lose him again, Nan? *Where immortal spirits reign.*' she cried.

Her grandmother stepped towards her, placing her hand on her forehead. April could feel a spark of sensation but no longer her grandmother's warm flesh.

You must realise, Little One, that you were once reunited. Only your soul knows why you chose to return. Richard is not here; he is in your heart. Look at that name; it says Annabelle; those bones lay in this earth, but Annabelle's soul, your soul, is inside you. Do you see?

Our souls, the love: we take it with us; they are the parts that remain. Richard will always be in your heart, just as he has always been in Annabelle's.

So, you must try to let go of Richard as he once was. That body lies here; you cannot bring it back.'

April's tears gradually faded, leaving smeared mascara down her flushed cheeks. She lifted her face from the tomb and looked hard at the writing.

'I love you, Richard John Henry Hardwick.'

April stood up on shaking legs, brushing the icy snow from her coat and trousers. She turned to where her grandmother had stood, but the spot was empty, leaving only the sight of the snow-covered gravestones and bare-naked trees.

April meandered the headstones back to the path while the snow fell. The tall gentlemen stood beside the black limousine beneath a snow dabbled umbrella. As she carefully approached, he opened the car door.

April stopped and stood under the umbrella a moment, looking up into his sombre eyes.

'Thank you for waiting for me,' April smiled.

His voice was smooth and low as he leant down. 'My pleasure, young lady; did the elderly lady get a lift back in one of the other cars, or shall we wait for her?'

For a second, April stood startled, and then she took a deep breath and replied. 'No, that's fine; I think she's made her own way home.'

CHAPTER THIRTY-ONE

'It's nearly half-past; we need to be there at quarter to.' Julia quietly knocked at the bedroom door, her ear close to the wood, waiting for a reply.

'I'm coming.' April appeared around a chink, her face pink and flushed. 'Mum, I don't think I can do this today.'

'I know, but we have no choice. We must go. Mr Walters will be expecting *all* of us.' Julia took her daughter's arm and guided her down the staircase.

They took the short journey along the footpath, turning right into the next street to the solicitor's office.

April sat down on the edge of the chesterfield sofa; her eyes travelled the original features of the oak-panelled walls, caught by an elaborate gilt clock on the mantelpiece, supervising the daily activities with its regimental ticking. It ticked through the moments as they waited.

'Mr Walters will be with you in a few minutes. Can I get you some tea while you wait?' The calm husky voice came from the reception desk. 'Maybe some coffee?'

'Thank you; coffee would be lovely. April?' Michael stood up and wandered over to the receptionist, turning to look at April on his way, 'Coffee?'

She shook her head, then turned back to the mantle clock and wandered over the fireplace. April watched as the hands crept around the clock and recalled her grandmother's words, suspended in thought.

'Time is nothing but a tick of the clock. It continues to pass; regardless, just as we do,' April uttered to herself.

'Quite true and very apt for today,' Julia replied. April spun to find her mother standing close beside her. 'I know you miss her; I miss her too. I've now lost both my parents.'

'I'm sorry, Mum.'

'What for, darling? It continues to pass, regardless, just as we do, remember. We all pass away at some time; it's the way of things.' Julia pulled her close in a hug. Tears seeped in a wet patch on the collar of Julia's black silk blouse.

'Hey, hey, it's fine; you still have your dad and me. But look, I know you both had a special… *bond*. I tried, but I could never compete. I'm not your nan, but I *am* your mum, no matter what; I love you more than life itself.'

'I love you too. It's just that...' April wasn't sure how to put it. How could she sum up these feelings?

'I know you've had a lot to deal with over the past couple of months. But, I promise, things will get easier. Come on; let's sit down. My coffee's getting cold. Besides, I should rescue that poor girl from your father,' Julia smiled, nodded behind them.

They turned to see Michael, animatedly gesturing to the interior panelling. The receptionist smiled, nodding when it seemed appropriate. Julia guided April back to the sofa, then took hold of her husband by the elbow and led him away, saying, 'Thank you very much for the coffee, it's kind of you.' Then, cast a knowing smile on the girl as they sat down.

The large oak door opened, and Mr Walters filled its frame.

'Julia, Michael, April, how nice to see you again. I just wish it were under happier circumstances.'

Michael stood up and held out his hand. The two shook hands with genuine friendship. 'Yes, quite so, quite so, John; it's been a couple of years. Sorry, we did not get a chance to talk properly at the funeral. How are you keeping? And the family?'

'Fine, Michael, all fine. It's good to have you back in town.' Mr Walters patted him on the back then turned to the receptionist. 'Thank you, Naomi. I have no more appointments until after lunch.'

They followed through the door, across the hallway and into another room. It was much the same as the reception area, with original panelling, a high ceiling and a fireplace, at one end, a mahogany table and matching chairs, about twelve in all.

Some people must have big families to leave their money to, not like us. The rest of my family is in another century, April thought. Within a few seconds, it hit how sad that was. She had her parents, but with now Nan was gone, everyone else she loved was long dead.

Mr Walters sat at one end of the large table and gestured to chairs on either side of him.

'Now,' he began. 'Let's get down to business.' He placed a large file on the polished surface, reached down to his glasses and slipped them on. 'As you know, Sarah, and Edward, have been good friends of mine, and I've always looked after their financial affairs.' He looked directly at Julia, smiled and continued. 'I do hope you will continue this tradition in the future with your own financial affairs.' Mr Walters opened the file and removed a few sheets of thick white paper.

Julia simply smiled while she fidgeted in her chair.

'So, this is the last will and testament of Sarah Lillian Parkinson.'

The sound of her grandmother's name brought stabbing pains to her chest. April sat back, resting her head on the high back chair and closed her eyes. They didn't need her for this. Reading the will only cemented reality, sealed it like a tomb — carved the words *new chapter*. But where was she to go from here? What was her path?

'To my daughter Julia I leave the sum of £5.8 million.'

April lifted her head, and her eyes opened in bafflement.

'Sorry, I thought you said five…?' Julia stuttered in a high squeak.

'Yes, Julia, £5.8 million,' Mr Walters cleared his throat and continued, not batting an eyelid. 'To my son-in-law Michael, I leave my husband's collection of vintage cars, currently held at Beaulieu Car Museum.'

'Cars... what cars?' Michael up sharply, with his hand over his mouth.

'Yes, currently at Beaulieu.' Mr Walters placed the papers on top of the file and removed his glasses, letting them dangle from the cord. 'Am I to assume you were not aware of the extent of the assets?' He turned to look directly at Julia.

'Extent? To be honest, John, I thought it would be a matter of the house deeds and the balance in her current account,' Julia shrugged in bemusement.

'Ah, the house deeds; we haven't quite got that far,' he replaced his reading glasses, peering down at the papers. 'To my only granddaughter April, I leave my house in Crown Street. This is for her to live in, as I know it is where she belongs,' he paused, raising his head and glancing at April.

'The house, Nan left me her house?'

'Your house, April,' Julia looked across the vast table at her daughter.

'Yes. To my granddaughter April, I also leave…' he coughed. 'Please excuse me... I also leave North House, the townhouse in Northgate Street. A plot of land on the North Norfolk coast...'

'Hang on, I'm sorry, but... but I don't understand any of this.' April sat with her head on her arms, her forehead almost touching the cold surface of the table. She shut her eyes tightly to block it out. Then, after a few moments, she quickly 'Was that Norfolk coast?'

'Yes, a plot of land on the Norfolk coast,' he repeated.

'That's Aunt Anna's place.'

'April? I don't understand,' Michael asked, mystified.

'Aunt Anna, she was Nan's great...' April looked past her father as she counted the generations, 'hang on, her great, great aunt. Anyway, Norfolk, that's where Anna lived, so it must be...' April continued, with all eyes on her. Then she stopped mid-sentence, her mouth still gaping, her eyes wide, her face draining of colour.

'Darling, whatever is it?' Julia gazed at her daughter with a very worried frown.

'Nothing, no nothing, it's fine,' she smiled at her mother and turned to the solicitor. 'Thank you, Mr Walters,' she nodded.

'Oh April,' he replied, 'we haven't finished by any means.' He cast her a warm knowing smile. 'Now, where was I? Ah… to my granddaughter, I leave… North Norfolk coast. The rental profits from North House are deposited quarterly into a bank account for her. I also leave the sum of £4 million in trust until her 21st birthday. All my other belongings, such as jewellery and items in the house, divided between my daughter and granddaughter as they see fit.' He quickly glanced around the table to find dumbstruck faces staring back.

Mr Walters sat back in his chair. 'I understand that it's a great deal for you all to take in, especially at this time. It's a great shock to accept the loss of a loved one. On a personal note, I know how close you all are.' He looked directly at April, his face calm and reassuring. 'In light of the shock Sarah knew it would be, she prepared a letter for each of you.' He reopened the file and removed three vellum envelopes.

April tentatively took hers. The envelope felt far too thick and stiff between her fingertips.

Mr Walters leant forward, elbows resting on the polished surface; he repeatedly pressed his fingertips together in a contemplating motion. 'You do know that I am here to help. Please, call me if you need anything. Of course, I will need to see you again to sign the paperwork, but I think we should leave that a couple of days just to let things sink in, so to speak. You all seem shocked, if I may say. Sarah was an extraordinary lady.'

Mr Walters stood, straightened his jacket, and adjusted his crisp, white shirt cuffs. 'She will be greatly missed. She made a profound impact on everyone she met.'

'Thank you, John, thank you for being so understanding.' Julia slid her chair out, ready to leave.

Mr Walters led the way back through the hallway to the front door. He shook Michael's hand. 'I shall be in touch, look after them.'

Outside, the air hit their faces with its icy fingers.

~

April drew her bedroom curtains, switched on her bedside lamp. A bizarre excitement had choked her all afternoon, battled with the emptiness in the hollow hole.

Propping up the pillows behind her head, April sat with her knees under her chin, her arms tightly wrapped around her legs.

'Well, Nan, it's now or never.'

The vellum envelope flipped in her fingers as hesitation kept her hands fumbling. Doubt niggled. After a few minutes, April sighed, slipped her long fingernail under the corner of the flap, and ran it along to break the seal. April unfolded the sheets of crisp paper. Cautiously she began to scan and digest the blue ink.

My Little One

Please don't be sad; it was my time to go. It was time to be reunited with your grandad.

I know how you feel, the emptiness that sits in your stomach, and the loneliness that lives in your heart. But it will pass. Each day things will get a little easier. Soon, you will feel lighter, and when the weather warms, everything will be easier.

I knew I'd lost a dear friend when I lost my grandmother. I was so young that our friendship was short-lived, but I felt the gaping hole in my world when she left. I had to wait over fifty years, but she did return. When you were born, the very first moment I held you in my arms, I just knew. I don't know how, only that my heart recognised you.

I know you very well; you are now sitting, asking me how and why. How I kept it a secret, why I hadn't told you before? The truth is, I knew that one day you would know, that you needed to go on this journey. One day, you would return home to where you belonged. I only ever tried to guide you, to help you through this bumpy roller coaster of emotions.

My darling, I'm not sure if you realise how special you are. What a unique gift you have. You can remember your past life, to relive another time and another life. Some people would give anything to live with that knowledge every day, to have that ability. However, with the gift comes a burden. I know and understand the sorrow and traumatic memories you are reliving. You must remember, these are only memories that have already happened long ago; you can do nothing to change that. All you can do is learn from them, and the wounds will begin to heal. I know you've lost those who were important to you, but you have so much life ahead of you, so many new loves to find along the way.

There is something I must confess. I had an encounter with Emily before, many years ago. I know I should have told you, but you'd have wanted answers I didn't have. When I was a small girl, my grandmother would take me to the park; we spent many lovely times in the Abbey Gardens. When the weather was warm, she would make a picnic, and we'd sit by the river. I loved those days, just lying there in the sun. She would tell me stories of how she had brought my mother there when she was young. As a child of only about seven, it was hard to imagine my mother as a child herself: I could only see her as a grown-up, a serious grown-up.

One afternoon, we laid a blanket on the grass. I remember how the long grass was warm and soft beneath the blanket, how it was as inviting as my bed. I lay outstretched on my back, with the sun warming every inch of me. Through my closed eyelids, I could see the bright pink sunrays. We would play games; my favourite was closing my eyes and concentrating hard on the sounds around me to see if I could pick out each sound, one by one. My grandmother would say, maybe if you listen ever so carefully, you may hear the fairies flying in the wind and dancing in the grass. I loved the thought of that; my imagination was full of magical worlds, of dragons and unicorns, but most of all, fairies. I can now see how she fed those fantasies and how she loved my childhood daydreams.

On this occasion, we lay on the blanket together. I can remember every detail about that day, as if yesterday. I wore my best summer dress; it was the palest blue with a pretty, lacy collar and a large bow tied at the back; my hair was dark, not silver. My mother always kept it long. She would tie it in a ribbon to match my outfit. My grandmother always said how like my mother I was, right down to the auburn curls. My grandmother wore a beautiful dress with a large white collar and large buttons on the front. It was the loveliest pale green, and she always wore gloves; they were white and fitted just to her wrist. She was so elegant. I suppose that is the most memorable detail about her, how immaculate and refined she was. She never raised her voice; I loved her so much and relished our playtimes so much that I never gave her cause.

My goodness, I'm reminiscing again.

That day, as I lay listening, describing the sound of the birds and the trickling of the river, I heard something new. I opened my eyes and looked about. My Grandmother was lying beside me, and her eyes were tightly shut. She asked me what I could hear, but I couldn't answer for a second or two. I lay back again and strained my ears to hone in on the new sound. It was hard. The more I tried, the more the usual sounds bombarded my ears. Then, it got louder and more apparent. I can remember it was the most beautiful thing I'd ever heard. Despite the warmth of the sun, I had goosebumps all over my arms, could feel every hair standing on end.

Don't get me wrong, I wasn't afraid, just amazed. I was so young; I didn't understand what was strange. My grandmother sat up, shook my shoulder, and asked me if I could hear that. I just nodded; I didn't open my eyes; I wanted to get soaked up by the sweetness. After a few moments, I opened my eyes to see her looking straight at me with a terrifying look of astonishment on her face. I asked

232

her what the matter was. She didn't answer me at first. I asked who it was. I could see her mind trying to work out what to say, then she simply replied, it was an angel looking after me. I realised years later that I had heard singing. My grandmother, of course, heard it and knew straight away that it was Emily. I never saw her, but every so often, if things were tough, I'd hear her singing. I don't think I am the only person who has heard her either.

Now, I suppose, I should get to the will. I know what's going through your mind. You must be confused and bewildered, full of questions, like where did it all come from? Some things you'll already have the answers.

Now, as you will know, I've left you the house. It belonged to you long before I was born, so I am returning it to you and therefore returning you to where you belong. This includes everything in the house, for you and your mum to do as you wish. I can hear your voice right now, 'I don't want to change a thing!' Just don't hold onto unnecessary bits and pieces that you don't need or don't even like. This is your home now, yours for you to live in.

As for North House, a lovely family has rented the house for the past twenty years. I don't think they have any thoughts of moving, so the income from that is enough for the upkeep and running of your house and, of course, plenty for you to live on. Mr Walters will look after the dull money side of things for you. You can trust John; he is a dear friend. I've made all the arrangements for him to continue on your behalf. If you have any questions about any of it, please ask him. He will always help. As you've guessed, this was my grandparent's home, so it is yours anyway. It was yours and Richard's home.

That's all the obvious things out the way.

The land in Norfolk is a lovely seaside plot and is quite large about two acres, so enough for a lovely cottage and garden overlooking the sea. Perhaps, in the future, it may be nice to spend time there in the summer months. I can imagine you in a lovely, quaint cottage with pink roses around the door and your children playing in the garden. I know I'm letting my imagination carry me away. My mother inherited this plot of land from her great-aunt.

I understand you must feel like your world is in turmoil. I am sorry, darling; I am so sorry; I know leaving you now was terrible timing on my part. Unfortunately, we don't seem to get a say when we go, do we? I suppose no time would be a suitable time. Cancer took hold last summer. The doctors hoped I had at least a year left, but never mind. Please don't be angry with your parents. I made them promise not to tell you, I hoped to be able to tell you myself, but then you had so much to deal with, it got to the point there was never the right time. You're strong, my Little One, far stronger than you realise. I have faith in you.

I know how terrible it was for you when you found out about Richard's accident. You cannot alter the past, no matter how painful. But you will find someone you can love. You will, I promise. My grandfather, Richard, was an only child, therefore, the sole son and heir of his family's fortune. They owned a large estate in the village where you just buried me. The cemetery has the Hardwick family tomb. I'm almost hesitant to mention it. But did you see it? I hope I managed to make it there on time. I'd got so ill that, by the time you fully understood Richard's fate, I was already bound to my bed.

After Richard's death, of course, he left Annabelle North House and a substantial sum of money yearly. Only two years after his death, Richard's father fell ill and passed away. After that, his mother soon followed. My mother said she mourned herself to death of a broken heart, but it was probably a heart attack. Then the manor house, the stables, and land were sold off. The sole beneficiary was my mother, Rose Hardwick; it was in trust until she came of age. Annabelle's money was more than enough to keep them both comfortable. So, that is where it all came from. I suppose you've probably worked most of that out for yourself.

April, you must remember that money must be respected, appreciated, and used well. That is why I never told you; you were to be so wealthy. You were never to be lavishly spoilt; I knew you would have it one day. Love is far more important than anything money can buy. I have complete faith in you. I love you more than you will ever know; it can never be put into words. We shall be together again one day, on this side or the other.

Sarah, your grandmother

April refolded the letter and placed it back in the envelope. The bedroom, her sanctuary, had dimmed as the night pulled the light out of the sky. She heaved her pillows back down under her head as she lay scrunched on her bed. Her arms tightly wrapped her body; she sobbed, salty tears of mascara-muddy puddles on her pillow. Her body shook in spasms as the sorrow seeped, bleeding into every bone of her body.

CHAPTER THIRTY-TWO

Winterton-on-Sea 1 mile.

April sat in the back of the car, the warm rush of comfort filling the void as they passed the sign. They were heading back home, where she had grown up, played and laughed, the place of security and assurance, the home of sandy beaches and magnificent crashing waves. The summer months were full of floral rainbow hanging baskets, window boxes and flower beds. The place of childhood memories, now she understood why.

'This is where the land is?' April's question was far more a statement. 'You mean, we lived in the very same village and never knew it.'

Her exhausted but enthralled brain mused over the possibilities. How many times had she walked the paths and sands where she had before, in another life? The pull of the waves and salty air tugged at her stomach as her soul soared with the exhilaration of being back.

Home: she mulled the thought over in her head, rolling it over in waves of thought. Home, that is what it had to be, but was it now? The longing to be back here by the sea, where the closeness to the elements, no matter how harsh they could be, soothed her soul and eased her mind. Yet now she knew the history, the families and hers, she understood where she belonged.

Michael slowed the car, pulling into the pub car park.

'How about we stop here for some lunch first? We can ask, see if anyone knows of it,' Michael said as he turned off the engine and opened the door. 'Do you know it's been at least a year since we've eaten in here? I wonder if they still do that fisherman's omelette.'

The wood-panelled interior welcomed them in its customary dark, gloomy way. April couldn't imagine it any other way, along with the regular half a dozen weathered locals in winter woollies and boots the speckled the bar.

'Hello there, what can I get you?' A middle-aged lady rested her palms on the wooden bar; the words rolled off her tongue with a familiar, slow, Norfolk droll.

'Hello there, how are you?'

'Ah, it's Michael, hey, how you all doing? It's been quite a time; thought you'd moved away? Didn't think I'd see that lovely old smile again in 'ere!' The barmaid moved closer, folding her arms resting her elbows on the bar. Waves of blonde hair with a wispy fringe mingled with her eyebrows as she fluttered her lashes.

Michael blushed as she winked. He unbuttoned his overcoat collar and loosened the paisley scarf around his neck.

Julia appeared a few steps behind him. 'Ah, hello Sandy, how is everything?'

'Not much differs 'bout 'ere, Julia,' she responded and wandered the length of the bar, gesturing to Julia with a flick of her head. 'How's your dear Mum? Will we be having the pleasure of her company this summer? I was shocked when I heard she was poorly,' her voice low with genuine concern. Sandy's long-drawn-out sentences made Julia squirm with the choking lump of her looming reply.

'Well, I'm afraid we lost her a few weeks ago, just after the New Year.' Julia wanted to add more to cushion the news for them both, but she could almost taste the emptiness.

Sandy reached out her hand and rubbed Julia's arm.

'Oh, I'm so sorry, Julia, really sorry. You know how much I thought of her... how much we all thought of her, lovely lady.' She winked as she puckered her pink lips and nodded to enhance her sentiments.

'Thank you, Sandy,' Julia sighed.

'Now, how about some lunch? You must be cold to the core, something to warm you all up; we've got winter vegetable soup on the specials, with warm crusty bread?' Her smooth Norfolk accent boomed over the bar.

April gawped at the special's menu scrawled in coloured chalk on the blackboard.

'Can I just have the cod n chips and a coke, please?' she called over.

April took a seat at a round table by the window, flung her jacket over the back of the chair, pulled down the sleeves of her jumper, held the cuffs and folded her arms elbows resting on the table.

April could smell the fresh furniture polish; it reminded her of her grandmothers' house. How long would it take her to come to terms with that? It'd always been Nan's house, and no matter how many times her mind went over the fact, it would always remain that way.

She inhaled the rich waxy smell again, taking pleasure in the remembrance. It didn't seem to matter what it was; everything conjured up those memories. She closed her eyes, tried to put it from her mind. Slowly, her ears began isolating the sounds around her; the wind whistling through bare branches of the winter-worn shrubs outside the window. Lonely, thin twigs thrashed against the glass, like fingers tapping a familiar tune, and a lone seagull screeched overhead to the sea. Then, a deep voice in a local twang drifted over it all.

'You all right there?'

The mellow tone came from the corner of the room. April opened her eyes and lifted her head. An old man sat on a red leather chair behind a coat stand two tables away. The mountain of waxed jackets and fishing hats hid him from the view of the bar. His cosy nook with a single table and a matching chair, its low sweeping back came round to form the arms, tarnished brass tacks that edged the old leather.

The man rested his right arm on the table, his left hand on his knee, as his leg juddered with the similar rhythmic tapping of his fingers on his trousers. The dregs of his *pint of best* in front of him. He nodded at April's bewildered expression.

'You feel all right, young'n?' he repeated. 'Mighty cold by that window, better move further in along the room if I were you. The coldest year in decades, so they say. Haven't had this much snow in over a hundred years.'

April grabbed her jacket and moved to the table beside the nook. A framed collection of fishing hooks and a large fishing boat painting hung over the man's head. The crashing waves and the dark stormy sky lightened by the shine of the lighthouse beam — it mirrored the ever-churning waves of emotion rumbling through her, only the dim glow of memories to light the future.

'Got the world on your young shoulders, have you? I can see it in your young eyes, but they don't seem that young to me,' he smiled and tilted his head to one side, examining April's face.

The man was wiry beneath his thick winter attire with thin white hair, and water blue eyes protruded from their sockets. However, there was something about this man. April felt pulled into his welcome — fascinated.

His eyes remained fixed on hers.

'You've trouble and unrest in you. I think you're hoping you'll find it here. Maybe you will,' he shrugged. 'Maybe you won't.

The profound observation jolted April. 'Sorry, find what?'

239

'The answer of what's missing, I presume.'

'What makes you think I'm looking for something?' she added.

'I know your look, the expression in those young eyes.'

April sat mystified. She couldn't say she would have taken any notice of him usually, but as he spoke, one else seemed to exist.

'I don't think we've ever met before. Have we?' April leant across the table as though to disappear from the view of the bar.

'I don't think we've ever met, no. But, I know, I know,' he responded with a smile.

'Do you?'

'I know, I know your face.'

'Well, I grew up here in the village.'

'I know I recognise those eyes of yours, *just like hers*. You've no idea just how alike you are. They don't know. No one knows. But, I know, only me,' he gestured to the rest of the pub.

The man continued, never moving his blue eyes from her. His words were odd, and her stomach leapt in summersaults in reaction. She felt something peculiar brewing and purely listened to his local drawl. She'd missed the place and its characters — the smell of the sea thick in the air, the noisy gulls, and the pastel-painted houses. Even in the coldest winter months, this place held a beauty, a peace that she loved.

'Know what? Who doesn't know what?' she asked after a while.

'You're searching for something, something that will help you and *her*. Although...' he paused. The man moved his arm from the table and scratched his chin with his fingers. The loose skin of his jawbone was thick with white bristles; the tips of his fingers massaged them in circular motions as he crumpled his lipless mouth. 'Although, 'he continued.

'Although, I don't think you have any idea what it is you're searching for, do you?' He looked directly into April's eyes.

April straightened in surprise, and it was a moment before she spoke. 'No,' she replied, as direct as the question. 'No, I don't think I do.'

Neither spoke for a while. Then, finally, April's eyes wandered about the pub. Her parents seemed to be musing over old times with the barmaid; sighs and quiet laughter were faint beneath the general din. The noise grew overwhelming. April covered her ears with her hands, rested her elbows on the table.

The old man began to jerk his knee again, and his fingers started up their tapping in a silent tune.

April sat bolt upright. 'Do *you* know what I'm looking for?'

'I don't have the answers, young'n. All I can do is see what's in your eyes. They're windows to the soul. Yours is good but troubled. I think you've been troubled for many years, but you can change it. I think you have a way. I think you know the way. I think...' He pressed his hand down on his knee, stopped it jigging. 'I think you've waited a long time for this. But you *know* that much, don't you?'

She shrugged. 'I'm not sure...'

'Of course, you do. You know more than you're willing to tell me, and that is how it should be. But you know.' He sat back in his chair and smiled at April, this time with a final smile, to symbolise the end of their conversation.

A voice called from the bar. 'Hey, Bertie, have you ever heard of a plot of land around here that's been neglected, or maybe...' Sandy's mellow voice carried through the bar room. 'D'you reckon that could be the land past...'

'Up by the round cottages,' interrupted Bertie, smiling at April. 'Yes, the old Warner place stood there, a long time ago, mind. It's about time someone did something; it needs

to be brought back to life… and a few things laid to rest.'
His eyes remained glued to April.

'You knew, didn't you? You knew. How?'

'It's in your eyes, young'n. They reflect your soul.' Bertie grinned. 'It's what you've been looking for.'

'But I know that we came to look for that. I inherited it.' She sat back in the wooden chair, her face disappointed.

'Ah, yes, you inherited it. But I wasn't talking about the land, young'n.'

'Just down the road, turn left past Rosebud Cottage and continue up the road...' Sandy explained with animated points and arm gestures. 'Keep going, just past the turning for the round holiday cottages. Be careful not to miss it, mind. It's just a field of overgrown grass, really.'

Julia put down her soup spoon and folded her paper napkin. 'I never knew it was there. I mean, I know that bit of land but had no idea that Mum owned it,' Julia expressed with realisation. 'My god, Mum owned that, and we lived not more than ten minutes' walk away for all those years. I don't understand.'

'I know, I never realised it belonged to your family. Sarah never mentioned it. She was a sly old case, wasn't she? Maybe she forgot or didn't realise until recently, or maybe thought it'd be a pleasant surprise,' Sandy laughed as she cleared away Julia's bowl.

'A surprise, all right! There's been quite a few of those lately, I can tell you.' Michael finished the last of his omelette and gulped the remains of his bitter lemon.

'So, April, what you got planned for the land then, girl? A nice fancy beach hut for all your friends to hang out. Great for summer parties! No neighbours really, not to speak of, not unless you count the seagulls, of course,' Sandy laughed.

April sat at her table, next to Bertie, who tucked into his ploughman's. She poked at the crispy batter, white fleshy

242

fish lay in flakes across the plate, and she lined up her chips in regimental rows.

'Cod not good?' Sandy called from the bar. 'I don't know, Julia, these young girls nowadays; they don't eat enough, do they? Never had that problem, I didn't.' She gestured to her ample figure, smoothing her ring-laden hands over her hips.

'Oh, sorry, no, the cod's lovely, thanks. And no, no beach hut and no parties. Maybe a new cottage.' April looked at Bertie. 'Thank you,' she mouthed quietly.

'What for young'n?' Bertie asked, as he stabbed a chunk of cheddar, 'I ain't done nothin'.'

'You understand. You seem to without even knowing anything, how?' April dropped her fork, giving up the cod as a lost cause. 'How do you know so much?'

Bertie took a long gulp of his fresh pint, wiping his mouth on his cuff. 'When I was a boy, a long, long time ago, mind,' he grinned. 'I saw things others didn't, I think that some saw them, but most were too busy going about their own business to even worry about looking. I used to play on the beach in front of that cottage; the best bit, I thought; full of rock pools and great for crabbing.

'Sometimes, when the wind was wild, so strong I'd be blown clean off my feet. My poor little legs were so skinny the wind would whip me up, and down I'd come,' he chuckled. 'It was on days like that I loved the beach the most. It was days like that when *she* would be there, watching the sea crashing down and churning the sand up into the foamy waves.'

His story-telling tone continued as he leant further towards April. She shuffled with her chair closer and eagerly nodded for him to continue.

'I'd sit and watch her. Couldn't help meself, so lovely she was, *a vision of loveliness*, you might say,' he chuckled again, paused a moment, slicing ham and another swig of beer.

'She'd sit on that bench for hours, never moving, never even flinching with the wind — well, why would she, no difference to her, but my goodness, she was lovely. As true as I sit here, she was the loveliest thing I'd ever set my eyes on, and... well, I see those eyes right now. I see those eyes; they're yours. I knew it the moment you walked in. I've seen you over the years, I remember you playing in the village as a kid, but now, you've grown up. Now I can see her in you.' Bertie leant forward, almost touching April with his nose. 'Yeah, that's 'em. There's no mistaking that.'

'You saw Emily? Have you seen her... you know, since?'

'Ah, no, not for many a year, come to think of it, not for a few decades. I stopped going down the beach, too many people, especially in the summer. But... I don't think she's there much anymore.' He beckoned to April as if she could get any closer. His old nose twitched an inch from hers. 'My old grandad, long gone now, he passed when I was as young as you, he used to tell me stories 'bout her, how she would sit there with her sister. They'd never talk, he'd say. Just sit; her sister would hold her in her arms, and she'd watch the sea. So many times, he'd tell me the story of when she went, the sadness it brought upon the family — mind you, not that he had much to do with the family. But sometimes, he'd take her sister into the village in his cart... lovely old horse, Dolly, her name was, a lovely grey dapple,' he beamed. 'Not that I remember her, but those stories; never the same after she'd gone and her sister left, but he knew it was no place for her here, not after all that.'

April edged to one side, her cheek in her hand and elbow on the worn table. 'Bertie, you're saying your grandad knew them?' April pressed.

'Oh yeah, young'n, course, everyone knew each other in the village in those days, not like nowadays, all those city couples comin in, buying holiday homes. Grandad did errands for the Warner's, the good sort they were, good stock, just look at you, young'n. You've got a good soul, *an old soul*, mind, but a true one.'

'You ready, April?' Julia rose from her bar stool, straightened her long skirt, and wrapped her cardigan tight. 'Ready?'

April stood up. 'I think it's time we were off. Thank you, Bertie, *thank you*.'

'You take care of yourself, young'n. I knew Sarah, you know.'

'You knew my nan?'

'Fine lady, Sarah, fine lady. Good man, Edward. Looked after Sarah well, he did. But, of course — the best man won and all that. Well, that's how it goes.' Bertie picked up his fork and stabbed a large, pickled onion, squirting vinegar across the table.

April left the pub, a little dismayed at Bertie's last comment.

They left the car parked and strolled up the hill. Seagulls whooshed overhead, diving down towards the sea and back to the land.

'Rosebud Cottage, that's Mrs Carter's place, isn't it? Do you remember, April? She used to run the Brownies at the village hall. Not that you lasted there very long, did you?' Julia pointed to a small, thatched house with candy-pink plaster.

'Not long, a week, I think. Too many kids.' April shook her head and crinkled her top lip.

'You were only nine; you *were* a kid,' Michael laughed.

'No, I don't think you were ever a child, April.' Julia clasped her hand in April's arm, and they meandered through the village.

They stopped a couple of hundred yards later, just short of an old rotten fence.

'Well, darling. This is it.' Julia stood, her hands on her daughter's shoulders, her head resting on hers. 'I can't believe your Nan kept this a secret all these years.'

'I don't think she kept it a secret, so much as didn't bother to mention it. She knew I'd have it one day, I suppose.'

April looked at the expanse of land in front of her. An old, wooden gate hung from rusty hinges; remains of some white paint flaked into her hands as she wedged it open on the thick grass. The remains of the old cottage stood amid the rambling weeds and brambles.

Ornate wrought ironwork, organic tendrils and leaves, adorned the neglected garden bench. April stared at the tangible object of her memories. Then, tentatively, she sat down. The view as she remembered. The cold February wind thrashed and flogged the sand with the wild North Sea.

The sheer magnificence of the natural energy that surged through each drop made April's body fill with emotion. It started in her toes, travelled her legs until it reached the pit of her stomach; churning whipped up a frenzy of sensation that bubbled up into her chest and lurched into the cold atmosphere. She sobbed and wailed.

Not uttering a word, Michael wrapped his arms around her. Julia sat on the other side.

The tempestuous North Sea rolled in white waves, lashing, beating the sand into submission as it tossed it over with its power.

April wept until there were no tears left, no strength in her body, her mind left drained and empty.

Julia pulled a tissue from her handbag. 'Here, darling.'

April held it to her eyes and wiped her cheeks to remove any mascara smudges.

'Can we go to the church? I think I need to.' April stated croakily.

'Of course.' Michael took her hand.

No one spoke as they paced back down the quiet village roads. Streams of grey smoke flowed in frayed ribbons from the chimneys while thick curtains were closed, protecting the residents from the February chill.

'I always did like it here,' April announced. 'I think I'll have the cottage rebuilt. Part of me still belongs here.'

'I agree,' Julia smiled as they walked to the church.

The parish church was only a few hundred yards down the road. The enormous tower was visible from across the village, valued by the locals as *a herring-and-a-half higher* than any nearby.

April stopped, her hands running over the flint boundary wall. 'There's something I need to find.'

'We'll wait here for you if you want. You go.' Julia perched on the edge of the wall and wrapped her arms around her body. Michael leaned beside her and placed his arm around her shoulders, briskly rubbing his hand up her arm.

April rambled through the myriad of grey headstones; the causal rows spread across the flat grass, dozens lopsided and leaning, filled the churchyard, boundary to boundary.

Stopping dead, she closed her eyes tight and listened; for what, she had no idea. Gulls drifted, along with the distant crashing waves. Isolated each sound, she counted them away until nothing. Silence.

'What way? What way?'

Annabelle.

'Emily.' With eyes still tight, April tuned and followed her instincts.

Looking down at her feet, they moved with no conscious thought. She found herself at the far side of the churchyard, where the flintstone wall dripped with ivy. By it, a row of gravestones. Her heart found an arched stone, carved with a rose, severed and broken and framed by scrolled coils.

April fell to her knees, pulled the damp hanky from her pocket and began frantically rubbing at the stone. Slowly, as she cleared away the moss and dirt, the words grew defined. April wrapped the tissue around her forefinger and traced the tip over the inscription.

In memory of Emily Rose Wright,
beloved Wife, Daughter & Sister
Passed away February 25th, 1901, aged twenty years.
This lovely bud, so young, so fair, called hence by early doom,
just came to show how sweet a flower
in paradise would bloom.

'I found you; I've lived here with you all my life,' she wept. 'And I know I felt your pain and sadness. I understand why you loved it here; I understand how the sea soothes your thoughts and helps wipe away your worries. But it's time I went home.'

CHAPTER THIRTY-THREE

April's birthday came and went with little fuss. Julia bought a chocolate cake — Nan would have baked one — but it was tasty and packed in one of Nan's cake tins. Along with a flash of coffee, they all headed to the park.

The early March morning was icy, a bone-stinging chill in the air, but as the blue sky chased off the last of the night's drowsy clouds, the sky gazed down, optimistic with the promise of some sun. They sat by the river, hugging their mugs tightly.

April could feel Nan there with her, the lady in her green coat, arm tucked snugly under hers as they watched the ducks scramble at their feet, eager for crumbs. She could feel her head resting against her shoulder. She was always there.

~

Longer days, lighter hearts.

Julia pulled out a black crepe evening bag with a crystal clasp. 'My goodness, I had no idea your Nan had so many handbags…' she opened it and looked at its label. 'Yes, it's original 1920's. Can you imagine it using this in some casino in Monte Carlo?'

For hours, they organised, cleaned, and tidied the house. Room after room, April discovered treasures, inherited, collected and hoarded over the decades: cupboards brimmed with boxes of new china; canteens of cutlery that had never seen the light of day, and drawers wedged full of damask tablecloths and runners.

'Shall we make a start on the spare room?'

'*My* room?'

'I've always known it as the spare room, not that I was ever really allowed in there. '

'Actually, mum, it was Emily's room.'

'Sorry, I can't get used to that, having a great-great-aunt whom we knew nothing.

The curtains grew pink with the dusky evening light. April sat down on the chair inside the bay window — her favourite spot, one for thinking. So much had happened over the past months.

'Hmm, I suppose it has put a whole fresh look on the family history, hasn't it?' April paused as Julia sat on the bed. 'Mum, she isn't your great-great-aunt, though. She was your great-grandmother.'

Julia lounged on the bed, her head in hand 'Great-grandmother?'

'Annabelle couldn't have children, the baby she brought up Rose, she was Emily's baby. Emily died in childbirth. So, Annabelle raised her as her own' April laid her head back and lifted her knees under her chin.

'Hang on a minute. Rose inherited everything, all the Hardwick estate, the lot!'

'Yes, everything.'

'But, oh...' Julia paused, not sure of how to finish her sentence.

'She was Richard's daughter.'

'Oh, poor Annabelle...' Julia sighed.

'Yes,' April finished.

'Well, I think it's time you put those photos up in the house. They shouldn't be locked away in this box.' Julia sat up on the end of the bed. 'Not anymore; they mean so much. They mean so much to you.' She wandered over to the dressing table and lifted the marquetry box. 'Come on.'

April unfastened her silver bracelet, resting it and the box in her lap. She inserted the key, and with a firm twist, the lid released.

Julia delighted in the photo album, remarking on how beautiful Emily was and how handsome James had been.

'Oh, she was beautiful, wasn't she?' Julia gently turned the heavy pages, their intricate gold embossing around each photo. 'My goodness, it all makes sense now, doesn't it? Look at Emily, look at her hair, and her smile. Tell me what you see?' Julia pushed the photo towards her daughter. 'Look.'

'I see it,' April smiled.

'Yes, you look just like her. *She* was your great-great-grandmother.'

'She was, and more.'

'James...' Julia stopped the words rolling off her tongue. 'What about James?'

'Emily lost him at war. The telegram said: *Missing, presumed dead*. She mourned herself to death. I know she died in childbirth, but I think she actually died of a broken heart.'

'I'm getting the picture, poor Annabelle.'

'Poor Emily, Mum.'

'But her own husband!'

'Everyone was grieving. I don't blame Emily or Richard; it was *my* fault for shutting them out.' April lost herself, swallowed by loss.

Julia sat and watched, baffled. After a moment, she looked back at the photo. 'James, he was a dashing young soldier, fair, and strapping,' she said, turning the page. 'Then, there's Richard.'

April's eyes were on her lap, occupied by the charm bracelet. 'Yes, he was. He was... everything.'

'You love him.' They stared at each other. 'It's all right, your nan told me. Not everything, she said you would in time. But I understand more than you think. Just so you know, I'm here to listen whenever you are ready.'

April gave an easy smile, the first happy smile in many months. 'I know you are, Mum.'

'Well, anyway, shall we make a start on that wardrobe? God only knows what your nan tucked away in there!'

Julia wandered over to the far end of the room to the large mahogany wardrobe. She ran her fingers over its polished surface down to the brass lock. 'Oh!'

'What is it? Ah, there's no key in that one. I've looked, but Nan never knew where it was either.'

'Well, I have an idea....' Julia dashed from the room. April stayed at the window, her thoughts occupied by Richard for the thousandth time that day.

'Here we are, let's try this one,' Julia returned with a brass key in hand. 'It's the one from your nan's. I think it'll fit; they all look the same.' The lock made a loud click, and the door swung open on its creaking hinges. 'Yes, there you go.'

Julia ran her hands over its contents; the rail was crammed full.

'Look, April, look at all these. I've never seen any of them. Have you?'

April strode to the wardrobe, packed with coats and evening gowns

A mink stole, draped over a beaded dress, gold iridescent beads and sequins, from neck to hemline. April lifted the hanger, gave it a shake to release the dust and cobwebs.

'My goodness, feel the weight of this!' April laid the dress on the bed. The detail of the artistry was intricate; the hemline fringed with long beaded tassels. 'Mum, I've seen this dress before.'

Julia stood beside her daughter. 'Yes, I think you have. Of course, it's the one Annabelle wore to my nan's wedding.'

'It's mine! It's my dress.' April took a deep breath and steadied her mind and her feet. 'Mum, I think I should tell

252

you. I'm not sure how. Or whether you'll believe me, it'll sound like I need locking up…'

'Darling, if you need to say it. Remember, say what's in your heart.'

They were the words of her grandmother: the words, the phrasing, the sentiment, even the expression on her mother's face. For the first time, April could see the distinct resemblance between them.

'Mum, I think you should sit down.' April took her arm, guided her to the bed and sat beside her. 'Mum, I am Annabelle. Or at least I was once.' Julia held April's hand tightly in her lap, her eyes on her. 'Do you understand, Mum? 'Cos, to be honest, when I say the words, I sound crazy…'

'I'm so glad you finally said it. Do you feel better?'

'Mum? Hang on, did you know?'

'Sweetheart, listen. I know I'm not your nan, but I *am* your mum. I have always known, well, not that you were Annabelle exactly. But something. Since you were tiny, there was a connection between you and your nan. She was with me when you were born. I lay there in bed, absolutely shattered, as you can imagine. I still remember the look on her face, I can't put my finger on what was different, but as soon she looked at you…' Julia paused, wiping her eye with the back of her hand. 'She had been waiting for you.'

April felt the need to say something, though what could she add. So instead, she rested her head on her mother's shoulder and squeezed her arm.

'It was as if you belonged to her, and there was no way I could ever compete with that kind of love.' Julia's voice trembled. 'I loved you instantly, you were the only thing that mattered, *and still*, I could never come close to the intensity your nan felt. Do you see?' Julia sighed. '

'Oh, Mum, I'm sorry.'

'Why on earth are you sorry, don't be silly,' she soothed. 'But you do understand what this all means?'

April shook her head.

'It means we never leave, do we? We always come back, time and time again, back to the ones we love.' Julia beamed. 'Well, shall we have a good look through that wardrobe?'

Julia jumped to her feet; she seemed a new woman, a new *mother*. April had never looked at her like this before.

They rifled through the many antique gowns and furs that filled the wardrobe. Then, behind, in the dark depths, squeezed tight between the fur coats and the door, Julia pulled out a hanger covered in a white linen cover. She hung it over the top of the wardrobe door.

'What's that?' April stood close and ran her hands down the length of it. 'What's underneath? Shall we have a look?' She gently raised the covering up and over the top of the hanger.

'My goodness,' Julia said, touching the blue lace.

Stunned, dazed, April stepped back until her calves met the bed, and she fell onto the mattress. Her eyes fixed, unable to move, struck dumb. She had never imagined this; it had never occurred to her, never a possibility that she should find anything like this. She had slept in this room for months, and it'd never occurred to her. And, just as when she saw the key, there it was, under her nose, all the time.

'Darling, whatever's the matter?'

Slowly, April's voice, along with her reasoning, returned.

'Mum, this was Emily's dress and...' Desperate to keep her footing, April walked over to the dress. 'This is Emily's cameo, her Wedgwood brooch.' April lifted her hand to the high neckline; her fingertips tentatively touched the brooch. 'Oh Mum, we found it; it was here all the time.

'I'm not sure what that means, but I understand it's important.'

April ran to her bedside table, quickly grabbing the mother-of-pearl photo frame. 'Here see. Annabelle's wearing her charm bracelet. My charm bracelet.' April jingled her wrist. '… and, Emily, there, the cameo brooch.'

April sat down on the rug, her body weary, her head spinning.

'It's what she's been looking for. I just *know* it. She wanted me to find it for her. She asked me to find it, and it's here. It's right here on her dress.' April said through tears.

Julia sat on the floor beside her. They both gazed up at the blue lace dress, complete with the Wedgwood cameo brooch, right where Emily had left it.

'Hang on,' Julia said incredulously. 'You said she asked you to find it. Do you mean she asked Annabelle or you?'

'She's still here in this house. I think she has always been here, never able to leave, move on or whatever happens when we die. I think it has something to do with that brooch.'

CHAPTER THIRTY-FOUR

The evening was warm. April went to the window; wispy curtains swayed in the breeze. The garden had begun to resemble its summer glory. The grass was lush, and the tree boughs were wearing their leafy coat.

She sat on the bedroom chair, watching the evening from the bay window. Beyond the garden, the tree-lined path and benches. How different it looked from when she had sat with her grandmother. The memory brought a smile. She lay back on the chair, her head resting on her arm.

A fragrance. April inhaled instinctively and sat up. 'Emily?' she whispered.

The blue lace dress still hung over the wardrobe door, the cameo brooch glinting in the light. Emily stood admiring it.

'I found it. I found it for you.'

'Annabelle, thank you. I thought it was lost. I could not remember...'

Slowly, tentatively, April paced to the edge of the bed, her hand resting on the mattress. She wanted to move close, but her feet grew roots.

'I know everything. I remember,' April affirmed, her voice not her own.

Emily turned to face her, 'Everything?'

'I remembered to love you.'

'I know you did. I know you did.'

'You know?'

Emily smiled. 'I have watched you: so close, but so far away.' She turned her attention back to the dress.

'You've been here all these years, haven't you?

'Time is nothing to me. It is endless, it means nothing, and it passes, regardless of us all.'

April sat down heavily, her legs unable to hold her weight, and stared as Emily studied her dress, the fineness of the lace, the detail of the collar. Emily's hand reached out to touch the lace but withdrew, curling her fingers, resting her clenched hand at the mouth.

'I watched, I watched you, and I watched Rose. Dear sweet Rose. I was so near to her; I watched her play and sat by her side as she slept. Then grow into a young woman.'

'Emily?' April hesitated.

'Yes, I saw him.'

April's heart sank; she knew her thoughts. 'James?'

'My James did not die. I watched him. I would lie down with him at night. I would kiss his lips, but he could never kiss me in return. I was invisible to both his eyes and ears, no more than a memory.'

'Oh, Emily.'

'I have spent lifetimes waiting, watching everyone live, while I merely existed — invisible.'

'Emily, I'm so sorry.'

'I have been with you every day of your life. I knew you were true to your heart and Annabelle's soul,' Emily whispered, admiring the dress.

'Emily.' This was the only word April could utter.

'I am sorry for Rose.' Then, discarding the dress, she turned her attention fully to April.

'Rose? What are you sorry for?'

'For leaving you. I took everything from you.'

April listened as Emily tortured herself, just as she had done for decade upon decade.

'You were grieving. You were both grieving.'

'I took what was yours. But, grief takes us all.'

'You gave me Rose. She was your gift. She was all I had left of Richard; she was all I had left of you.'

'Richard, I am sorry, that emotion still runs through me like a hot knife. I only ever loved James. But we both loved you. I still love you; my heart is still full of love.'

They both gazed back at the blue lace dress.

'I cannot touch it. Can you read it for me?'

'Read it?' April rose from the bed.

'My letter!' Emily's finger pointed to the Wedgwood brooch, '...my letter from James.'

April walked over to the wardrobe. Emily stood within inches of her; her sweet aroma filled the room; she inhaled consumed herself with her sister. Gently, April unfastened the brooch. It lay in her hand, the shiny silver cold to the touch surrounding the blue Wedgwood cameo. April held it in front of Emily.

'Turn it over.'

April flipped the brooch over in her palm. Behind the Jasperware plaque, tucked securely within the silver mount, lay a small, folded piece of paper. April prised it free and carefully unfolded it, conscious of its fragile and flimsy quality, almost transparent at the creases.

> *My dearest Emily,*
>
> *If you are reading this letter, then I am gone.*
> *My death is no one's fault but a cruel truth war.*
> *My heart and soul will always be there with you.*
> *By day, I shall sit and hold your hand. Each night, I shall lay by your side and kiss your lips. I shall listen to you sing and hear you laugh. As each day passes, it will be a day closer until we are reunited.*
> *Do not grieve but remember the love we share.*
>
> *Yours forever and beyond, James*

258

April refolded the delicate paper, placed it back into the brooch and turned to her sister in tears. 'Oh, Emily.'

'I have waited so awfully long to hear those words,' she sighed. 'I am the one that watched, I am the one that lay by his side, I kissed his lips, and I waited and waited.'

April dropped her eyes to the cameo.

'I have watched everyone that I love grow old, then leave me. I waited for them, but they have gone, yet I am still here.' Emily stood, once again staring at her lace dress.

Emily, my love.

Emily turned as April looked up from the cameo.

A glow seeped into the dusky evening; a bright white light slowly flooded the room with its brilliance.

Emily, it is time.

James stood tall in his military uniform; his brass buttons gleamed.

'James? I have waited so long.'

It is time to rest now. There is no more for you to do.

James stretched his hand and stepped closer to his wife.

'Thank you, my dearest, Annabelle. Do not forget me.'

'I shall always remember to love you.' April watched as they faded and were gone.

CHAPTER THIRTY-FIVE

April hurled the last few sandwich crusts on the grass as a flood of ducks and geese gathered at her feet, flapping their wings, eagerly scrapping over the bread. Her back rested against the sun-drenched bench. She watched the birds feeding, the children playing, the couples walking, their hands clutched together.

The park was an abundance of life. A duck flew over the fence, landed on the river's mirrored surface, and swam towards the old Abbot's Bridge. The place she had once sat, dreamed of her future, a future that she had already lived.

April opened the leather flap of her handbag, reached in and retrieved the photo album that lay warm from the midday sun. The white envelope fell out, on the front, the words: *Little One.*

'Oh, Nan,' she breathed. 'I think it's time.'

April slipped her fingers under the seal; she eased out its contents with the very tips. A photograph: a beautiful woman and a young girl with long fair hair sat on a settee. Their dresses were light and formal. A young Annabelle sat perched upon her mother's lap, both peaceful and content. April turned it over, in black ink were the words: *Rose and Annabelle 1879.*

April stared, amazed at a photo of Annabelle before Emily's birth. Then, as she went to put the envelope down, she noticed something still inside, a folded piece of paper.

Dearest Little One

I never got a chance to say sorry. Annabelle passed away before I knew. However, she did not go for very long, did she? Now it is my turn to leave, but not before I tell you what I have waited so very many years to say.

I am so sorry, my Little One, so sorry for leaving you and your father. You both raised your sister into a beautiful young woman, and despite all the turmoil you both had to endure, you stayed loyal to Emily. And Rose, look how you loved dear little Rose.

I know that, in your heart, you still ache with loss. You have lost so many of those who have loved you so dearly. But you were always true to your heart. I am so proud of you for that. You were so small, but you always remembered, remembered to love.

Please don't ever look at this as a burden, these memories you have. It's our family legacy, and it is our gift.

Annabelle, you will always be my Little One.

April's heart sank.

'Oh Nan, I didn't know, how could I not see? It was there in front of me the whole time.'

She leant her head back and gazed up into the warm, sun-filled sky and closed her eyes. It warmed her face. For many moments, she remained basking in the revelation. Then, carefully folded the letter and enclosed the photo inside, placing them back in the envelope.

April reached back into her bag and removed her new leather diary and pen. The pages were pure and untouched.

'Perhaps it's time to start a new chapter, hopefully with some peaceful memories and thoughts for my descendants to read, maybe for you, when you return.' She sighed, closed the diary and hid it back in her bag. 'But later, it can wait.' Then opened the leather photo album at the wedding photo of Rose and Charles.

'That's a rather nice antique piece.' The voice came from beside her. 'Victorian, circa 1870s, immaculate condition, very sought after.'

'I beg your pardon?'

'Your photo album, it's an antique piece.'

'I'm sorry?'

'Your album.'

'I'm quite aware of what you said.'

April kept her eyes down, eager not to make eye contact with this stranger. Unsure why he frightened her. It wasn't him she feared, more the exchange of words with someone from her own time.

For a moment, she closed her eyes, hoping when they opened, he would be gone. But there he was, his feet uncomfortably close. She noticed the shine on his shoes, a rich tan leather, highly polished toes. Do men still buff their shoes like that, *a good spit and polish*; she could hear her dad's voice. The laces were neat, tied in perfect matching bows. Who ties a shoelace with so much accuracy?

She shuddered slightly as her eyes followed slowly up his legs, his trousers, expensive, she thought.

Unperturbed, he continued, 'I'm sorry. I didn't mean to startle you. It's just; I love old photographs — they intrigue me. The history of someone's life, suspended in time. You can tell so much about them, don't you think?'

'Do you think so?' *Why am I still talking to him?* 'No, I'm not sure you're right at all.' *Just walk away.*

'I must say, I know it's said there isn't much a woman doesn't carry in her handbag, but do you make a habit of carrying old photo albums around with you often?'

'You really have a cheek, don't you?' April barked.

'I didn't mean to offend you,' he quickly added. 'Let me assure you, I don't normally go around harassing young women,' he said in earnest, with a hint of humour.

'No, I'm sorry, I didn't mean to snap. You didn't offend me. I just don't think you can tell as much about someone's life as you think. Life looks so perfect and idyllic in a pose for a camera.' April sat, bewildered by the conversation but compelled to continue, all the while her eyes were on the album.

'They look pretty perfect to me. Look at the way he holds her hand and the love in his eyes. They say that the eyes are the windows to the soul.'

'Do they?' *Stop talking to him.*

'Yes. Look at her, a true beauty. I don't mean just because she's attractive, but she has beauty from within.'

April kept her eyes on the photograph, tracing the outline of Richard's hand, the look on his face, how his eyes twinkled back from the photo. 'Maybe you're right.' April closed the album with a snap, quickly packed it away in her bag and stood up.

'I'm sorry. I didn't mean to offend you. Sorry, where are my manners? I'm…' the man's voice was strangely alluring, mellow, slightly husky.

'I'm leaving anyway. I'd better get back to work,' April interrupted quickly.

Walking past the ducks, she kept her eyes in front, anxious to separate herself as far from the stranger as possible. She followed the broad path through the flowerbeds until she reached the Abbey Gate, leaving the stranger and their obscure discussion far behind.

Within the archway of the Abbey gate, April turned to look back, dozens of locals with shopping bags, smart suits with newspapers and takeaway sandwiches. The tourists were now heading her way, but no stranger with shiny shoes as far as she could tell.

'Nice lunch, darling?' Julia stood behind the shop counter.

'Hmm,' she responded with an amused tone.

'Hmm; what does *hmm* mean?'

'Nothing, Mum, nothing, really,' she paused, putting her lunchtime episode to the back of her mind. 'I've decided: what do you think about putting all the photos in frames and hanging them around the house?'

'Sweetheart, you know my thoughts on that; it's about time. Your dad did a house clearance last week; he's sorted a lot of it out, but before the auctioneer comes to look at the furniture, why don't you see if any of the photo frames are to your liking?' They're out the back. Your dad's going through the last of it now.'

April wandered behind the counter; Michael stood amongst furniture, paintings, and endless boxes.

'Dad, Mum said I could have a look for some photo frames?'

'Ah, yes, they're here... somewhere. I could do with a hand sorting all this,' Michael gestured to the boxes. 'We've got a guy coming from the auction house to value the furniture and paintings in a while.'

'Yeah, of course.'

'There they are, in that box with some other silver bits.'

April pushed the box across the floor with her foot, perched on a wooden stool and began to rummage.

'Michael, Mr Taylor is here,' Julia called from the shop.

'Send him through, dear, send him through.'

Mr Taylor followed the direction of the voice. Michael stepped over a wooden crate and held out his hand.

'Nice to meet you, Mr Taylor. I'm Michael. Please come through. Watch your step there; sorry about the mess, as you can see, we haven't got much room out the back.'

Michael guided the auctioneer towards an antique armoire and large tallboy.

'These are the pieces of furniture. Oh, and those paintings as we discussed on the phone,' he stated, pointing to the framed oils beside April. She remained silent, preoccupied, her head low over the box.

'So, Mr Taylor, please don't think me rude, but you're quite young to be interested in old objects,' Michael inquired with a slight laugh. 'Not that I see anything wrong it that.'

'Ah, I'm not sure that age has any relevance to the passions we acquire. I've always had it, my mother was always on at me to go out and play with my mates, but I'd rather read or be hunting junk shops,' the auctioneer replied with a grim.

'Do you know, I think we shall get on very well, you and me. So, getting down to business, what do you think?' Michael stood casually, his arm resting on a heap of leather-bound albums.'

'Well, we would be interested in the furniture, they are good examples. And of course, the paintings, not a particularly well-known artist, but local which is always nice to see, and fine pieces of work all the same.'

Mr Taylor glanced again over at the paintings, close to April. She continued to search through the box, her long auburn hair tousled over the frames. She had already made her judgment on those paintings, not worth the wall space of the shop.

'I was wondering if you were interested in selling those leather albums?' Mr Taylor continued. 'Could I have a look?' he pointed to Michael's elbow.

'These, of course,' Michael removed his arm and placed them on top of the chest of drawers.

'I have a passion for old photographs, you see. I can't seem to help myself. I had boxes of them as a boy, you know, under my bed. Probably where normal boys may hide something else if you know what I mean,' he grinned.

April placed her hand inside the box, but it dangled there, paralysed at his words. She slowly looked up. The auctioneer stood with his back to her; he was tall and wore dark, perfectly tailored trousers and a crisp white shirt. April's eyes continued to travel to his hair, dark and lustrous, with just enough length to sit upon the collar in polished curl.

'Ah, your passion for old photos is much like my daughter's.'

Michael pointed in the direction of the wooden stool, about to introduce her, but April was already on her feet, her legs shaking slightly as she rubbed her dusty hands down her jeans.

She took a tentative step closer, her heart obscurely pounding in her ribcage, as she recalled her lunchtime encounter.

Mr Taylor turned to face her, 'Ah, hello again,' he smiled.

'You two met before?'

'Lunchtime in the park, although we didn't get the chance to be properly introduced, your daughter was so eager to get back to work.'

He stepped forward. The daylight from the shop window reflected off his shirt in a glow.

'Ah,' Michael laughed. Well, then, this is my very conscientious daughter, April.'

'It's very nice to meet you, properly, April. I'm…'

'You're Mr Taylor, an auctioneer with a very annoying lunchtime habit.'

'Well, you have me there,' he laughed. 'So, April, as someone who knows me well already, then, we shouldn't be so formal, I'm Richard, but my friends call me Rick,' he said warmly, his hand outstretched.

April moved closer into the beam of sunlight. Her eyes were constantly on his hand as it lay open, waiting. Then, in a peculiar sensation of slow motion, April placed her hand in his open palm. Her fingers looked small as he enclosed his around them. A tingling started in her fingertips, smoothly flowed through her arm and whooshed through her body, flushing her cheeks.

She looked up into his face, handsome, she thought, but it was his bright green eyes that pulled the air from her lungs.

'Rick?' her lips tingled. 'Richard. Of course, you are.'

THE END

ACKNOWLEDGEMENTS

First, I would like to thank you, *the reader*, for picking up this book. If you enjoyed *Remember To Love Me*, please leave a review either where you purchased it or on Goodreads (or both); they genuinely are the author's lifeline.

Behind every book is a writer bleeding from their fingers, eager to create something of note. But behind them is a support network who give time and expertise — all to steady the madness.

Firstly, my thanks go to my incredibly supportive husband, James, who is there with me every step of the way, endless cups of coffee. I couldn't ask for a better wingman or someone to *help me hide the bodies!*

To the wonderful Kayleigh at Full Proof Editing for her brilliant editing and proofreading skills, I could not have achieved this without her.

Becky Wright is an author with a passion for history, the supernatural, and things that go bump in the night.

Blessed, she lives in the heart of the English Suffolk countryside, surrounded by rolling green fields, picturesque timber-framed villages, country pubs and rural churches. She is married with children and grandchildren.

Family bonds and the intricacy of relationships feature strongly in her books. With her lifelong fascination for the supernatural, Gothic fiction and the macabre, her stories tend to lean towards the dark side.

For information on all Becky's books, writing and updates, please go to her official website. You can also follow her across all social media platforms.

www.beckywrightauthor.com

Printed in Great Britain
by Amazon

74482781R00166